PRAISE FOR
HELEN HARDT

"I'm dead from the strongest book hangover ever. Helen exceeded every expectation I had for this book. It was heart pounding, heartbreaking, intense, full throttle genius."
~ **Tina at Bookalicious Babes Blog**

"Proving the masterful writer she is, Ms. Hardt continues to weave her beautifully constructed web of deceit, terror, disappointment, passion, love, and hope as if there was never a pause between releases. A true artist never reveals their secrets, and Ms. Hardt is definitely a true artist."
~ **Bare Naked Words**

"The love scenes are beautifully written and so scorching hot I'm fanning my face just thinking about them."
~ **The Book Sirens**

Melt

STEEL BROTHERS SAGA
BOOK FOUR

This book is an original publication of Helen Hardt

This is a work of fiction. Names, characters, places, and incidents either are the product of the author's imagination or are used fictitiously, and any resemblance to actual persons, living or dead, business establishments, events, or locales is entirely coincidental. The publisher does not assume any responsibility for third-party websites or their content.

Melt

STEEL BROTHERS SAGA
BOOK FOUR

WATERHOUSE PRESS

DEDICATION

For everyone who has ever left me a five-star review—
thank you! I'm so glad you enjoy my work.

WARNING

This book contains adult language and scenes, including flashbacks of child physical and sexual abuse, which may cause trigger reactions. This story is meant only for adults as defined by the laws of the country where you made your purchase. Store your books and e-books carefully where they cannot be accessed by younger readers.

PROLOGUE

Jonah

"What is it, Tal?" I walked into the kitchen of the main ranch house, where Talon, his girlfriend, Jade, and our sister, Marjorie, were sitting at the kitchen table. Our younger brother, Ryan, was also there.

Talon raked his fingers through his dark hair. Dark circles rimmed his eyes. He looked like he hadn't slept in weeks.

"I came as soon as I got your text."

"Thank God you're here," Talon said.

"So what's going on?" I asked. "You look like hell."

"Take it easy, Joe," Ryan said. "He's freaking out."

Ryan always had Talon's back. The two of them were close in a way I would never be close to my brothers. I was the oldest, the one doling out dictatorial commands when they wanted to play. And then of course there was the fact that Talon had protected Ryan the day of his abduction—a courtesy I had been unable to extend to Talon as his older brother.

I spent a lot of time thinking about that, thinking I was a piece of shit.

"You want some coffee, Jonah?" Jade asked.

I nodded. "Don't get up. I'll get it." I helped myself to a mug, filled it, and sat down at the table with the other four. "What's going on?"

Talon paced around the table, clearly agitated. "Someone's been in our house. *This* house."

I raised my eyebrows. "What are you talking about?"

Marj hunched her shoulders. "I'm terrified, Joe."

Jade nodded. "It's really scary."

Frigid fingers trailed up my spine. "Would somebody please tell me what the fuck this is about?"

Talon looked at Jade. "You guys are well aware what happened between Jade and me a while back. When I asked her to leave the house." He winced.

"It's okay." Jade stroked his arm.

He rubbed his hands together. "Evidently, sometime while Jade was in the shower, someone got into the house."

"Again, please explain what you're talking about." My nerves were on edge, and I was growing impatient.

Jade cleared her throat. "After I came out of the shower, I found this on my pillow." She opened up what appeared to be a law dictionary and pulled out a flattened red rose. "I never mentioned it because I thought Talon had left it."

Marj piped in then. "Yeah, Jade told me about the rose. I thought it was kind of weird at first, because we don't grow roses here on the ranch. But maybe Talon had gone into town and gotten it for her. I didn't know."

"Neither of us thought anything about it at the time," Jade said.

Talon cleared his throat. "Then, just this morning, Jade mentioned it—that I had left a red rose on her pillow. But...I never left her a rose."

Marj shivered, running her hands up and down her arms. "I don't feel safe here. It's...a violation."

Talon darted his eyes back and forth. "We need to find out

who it was. I can't have Jade and Marj at risk in this house."

"Absolutely, I agree," I said, my skin cold. "Have you called the cops?"

Talon shook his head. "Not yet."

"The only evidence we have is the rose," Jade said. "And obviously it's all dried out now."

"I'm glad you kept it," I said. "Maybe the cops can get prints or something."

"I don't know how they'll be able to," Jade said. "I'm sure my prints are all over the stem. And getting something off the petals would be impossible."

"Still," I said. "It's all we have."

Talon sat down at the table, finally, and then punched the wooden surface. "Damn! Just as we'd all agreed to move forward. Just when I was starting to feel like I could have a life with my family and the woman I love."

Ryan turned to Talon. "You can still have that, Tal. This is just a minor setback."

"A minor setback?" Talon's eyes lit with fire. "Someone was in our fucking house, Ryan. The house I now share with my girlfriend and my sister, the two most important women in my life. I will not have them in danger."

"Do you think it could have been Colin?" Jade asked, referring to her ex-fiancé.

"I wouldn't put it past him," Talon said.

"Of course, no one knows where he is," Ryan said.

"He's dead," Talon said. "Larry Wade killed him."

"I'm not sure he did," Jade said. "Don't get me wrong. I don't have any love lost for Larry Wade. I'm glad he's going to prison for a very long time. But when I talked to him recently, he swore up and down that he had nothing to do with Colin disappearing. That someone had planted Colin's personals on him."

"Colin could definitely be the culprit," Marjorie said. "He turned out to be a bad seed. How did I spend four years with him at college and not realize that?"

Jade shook her head. "You're telling me. I spent seven years with him. I was going to marry the creep."

"Colin." Talon hit the table again. "He wanted you back. Somehow that motherfucker got into our house."

"What about Larry Wade?" I asked. "It could have been him."

"Why would Larry leave me a rose?" Jade asked.

I let out a sarcastic laugh. "Why would Larry molest his nephew?"

Eight eyes met mine, all widened. Perhaps I shouldn't have said such blatant and tactless words, but really, the time for pussyfooting around this subject was long past. "Look, I'm sorry if that upset any of you. I really am. But this is no longer a secret. Everybody knows why Larry is sitting in a jail cell. It made the news, and this time Dad and Wendy Madigan weren't around to cover it up. Maybe I should have quashed it. In truth, I thought about it, but what good would that do any of us now?" I zeroed in on two of the eyes. Talon's. "Did I do the right thing, Tal? Did I do the right thing by not covering it up?"

He met my gaze, and his expression softened. A bit. "I would've covered it up myself if I'd wanted to, Joe. As humiliating as it is, I know it wasn't my fault. Maybe my story will help someone. Who knows? That's the least of my concerns right now. Right now, I want to know who the hell broke into my house and put a flower on my woman's pillow."

CHAPTER ONE

Jonah

In the end, I knew the guilt would eventually kill me.

As I lay on the harsh pavement in a dark alley, guilt—in the form of a couple homeless vagrants booting me in the kidneys—was kicking my ass.

I always protected my face. I couldn't risk my brothers seeing evidence of what I was up to. Anything from the neck down was fair game though. Sometimes I even threw the guys a couple bucks for their trouble.

Tonight, though... Nope.

Tonight guilt would end my life.

And I welcomed it.

★ ★ ★ ★

"Joe! Thank God!"

My sister's voice. I opened my eyes. Marjorie's form was a blur, but it was her. Her dark eyes shone with concern. Where the hell was I?

I groaned. My lower back throbbed, and I inhaled sharply. Big mistake. Damn, guilt had gotten a few of my ribs, too.

But I was alive.

Still alive.

"Thank God you woke up. I'll go get Ryan. He just stepped

out for a minute to take a call."

Marj's blur was replaced with a blue blur I didn't recognize.

"How are you feeling, Mr. Steel?"

Like shit, thanks. I wasn't sure if I'd said it out loud.

"I'm going to check your blood pressure. You might feel some squeezing."

Not likely. I couldn't feel anything over the bass drum beating on my back.

"You've been beaten pretty badly," the blur said.

Not badly enough, apparently. I inhaled again, and a knife sliced through me. Damned broken ribs. Nothing I hadn't experienced before many times. This was the first time I'd ended up in the hospital, though. As I tried to focus on the blur through slitted eyes, my heart sped up.

What had I been thinking? I didn't want to die.

I had this revelation every time after I let myself get beaten up. Each time would be the last. I swore it. Well, this one would truly be the last. Even though she'd been a blur, Marj's voice had cracked with fear. I couldn't take that sound in my baby sister's voice, nor in the voices of either of my brothers.

I breathed in again, wincing at the sharp, knifing pain.

Never again, goddamnit. This dangerous self-indulgence was over.

"Hey, you gave us a pretty good scare, Joe. Thank God you managed to crawl to that bar and get help. What were you doing in that neighborhood? What the hell happened?"

Ryan's voice. A bar? I'd been at a bar? The last thing I remembered was blacking out in the alley. I opened my mouth to speak, but only a crackled croak emerged.

"It's okay, bro. Don't try to talk. Looks like you're going to live."

★ ★ ★ ★

Dr. Melanie Carmichael sat across from me in her office decorated in dark wood and hunter-green. She was as beautiful as I remembered. She and I had met months ago in a hotel bar. We'd both been staying at the hotel for different conferences. Her golden-blond hair had fallen in gentle waves against her shoulders as she sat next to me, sipping a cocktail. She wore it up today, pulled back in a tight bun at the top of her head. She was still gorgeous, even with the severe schoolteacher hairstyle. Piercing green eyes, though—they were the same. I hadn't been able to look away from them that night in the bar, and I was having a difficult time trying to do so now.

How was I supposed to tell this woman my innermost thoughts?

My brother Talon had, and he was on his way to healing from a horrific childhood trauma of being abducted and held captive by three men when he was ten years old. Once I had regained consciousness in the hospital, Talon had come and begged me to make an appointment with his therapist.

So here I was, three weeks later, my ribs still aching a bit, sitting in a supple leather recliner. My brother had sat in this chair, no doubt, and told this woman his deepest secrets. Now it was my turn.

"I'm not sure what to say."

She smiled. My God, she had a beautiful smile. Her lips were full and red, the color of a ripe currant. "Say whatever you feel like saying, Mr. Steel. This time is for you."

"First of all, no Mr. Steel. Only Jonah. Or Joe. Whichever

you prefer."

"Okay, Jonah. Why don't you just start with what brought you in to see me today?"

I felt like a fraud. My brother had been through so much, and here I was, seeing a therapist when there was nothing wrong with me at all—nothing except the guilt that lived inside me like a parasite, killing me from the inside out.

I looked around the room, playing for time. On the wall behind her desk were her various degrees. I was surprised to see a medical degree.

"I thought you were a psychologist," I said.

"I am."

"But you went to medical school? Wouldn't that make you a psychiatrist?"

She cleared her throat. "Technically, yes. But I also have a master's degree in psychotherapy, which is what I practice. Because I rarely prescribe medication, I prefer the term psychologist or psychotherapist."

I shook my head. "That's a lot of schooling."

She tilted her head back a little. "Yes, there were times when I thought it would never end. Being a psychiatrist has some advantages, too. I have admitting privileges at Valleycrest Hospital, in case any of my patients need more day-to-day care. But I consider myself more of a psychologist than a medical doctor."

I nodded, continuing to peruse her office.

"So do my qualifications meet your approval?" she asked.

I turned back to her abruptly. "Of course. I was just curious."

"You mean you were desperate for something to talk about other than what brought you in here today." She smiled.

Guilty. She knew as well as I did. No need to prolong it. "I... Well, you know my brother's story."

Dr. Carmichael nodded. "I do. And he has given me permission to discuss his case with you if we need to."

My neck chilled. I wasn't sure I wanted to know what Talon had told the doctor. Hopefully this wouldn't get to that.

"It was Talon who suggested I call you and make an appointment."

"I know. He told me. And he talked to me a little bit about you."

Christ. God only knew what Talon had said. He knew I'd gotten the shit kicked out of me by a couple thugs in a dark alley. What he didn't know was that I'd been there on purpose, that I intentionally hadn't fought back, that I'd actually started the fight. Thing was, I wasn't a coward. I could've made quick work of the vagrants who'd attacked me. And I sure as hell didn't want to tell this beautiful woman across from me that I'd *let* them beat me to a pulp.

Then the word popped out of my mouth.

"Guilt."

"I understand," Dr. Carmichael said. "You have a lot of guilt about what happened to your brother."

I swallowed and nodded.

"Let's talk about that," she said. "Why do you feel so guilty?"

"Because I'm the older brother. I should've been able to protect him that day. I should've protected him the way he protected Ryan. But I wasn't there, and he paid the ultimate price for my failure."

"You do understand that Talon doesn't blame you for what happened, don't you?"

I understood that, all right. He'd told me enough. But that didn't seem to matter. Still, I blamed myself. "I do know that, Melanie." Shit, what a blunder. "I'm sorry. Dr. Carmichael."

She smiled again, and my heart did a little dance. What a gorgeous smile.

"If you're more comfortable calling me by my first name, please feel free to do so. After all, I'm calling you Jonah."

For some reason, she was Melanie to me. Maybe because we'd met before. I didn't know. "All right. If you don't mind."

"I don't."

"So anyway...Melanie, I know he doesn't blame me. But I also know he resents what happened to him."

"He may have in the past, but he no longer feels that way. And even if he did, it was completely subconscious. We've talked at length about that."

I looked down at my hands. "God, it's so weird for you to talk to me about this."

"As I told you, Talon gave me carte blanche with you. He's very concerned about you and the guilt you feel. He wants you to get help, and if his sessions with me can assist you along the way, he wants that to happen."

"It just feels so..."

Melanie nodded. "I understand. So if you would rather I not share Talon's sessions and feelings with you, we can go that route. Either way, I'm here for you, Jonah, just as much as I am for your brother. I can also recommend another therapist, if you'd rather deal with someone who doesn't know Talon's history. I have several colleagues, both male and female, who are excellent and who I think could help you."

I shook my head. "No, then I'd just have to explain the whole story to them. You already know it, so we don't have to go there. But yeah, I would rather not discuss Talon. I mean, at least not his sessions with you. That seems too private to me. But we can discuss Talon from my perspective. His situation is why I'm here, after all."

"I completely understand. So tell me, how did you find yourself in that situation? In a dark alley, getting beaten?"

Embarrassment flooded through me. The last thing I wanted was for Melanie to think I couldn't take care of myself when I encountered a couple of thugs. Of course I could. I could've sent both of them into tomorrow. God knew I had before when someone else was at stake.

Just not me.

Thing was, I knew exactly what I'd been doing. I was punishing myself. Seemed the only way to get rid of the guilt was to inflict so much physical pain on myself that I could no longer feel the emotional pain. I didn't need Melanie or any other therapist to tell me that. Sounded pretty textbook to me.

"Do you want to talk about something else?"

"No, this is what I came here for. I hope you don't think I can't handle myself."

"Of course I don't think that. Even if I did, I'm not here to judge you, Jonah. I'm here to help you."

Knife in the gut. She didn't think I could handle myself. Well, I'd have to take care of that. I just wasn't sure how to at the moment.

"Do you want to tell me how you got into that situation? Or like I said, we can talk about something else."

Something else. If only...

"It's the guilt, Melanie. It's eating me alive."

She nodded, her countenance grave. And something else laced her eyes.

Pity.

I didn't want pity in any form. I didn't deserve anyone's pity. Nothing bad had happened to me, at least nothing I hadn't walked into myself. Not like what had happened to Talon.

"Please. Don't look at me that way."

She widened her eyes. "What way do you mean?"

"With sympathy. I don't deserve it."

"I think you may have misread my facial expression. I'm only feeling concerned."

Right. I didn't believe her for a minute.

"But let's attack this from a different angle," she said. "How are you feeling? Physically? You took a pretty bad beating, but you look great today. There's certainly no indication on your face that anything happened."

Of course there wasn't. I always protected my face.

"I feel okay. Still a little achy where my ribs were broken." I'd taken some nasty boots to the back as well, but luckily they hadn't done any lasting internal damage.

"Well, that's good news."

Silence reigned for what seemed like an hour. She didn't seem to know what to say to me, and I sure as hell didn't know what to say to her. Finally, I stood.

"I think this might've been a mistake. I'm not certain I'm ready for therapy. I'm not sure I need it."

"All right, but feel free to change your mind," she said. "My office is open to you anytime if you ever want to come back."

She moved toward me, and electricity surged through my veins.

She was so beautiful, and I wanted to rip her blond hair out of that bun and watch it flow around her creamy shoulders.

Of course, if I wasn't going back to therapy, what was

stopping me? She wasn't going to be my therapist...

I walked toward her, closing the distance, and met her emerald eyes.

Her lips trembled—such gorgeous, kissable lips.

Then I turned.

I walked out of her office.

CHAPTER TWO

Melanie

I stood, alone, in the middle of my office, shuddering.

It was better that Jonah Steel hadn't kissed me, but for a millisecond I had been sure he was going to. ·

And I had wanted him to.

I shook my head to clear it. I'd been a practicing psychotherapist for over ten years now, and never had I let my feelings get in the way of the doctor-patient relationship. Certainly, I'd found some of my patients attractive—Talon Steel was gorgeous, after all—but I hadn't let the attraction color my work. I had never harbored personal feelings for any of them beyond friendship.

Perhaps it was best if Jonah Steel did not come back for more therapy, at least not with me. Something about him called to me. He looked a lot like his brother—same dark hair, only with a little gray at the temples. He wore a few days' growth of beard, also laced with silver. What would that stubble feel like against my cheeks?

"Stop it," I said aloud. "He's a patient, nothing more."

I sighed and walked over to my desk. My last appointment for the day had canceled. I logged in and checked some e-mails, responded to a few, and then closed up shop. I hadn't had an hour off in the afternoon for a while, so I decided to do some shopping. I locked up my office, gave my assistant, Randi, a quick update, and headed down the elevator to the street. I worked in downtown Grand Junction, and there were plenty of shops to choose from.

So I wasn't sure why I entered the lingerie shop.

A twenty-something woman with bleached-blond hair came forward. "Can I help you find anything today?"

I shook my head. "Thank you. Just looking."

For what? I didn't know. I never came into this shop. I was a cotton bikini kind of girl. Even my bras were lace and ribbon free. No need to accentuate a B cup.

Purple. A display of purple satin and lace drew me. I rarely wore purple, so I wasn't sure why the color beckoned me. The fabric was soft and smooth beneath my fingers.

"That's our new Midnight Reverie line." The blonde came up behind me. "What size are you?"

My cheeks warmed. I was tall and lean, a basic size six, with basic thirty-six B boobs. Nothing special about me or my body. Certainly not special enough for the Midnight Reverie line. Besides, all the purple would clash horribly with my green eyes.

"The color would be great on you," Blondie said.

I turned toward her. "I never wear purple. It doesn't look right on me."

"Are you kidding? With your skin tone and blond hair, you'd rock purple." She eyed me up and down. "And you sure do have the body for it."

Now I was really uncomfortable. She was looking me over as if I were her dessert.

Why had I come in here again? "If you'll excuse me, I really must be going."

Blondie was not so easily swayed. "If you open a line of credit today, I can get you twenty percent off. Honestly, this line is perfect for you. The man in your life would adore you in it."

She had said exactly the wrong thing. I looked at her squarely. "I have no man in my life."

I walked swiftly out of the store.

What had I been thinking going in there? I walked along, gazing in some store windows. My reflection stared back at me. My hair was a mess. A couple strands were falling out of the updo I'd worn.

My body was...okay. Perfect for a purple lace lingerie line? Not even. Blondie was a good salesperson. A lot of women probably fell for her line.

But not me. Nope, nothing special about me or my body. Nothing special about me, period.

I sighed. Why had I been looking forward to shopping? Why not just go home and take the extra time to relax? I walked back to my office, took the elevator to the parking garage, and left.

★ ★ ★ ★

Talon Steel sat in my office, his hands on the arms of the leather recliner where he always sat.

"It's been a couple weeks," I said.

"Yeah, I'm sorry I haven't been in. Harvest time at the orchard is finally dying down, and I'll have more availability. I know it's important to continue my sessions. I know I'm not fully healed yet."

Did anyone ever fully heal? I wasn't so sure. "How is

everything going?" I asked.

"Pretty well. I still have a dream about once a week, but they don't matter so much anymore. Jade moved back in, and she shares my bedroom."

I smiled. "And you no longer fear sleeping with her."

He maintained eye contact, something he'd had a hard time with at first. "No. I look back now and wonder why I ever did. I know I would never hurt her."

I nodded. "I know."

"How did things go with Joe the other day?"

I bit my lip. "I'm not at liberty to say. Although you gave me permission to share your sessions with him, he didn't give me that same permission."

"Sorry. I didn't think about that."

"There's no reason why you should have. You're just concerned about your brother."

"I am. It's not like my brother to get the crap kicked out of him. He's a big, strong man. He should be fine on his own."

I agreed. What could I say? "He has things to work through, Talon, just like you do."

"I just never understood why both my brothers were so affected by what happened to me. They both seem to carry a lot of baggage from it."

"What they're going through isn't uncommon. But you can't take on their healing as well. They have to take that initiative."

"I guess you're right, but it's hard, Doc, watching them struggle."

"I'm sure it is. I'm sure it was just as hard, maybe harder, for them to watch you struggle all those years."

Talon nodded. "I always forget that. I always forget that

what happened to me also happened to them, but in a different way."

"You're absolutely right. But as I said, you can't do their healing for them."

"I know. I wish I could help."

"You can. You can take care of yourself."

He pressed his lips into a slight frown. "Doc?"

"Yes?"

"How do you think I'm doing? I mean, really."

"I've told you before, Talon. Your progress is amazing. You're doing great."

"Do you think I'm ready for..."

"What?"

He fidgeted, steepling his fingers. "I'd like to ask Jade to be my wife."

I couldn't help a broad smile. "I think that's wonderful."

"Do you think I'm ready? To make that kind of commitment?"

"Only you can answer that question. Just that you're asking, though, is huge. Remember, when you first came in here, you weren't sure you could even have a relationship with Jade."

He nodded. "True."

"If you're considering marriage now—I mean, if you are *letting* yourself consider it—then yes, I think you're ready."

He sighed. "I really want to put a ring on her finger. I want the world to know she's mine. And I do want to get married. I want her to be the mother of my children." He shook his head. "Children. Man, I never thought I wanted to bring children into this world. But now, with Jade, I do, Doc. I want children."

"That's wonderful. I think you'll be a great father."

A wide smile spread across his handsome face. "I don't know. But with Jade by my side, I feel like I can accomplish anything."

"You *can* accomplish anything. And it has nothing to do with Jade being by your side, although I know what you mean. Remember, you can do anything you set your mind to. Look how far you've come already."

He looked at his watch. "I have to cut our session a little bit short today, Doc. I have an appointment to meet a guy. The tattoo guy I told you about."

I nodded.

"He says he found some of his old records. I'm hoping maybe I can track down the man he did the phoenix tattoo on. I need to prove that Nico Kostas was one of my abductors."

Talon had already decided who two of his abductors had been. Strange thing was, he'd turned out to be right about one of them—his half-uncle, Larry Wade. What were the chances he was right about the other? Slim to none. But he knew my feelings on the matter. "I wish you the best of luck. I know it's important to you that you find them."

I watched as he walked out the door.

Talon Steel was a handsome man, no doubt. But he didn't make my heart flutter the way his brother Jonah did.

CHAPTER THREE

Jonah

I finished a hard day on the back forty, and after I had taken a quick shower, I decided to go for a swim. I lived in my own ranch house that I had built a while ago, before my father passed away. Things had gotten pretty cozy in the main house. The house might be five thousand square feet, but with my father, two brothers, and my sister, it was hard to get any alone time.

God knew I needed my alone time.

It was the only time I could think about things. Things I didn't want to talk about, that my brothers and sister would have seen on my face. I hated them asking what was wrong all the time.

I gave my golden retriever, Lucy, a quick pet, and then I dived into the cool water. I had always loved swimming. Truth be told, I preferred swimming to horseback riding. I rode with my brothers every so often, and of course I rode nearly every day taking care of the ranch, but it was really more my brothers' thing than it was mine. I preferred being surrounded by water. Many times I'd wished I lived by the ocean instead of in the Rocky Mountains. Not that I would trade my life for anything. I loved working the ranch. Sometimes I wondered if I had been some kind of sea mammal in another life, the way I loved the water so much. Water took my weight away, not only physically but emotionally and mentally as well. The guilt that consumed me on land washed away in the water.

I did two laps of freestyle and then switched to the backstroke, looking up into the sunset. Autumn was on the way now, and the days were growing shorter. I went on to the butterfly and then to the sidestroke, and then I rested, doing a few laps of the elementary backstroke. I could swim forever. And I loved every minute of it.

When my skin got pruny, I left the water and grabbed my towel.

Melanie Carmichael popped into my mind.

I wanted to see her again. And not for therapy. But she knew all about me and my fucked-up life. She would never be interested in seeing someone like me socially. So there was really only one way to see her. I had to make another appointment for therapy.

I'd give her a call tomorrow morning and set up an appointment.

I toweled off and lay down on a chaise longue, stretching. Lucy lay down beside me. I closed my eyes. What a day.

★ ★ ★ ★

"Hey, Joe," Talon said. "I want to go over to the Walker ranch and look around after school."

"What for?"

"Just want to find out what happened to Luke. It's not sitting right with me. He doesn't seem like the type who would run away."

"Of course he would run away," I said. "Those bullies are

always giving him a hard time. Why would he want to stay here?"

Talon shook his head. "Like I said, it just doesn't sit right with me. Sure, it's harder with the bullies, but...he's not the type to run. He takes it, you know?"

"You'd best go home. You'll get your ass whooped if you don't get your chores done."

"I'll get them done when I get home. I just want to figure this out."

"You don't even like the kid that much."

"I like him fine. And I hate what the bullies do to him."

"Best leave things alone," I said, shaking my head. "He'll make his way home soon enough."

"I want you to come with me, Joe."

I shook my head. "Heck, I've got major work to do this afternoon at home. And homework. I can't do it."

"I'm going anyway."

"Suit yourself."

Our youngest brother, Ryan, tugged on Talon's hand. "I'll go with you, Tal."

★ ★ ★ ★

My eyes shot open. It wasn't the first time I'd nodded off and relived that day. It wasn't a dream. It was a flashback to the day Talon had been taken. The day all our lives had changed.

If only I had gone with him...

★ ★ ★ ★

"I was surprised to get your call," Melanie said.

I let out a breath I hadn't realized I'd been holding. I

squirmed in the leather recliner. What to say? *I wanted to see you again, so I made an appointment for therapy I don't want?* Nope, that wouldn't do.

Again, silence.

"So why did you call? What would you like to talk about?"

Her hair was down today, falling in a silky cascade against a green satin blouse that matched her eyes.

"Honestly, I don't know."

She smiled. "Okay. Why don't you tell me about yourself? What's a normal day like for you, Jonah?"

I wasn't sure how talking about a normal day would help me, but she was the doctor. "I keep pretty busy. I'm in charge of the beef ranch. You probably know that Talon runs the orchards and Ryan the winery."

She nodded. "Actually, Talon and I have talked relatively little about his work. But yes, I did know that he handled the orchard. He brought me some of his luscious peaches. They were delicious."

Luscious peaches. I shot my gaze to her chest without meaning to. She wasn't huge like Jade, but damn, just the size of those large peaches from our orchard...and most likely just as succulent. What might Melanie taste like? A juicy peach? Maybe not. Maybe something completely unique. Yes, unique.

"I guess when he came in, you knew exactly what to talk about."

She chuckled. "Actually, no. He didn't really know what to talk about either. What you're experiencing is completely normal. So I try to start with something familiar, like your daily life. Usually we end up where we need to be."

"But you didn't do that with Talon."

"Of course I did. I just didn't start with his daily routine."

"What did you start with his first time?"

"Last time, you told me you didn't want to talk about my sessions with Talon."

True, I had. So why not just answer the question she asked?

"My life is pretty routine. I get up early, around five a.m., meet my foreman and several others in my office and get a look at the day's work. Sometimes I go out into the pastures myself. Other days I'm stuck doing paperwork all day."

"So you guys have a pretty big operation."

"Yes. The most successful ranch in Colorado. We have just under half a million acres, and we employ hundreds, and that's not counting seasonal work."

"Then you have a lot of responsibilities."

"Yeah. I mean, I'm mainly responsible for the ranch, but..."

"But?"

I stiffened.

Melanie continued, "But you feel responsible for everything, don't you?"

She was right. I did. I was the oldest, after all.

"If you take care of the beef, Talon takes care of the fruit, and Ryan takes care of the wine, what does your sister do?"

"Marjorie is a lot younger than we are. Right now, she just fills in and helps where she's needed. At some point, she'll probably decide whether to stay on the ranch and help us or to leave. Her true love is gourmet cooking. But she does own a quarter of the ranch. My father left it to all of us in equal portions, so she'll always have a cut."

Melanie nodded. "So tell me, if your siblings own three quarters of the operation, and you're all adults, why do you feel responsible for everything?"

Why did I? "Because I'm the oldest, I guess."

"Because you're the oldest. I see."

What did she see? I opened my mouth to ask the question, but she began speaking again.

"Jonah, you don't have to be responsible for everything."

"Oh, I know. My brothers both do their fair share. They work really hard, and Marj does whatever we ask her to. Whenever there's extra work to do, she's right there to lend a hand."

"Still, you feel responsible."

She was right. I did. Because I was the oldest. My father had told me that enough. *You're the oldest. You need to take care of things. Take care of your brothers and sister.*

I hadn't done a very good job.

"Tell me about your father," Melanie said.

Could this woman read my mind? After all, that was her job. Get inside my head. I still wasn't very comfortable with that.

"What does my father have to do with any of this? He's been dead for nearly eight years."

"You got the sense of responsibility from someone. Your father is as good a place as any to start."

"All right. My father was...pretty domineering. Very loving as well, don't get me wrong. He was a good father. He taught us all from a young age about ranching, about responsibility."

"But he taught you more about responsibility than the others."

I nodded. "I was the oldest. Of course I was expected to be the most responsible."

"And your father? Was he the oldest of his siblings?"

"He only had one brother, but yes, he was the older."

"That makes a lot of sense."

"How so?"

"He was most likely taught to be responsible as the older child, and because you were his oldest, he passed that on to you."

Did he ever. "Yes, he did."

"Did you ever resent being given such a large amount of responsibility at such a young age?"

"Maybe a little. But in a way I liked it as well. I was the oldest brother. I like being the oldest. I got to learn how to ride a horse first. I got to learn how to ride a bicycle first. I got to learn how to drive a tractor, a car. I got my own room, when Talon and Ryan shared one."

"Didn't you grow up in a large ranch house?"

"Yeah, but the two of them liked sharing a room. At least until after..." I cleared my throat. "Talon wanted his own room after that. But me, I always wanted my own. I like alone time."

"Alone time. Why do you think that is? Why do you like being alone so much?"

"I don't know. I always have."

"Do you think it was because it let you escape the responsibility of being the oldest brother sometimes?"

My palms began to itch. Damn, this woman was getting inside my head, and all my defenses were yelling at me to make it stop. I clenched the arms of the recliner, getting ready to stand.

"Going somewhere?"

"What do you mean?"

"You're bracing to leave. Your body language is speaking volumes right now, Jonah."

She was in my head all right. Well, that was what I was

paying for. How was I supposed to let her into my psyche when all I could think about was getting her into my bed?

I forced myself to relax. "You must have misread me. I'm not planning to go anywhere."

She smiled. "All right."

She was pacifying me. I could tell. She didn't believe for a minute that she had misread me.

And of course she was right.

"So let's get back to you and your alone time. Do you still like your alone time now?"

I nodded.

"What you do during your alone time?"

"Sometimes nothing. Sometimes I swim. I have a lap pool at my house. I've always loved the water."

"I see. What is it that you love about the water?"

"I don't know, really. I guess I just like the way it wraps itself around me."

"Like a shield?"

"I don't know. Maybe. It seems to..."

"What?"

"It...soothes me. Takes the weight away."

"I see. That makes a lot of sense. What else do you do while you're alone?"

Well, I jacked off a lot. But I sure as hell wasn't going to tell her that. It had been way too long since I'd had a woman. Even though I'd had girlfriends in the past, I'd never had what I thought was a serious relationship. Only one of us had—before Talon and Jade, that was. Ryan had been with a woman named Anna for several years, but they'd ended up calling it off.

"Sometimes I read up on ranching, agriculture."

She laughed softly. "That's part of your work. I'm talking

about your free time. Your alone time. What do you do besides swim?"

I honestly didn't know how to answer her. If I wasn't swimming or sleeping, I was doing something involving the ranch, whether it was reading up on new techniques, attending a conference, or talking to my brothers or my foreman. God, had I really become so involved in my work?

"I...hang out with my brothers and sister."

"What about friends? What about a girlfriend?"

"Talon has a group of guys he plays poker with. Ryan joins them sometimes."

"But you don't?"

"No. I don't really believe in gambling."

"Why not?"

"I just don't."

"Why do you think that is?"

I had no idea what she was driving at with this line of questioning. "Isn't it better not to gamble, Melanie? I mean, it can lead to addiction, right?"

"Do you think you have an addictive personality?"

This was getting way off track. "Of course not."

"All right. I'll move on, then. What about dating?"

Was it my imagination, or did her cheeks turn pink just a little bit at the mention of dating? "I don't have time. Plus, I haven't met anyone I'm interested in." Until now, that was.

"Friendships?"

"Again, I grab a drink with some of the guys on the ranch sometimes, sometimes my brothers."

"No one else?"

"Well, my best buddy from my childhood just came for a visit. He's actually the cousin of one of the kids who was killed back when Talon was abducted."

"I see. So you've spent some time with him, then?"

"Yeah. He's still here. He has a ten-month-old little boy who's really cute."

"How old are you, Jonah?"

"I'm thirty-eight. How old are you?"

I shouldn't have asked that. I wasn't sure why it had popped out.

"I'm forty."

I hoped my shock didn't show on my face. I'd have pegged her for much younger, but all that schooling...and she'd been in practice for a while. Of course she was older.

She continued, "But we're not here to talk about me, are we?"

"I'm sorry. That was personal."

"No worries. I'm not one of those women who gets weird about her age."

"No reason you should. You look great. I'd take you for late twenties."

She blushed again, this time all the way down her neck. Her skin was fair, and the rosiness erupted like pink petals against her flesh.

My groin tightened.

"Thank you. Let's get back to your friendships. You mentioned that your friend has a little boy. Do you ever think about having a family?"

I tensed up. "For a long time, I didn't. But now I see what Talon and Jade have together, and I wonder..."

"What do you wonder about?"

"I wonder if...if there's someone like Jade out there for me." And I also wondered if she might be sitting across from me.

"I mean, if Talon, with all of his past, can make a relationship work, maybe there's hope for me."

"I think there's plenty of hope for you." She looked at the clock on her table. "Our time is up for today. I want you to think about something before we meet again."

"Sure. What's that?"

"I want you to think about what your responsibilities truly are, and the next time you come in, we'll talk about that."

"Easy. I'm responsible for everything. It's my ranch."

"It's one-*quarter* your ranch. Let your siblings do their jobs. When you come back next time, I want to know what you're truly responsible for. Not what you think you're responsible for, but what you actually *are* responsible for."

Seemed like a simple enough question. So why did I have no idea where to start?

CHAPTER FOUR

Melanie

I sat down in my chair, shaking, after Jonah Steel left my office. The poor man felt the weight of the world upon his shoulders, and I wasn't sure how to help him realize that it was not his responsibility. I specialized in treating victims of childhood trauma, and in his own way, Jonah was a victim of childhood trauma. But I had the feeling that his problems went further back than Talon's abduction. Somehow he had grown to believe he was responsible for everything in his life, and I had to figure out how to disavow him of that that notion.

More importantly, if I was to truly help, I had to get rid of my sweaty palms and quivering body. Jonah was the most attractive man I'd met in some time, and I didn't mean just his amazing physical looks. I was a sucker for someone like him—a man who had so much honor that it became his nemesis. Jonah wanted to protect everyone, but he couldn't. He was only one man. And twenty-five years ago, he was a thirteen-year-old boy.

How I ached to help him. But I wasn't sure I was the right therapist for this job.

I riffled through the papers on my desk, looking for Brad Logan's number. He might be a better fit for Jonah. For some reason, his number wasn't in my phone or in my paper

Rolodex on my desk. I hadn't seen him in over a year, but he'd given me a business card then. I wouldn't have thrown it away. My desk was an infernal mess, of course. I was as disorganized as anything. It was a wonder I ever got anything accomplished. Paper after paper after paper. I'd have to have Randi go through all this stuff. Normally my office was my sanctuary and Randi did her work out in the reception area, but this was more than I could handle. I picked up some folders to take them out to her desk for filing, when a piece of paper slipped out of one.

I glanced at the floor, and my heart sank. I knew what it was before I picked it up.

The piece of stationery was pink and tear-stained. Whether they were my tears or Gina's, I wasn't sure. The pain was still new and raw.

Six months had passed, but I hadn't dealt with all these emotions. Oh, I put up a good front. I told the few who knew that I'd made peace as best I could with what had occurred, and I repeated my own advice—advice I gave to all my patients— in my head. *You have to want to heal, and you have to do it for yourself.* Did I *not* want to heal on some subconscious level? Many times I'd thought about calling Brad for my own benefit, but I hadn't. I resisted.

Physician, heal thyself.

I glanced up the wall behind my desk. My MD was framed there, along with my master's in psychotherapy.

I should be able to get through this. I knew that.

Could a doctor ever get over losing a patient?

My hands trembled as my gaze, seemingly of its own accord, was drawn like a magnet to Gina's words.

Dear Dr. Carmichael,

I can no longer go on.

This isn't your fault. You did your best to try to help me, but I'll never be able to forget what my uncle did to me when I was so young. I tried, and I prayed that I could heal, but it's just not in the cards for me.

There's something else I need to tell you. This isn't easy for me, and I wish with all my soul that I had the courage to tell you in person.

I love you.

And no, I don't mean I love you as a friend or as a therapist. I mean I'm in love with you. I'm truly in love with you.

I don't normally fall in love with women, at least I never have before. The feelings I have for you are so strong that I'm not sure I've ever felt anything close to them for anyone, male or female. I dream of kissing your red lips, taking you into my bed and making love. I dream of you holding me in your arms, chasing the beasts away.

I don't expect you to return my feelings. I know you could never be interested in someone as horribly defective as I am. But before I leave this earth forever, I want you to know how I feel.

Please don't blame yourself. I know you did your best for me. No one on this Earth could have helped me. I'm too damaged. I wanted to be whole, but I know now that I never will be. I'm not good enough for you or anyone else. You deserve so much better.

That's why I must leave. Please don't worry about me. I've chosen a painless and cowardly way to die. For that's what I am, a coward. I don't have anything more to give to this life.

I will love you forever, even beyond the grave.

Yours,

Gina

I sighed as tears emerged in the corners of my eyes. I had a good record with my patients. I was able to help most of them, and the few I couldn't help, I always referred to someone else.

But I hadn't been able to help Gina Cates. She'd come to me about a year ago, suffering from night terrors and depression. She'd been repeatedly raped by her uncle between the ages of eight and thirteen. She never told anyone about the abuse, and the uncle was now dead. However, I'd been blind to the fact that she'd fallen in love and blind to the fact that she was suicidal. That haunted me to this day. Was it because I was a straight woman that I didn't recognize that another woman loved me? I'd been over and over it in my mind. I should've noticed. I should've had her hospitalized. I should've done a lot of things, but I hadn't.

If I had, Gina might still be alive.

She had closed herself in her garage, opened her car windows, and turned on the ignition. The carbon monoxide put her to sleep and killed her peacefully. She stayed in her garage for three days, until I received the letter. I alerted her parents and the police, saying I was concerned because she'd missed an appointment, and they found her.

I never told anyone about her letter.

I cradled my head in my hands, sitting down in my chair at my desk. I concentrated on holding back the tears that wanted to fall, until I jerked forward. Someone had knocked on my door.

I grabbed a tissue and wiped my eyes and nose quickly. I cleared my throat. "Yes, come on in, Randi." I stood.

But it wasn't Randi who opened my door.

Jonah Steel, in all his masculine glory, walked into my office.

"I'm sorry to bother you, but I think I left my—"

I ran into his arms, nearly knocking him over. The tears I'd tried so hard to hold back gushed forth, wetting his black cotton shirt.

He gently stroked my hair, saying nothing. I held on to him in a fierce clench. He was so hard, so solid...like a rock in the midst of a stormy hurricane at sea. I sobbed into his shoulder, soaking him, but still he stroked my hair, murmuring gentle sounds.

"It's okay," he said. "Whatever it is, it's okay."

Oh, if he only knew.

He moved backward, trying to release my hold on him. At the thought of him leaving, I grabbed him, wrapped my arms around his neck, and pulled his mouth toward mine.

Unprofessional, yes, but that was my last thought when his firm lips opened beneath mine.

He returned my kiss, swirling his tongue into my mouth. He tasted of sweet mint and cloves—so perfect and so right. I had dreamed of kissing him when I saw him at that hotel bar months ago. He was so out of my league, but right now he was responding to me. He pulled me closer, ground his hardness into my belly. *My God, is he as attracted to me as I am to him?*

When I pulled away, taking a needed breath, he bit my earlobe.

"I've wanted to kiss you like that since I first saw you," he whispered. "And today, sitting across from you, I could hardly think of anything else."

I melted against him. He wanted me? Truly wanted me the way I wanted him?

No more talking. I drew in all the oxygen I needed and pressed my lips back to his. He kissed me with fervor, passion, so deeply—more deeply than anyone ever had.

The kiss was trance-inducing, as if I'd never been kissed before. As if all the men who had ever kissed me were just leading up to this—the ultimate kiss, the only real kiss I'd ever been given.

I poured everything inside me into the kiss, wanting desperately to escape all my troubles. Jonah Steel was alone. Alone like I was. Struggling with responsibilities he felt he had neglected.

But no kiss, not even one this amazing, could make up for those neglected responsibilities. I was a therapist. I knew better than to be seduced into a physical break from reality. I forced my mouth from his, whimpering at the loss.

I stumbled backward, nearly losing my footing, but he caught me. I looked into his dark gaze. Fire burned within those eyes. Fire that I wanted to stoke with more kisses, more... everything.

"I'm so sorry." I touched my lips, so tender from his kiss. "I... I don't know what came over me. That was completely unprofessional. Please believe me. I've never done anything like—"

His lips came down on mine again, and all the sense I'd just had a moment before fled out the window. Again I opened for him, and again I took his tongue into my mouth. My nipples tightened against my bra, threatening to poke through the cotton fabric. Again his hardness nudged my belly. If only this could be. If only I could take what he was offering and escape— escape the responsibility for Gina's death and everything else that had gone wrong in my life. But again, reality prevailed. I knew better, better than anyone, that I couldn't run away from my problems.

Still, my body was ready. I throbbed between my legs, my nerves on edge. My senses were heightened, and I inhaled. He smelled of leather and musk, a little like the outdoors. He ravaged my mouth, taking and giving. And I gave back. I poured everything into that kiss, even though I knew it was wrong.

When I had to pause for another breath, he dragged me to him, whispering, "My God. Melanie, my God."

"I'm so sorry," I said again. "So very sorry."

He pulled back slightly again, and I met those blazing dark eyes.

"Why are you sorry? I'm sure not."

I took advantage of my position and pushed him hard, so his back hit the wall by the door to my office. I gasped. The office door was still open. Where was Randi? I looked out the door toward the reception area.

"No one's out there," Jonah said. "That's why I knocked on your door."

Randi had a dental appointment this afternoon. I'd forgotten. "Right. She left early."

Jonah smiled at me. God, he was gorgeous.

"I, for one, am glad she's not here." He came toward me.

I held up my hand. "No."

"Why? Aren't you enjoying it?"

I'd never enjoyed a kiss more. That wasn't the point. "It's unprofessional. I'm your therapist."

He smiled again, and my heart nearly melted right onto the floor.

"We can take care of that. I can find another therapist."

He was temptation personified. Such a beautiful man, so strong, so virile. I could have him. His erection was apparent beneath his jeans, and perspiration was slick on his skin.

But I couldn't do it. I just couldn't.

"After this, you probably need to find another therapist regardless. This was completely unprofessional behavior on my part, and I hope..." My lips trembled. "My only excuse is that I was looking at papers when you came in, some papers from a former patient. I was overly emotional, and I—"

He walked forward and covered my lips with his finger. "Shh. You don't need to explain anything. You're an amazing kisser, Melanie."

I warmed from my scalp to my toes. I looked down. My blouse was mussed, and my nipples were protruding right through my bra and the silky green fabric. I quickly crossed my arms over my chest. "Please, this is not something I normally do. I've never kissed a patient before."

"Do I look like I'm complaining?"

"Professionalism is very important to me, Mr. Steel."

"Now we're back to Mr. Steel?"

"Uh...Jonah." His name left my lips as a soft caress. Jonah. What a beautiful name—a rugged, masculine name for a rugged, masculine man. "Please, I need you to accept my apology."

"Fine, if it makes you feel better. I accept your apology. And I'd love to accept another kiss."

God, so would I. But that wasn't going to happen. I fussed with my blouse a bit, willing my nipples to soften. I cleared my throat. "I'm sorry. Why did you come back?"

He stalked toward me, a feral look in his dark eyes. "My cell phone seems to be missing. Otherwise I would've called you before I barged back in."

I nodded. "Go ahead and have a look."

He headed toward the chair where he'd been sitting, and

sure enough, a few seconds later, he held up his phone.

I shook all over. More than anything, I wanted him to kiss me again.

His eyes were so full of fire. So full of want and need. The air between us was thick with lust. Or was it my imagination?

All I knew for sure was that if he didn't leave my office this instant, I would launch myself at him again. I dug my feet into the carpeting, forcing them to stay where they were. Turned out it was futile, because he came toward me.

"Melanie," he said.

My name from his lips sounded beautiful. A verbal caress. Still, I forced my feet not to move.

"No." I held up my hand. "Stop right there. Don't come any closer to me."

Still, he stalked forward. "Why? Why do you want to deny whatever this is between us?"

"I... You're a patient. You're not available to me. And even if I wanted you to be available to me, I'm not in any state to begin anything with anyone."

"I told you before. I'll find another therapist."

"Jonah, you're not hearing me. I'm a mess. And I'm not looking for a quickie on my desk."

"Who said anything about a quickie?"

"I... Just the way you're looking at me." Visions of him swooshing the disorganized papers from my desk and thrusting into me atop it littered my mind. My nipples puckered, and again I throbbed between my legs.

How long had it been for me? I hadn't had any kind of relationship in over five years, and other than a few one-night stands, which I wasn't particularly proud of, I hadn't had any sex either.

A quickie with Jonah Steel wasn't the worst idea.

But not now. He was a patient. His brother was a patient. It was just all too wrong.

As he closed the distance between us, I crossed my arms over my chest again, wishing I formed a more imposing presence.

"You just stop right there. Don't come any nearer to me. I swear to God, I will scream."

CHAPTER FIVE

Jonah

I stalked toward her. "Who's going to hear you? You said yourself the secretary is gone for the day."

"There are people in the offices adjacent to mine," she said, chewing on her lip.

I closed the distance between us with one more stride, grabbing her hand. I placed it on the bulge beneath my jeans. "You feel that? Feel how much I want you?"

Her hands trembled against mine.

"Tell me you don't want me. Tell me you're not wet for me right now, and I'll never bother you again."

She shivered against me, and her nipples poked out from the green silk of her blouse. I reached toward her and fingered one.

She groaned, closing her eyes.

"It's been a long time since I've had a woman, Melanie. A long, long time. I want you. Tell me you want me too."

She shook her head, still biting her lower lip. Her skin turned that rosy pink I had seen during our session.

I lowered my voice, moving to her ear. "Just tell me. Tell me you don't want me, and I'll go."

She pushed me backward. "I can't. Don't you understand?"

"From where I'm standing, Melanie, we're both consenting

adults. You told me your age. So what's so wrong about it?"

"I... I can't do this anymore." She grabbed her handbag from the corner of her desk. "Please, let yourself out."

Within seconds, she was gone.

★ ★ ★ ★

I met my buddy Bryce Simpson at Murphy's Bar in Snow Creek later that evening.

"Who's watching the kid tonight?" I asked, referring to his ten-month-old son, Henry.

"My mom and dad. They're crazy about the little guy."

"Are you still staying at the house with them?" Bryce's father was the mayor of Snow Creek.

"Yeah, for now. I'm looking to find a place of my own. I think Henry and I might stay here for a while."

"Really? That would be great. I was just telling—" Whoops, I had been about to say that I had told a therapist that I had very few friends. So didn't want to go there. "I was just thinking that it would be nice to have you around."

"I hear Talon has a girl."

I took a sip of my CapRock martini and nodded. "Yeah, she's very nice. Young though. Only twenty-five. Marj's age."

"Wow, that *is* young."

"She doesn't seem young though. She's the city attorney."

"Yeah, I heard. That's crazy what happened with Larry Wade."

I nodded. "News travels fast."

Bryce's eyes went glassy. "I'm sure sorry about what happened to Talon. I had no idea."

I still didn't know how to respond to things like this. I

wanted to squirm and pretend I hadn't heard Bryce. I could only imagine how uncomfortable it was for Talon. "No one did. It was very hush-hush."

"Why? Why didn't your parents try to find out what had happened?"

"That's what we're all trying to figure out. They had their reasons for keeping quiet, I guess. But at least one of those motherfuckers will come to justice."

"Pretty scary," he said. "It could have been either one of us."

True that. It had haunted me since it happened twenty-five years ago. I swallowed the lump that had formed in my throat. "Yeah, it should have happened to me."

"What the heck are you talking about?"

I cleared my throat. Bryce was my oldest friend. If I couldn't be honest with him, I couldn't be honest with anyone. "The day Talon was taken, he went out to the Walkers' ranch to look for clues. He asked me to go with him, but I refused. If I had gone..."

"If you'd gone, they'd have taken both of you."

I shook my head. "Ryan was with him, and he got away. He got away because Talon protected him. He protected his little brother, like I should've protected mine."

"You can't hold on to something that happened so long ago, man."

If only it were that simple, but I didn't think for a minute Bryce would understand. Then again, maybe he would. Luke Walker, the boy who had been kidnapped before Talon, was Bryce's cousin. Talon had told Ryan and me what had happened to Luke Walker. Two of the kidnappers had chopped him up into pieces while they forced my brother to watch. I chilled to the bone. I couldn't be the one who told Bryce that horror story. Still, he might understand my feelings about failing to protect Talon.

"Do you ever feel guilty about what happened to Luke? He wasn't your brother, but he was your cousin."

"I missed him, even though we weren't overly close. We didn't have a lot in common." He shrugged. "But guilt? Not really. Maybe I should have. It was horrible that he disappeared and was never found. I was bummed when he disappeared, but nobody knew he was taken. We all thought he'd run away at first and that he'd eventually show up."

"But then Talon disappeared."

"But remember, none of us knew about Talon. It happened during the summer, and by the time school started up again, Talon was back. Then your parents covered it up, so no one knew."

He was right, but then something shot into my mind. "You know, I never thought of this before, but after Talon, no one else was taken. At least not from around here."

Bryce nodded. "You're right."

Larry Wade had been caught, but the other two hadn't. Those two could have kept abducting kids. "My parents knew Larry Wade was one of Talon's kidnappers, and they let him get away with it. I sure as hell don't know why. Larry claims he helped Talon escape, and maybe he did, but I still don't get why my parents let him go."

"Have you asked Larry?"

"I haven't gone to see him. Only Jade has. I'm not sure Talon could hold it together. Hell, I'm not sure I could either."

"Did Larry tell Jade anything?"

"No. Larry won't say a word about the other two. He's

scared to death of them. We don't know who the hell they are, and he won't roll over on them."

"That is a pickle."

"A pickle?" I laughed, despite the somber subject.

"Just a phrase my mom uses," Bryce said. "I'm sure you've heard me use it before."

I shook my head. "I'm certain I'd remember that. But seriously, I don't know. Maybe I *should* go talk to the SOB. I can force myself to hold it together. God knows I've done it before. Nothing to lose, except a couple hours of my life."

"I'll go with you, if you want. I'd like to pick his brain about Luke. My cousin could be alive somewhere for all I know."

Poor Bryce. I'd have to tell him the truth about Luke at some point. But not right now. I loved the idea of him going with me, though. Facing Larry alone was more than I could stomach. "Would you really go along? I'd be grateful for the company, and I can't ask one of my brothers to go with me, especially not Talon. They have to go in their own time. But I should talk to Talon first. It's really his call whether I go. This is his story, not mine."

"That's true to a point. But we don't need his permission to talk to Larry. Why shouldn't we try to figure out what happened? We can help Talon all the better the more we know, and I'd like to find out more about what happened to Luke."

"It's a plan, then," I said. "We'll go see Larry. Does tomorrow work for you?"

"I set up a bunch of appointments to look at houses tomorrow. How about sometime next week?"

"Sounds good. God knows I have work to do around the ranch."

Something occurred to me then, something I hadn't yet

asked Bryce about. "Tell me about Henry's mother. What happened between you two?"

Bryce chuckled. "She was really hot, and I was drunk and in Las Vegas. That's about the sum of it. Not one of my finer moments."

"So how long were you two together?"

"About a year. She got pregnant the first night we were together. My own damned fault. I was shit-faced and forgot the condom. She gave me the 'Oh, honey, it's okay. I'm on the pill,' line. What a crock."

"She's not the first one to use that line."

"Yes, I should've known better. I'm not an idiot."

"No, you're not. But look at that cute little boy you got out of it. Is she in the picture at all now?"

"Not really, and it's just as well. She has no business having a kid. I requested custody, and she didn't fight me on it. It was a quickie divorce, just like it had been a quickie marriage."

"At least it was a relationship. It's more than I've had."

"It was no relationship, Joe. It was a one-night stand with consequences."

"What was her name?"

"Francine. Francine Stokes. She's a topless dancer."

I smirked. "Are you going to tell Henry about her one day?"

"Of course I will. He has a right to know who his mother is."

I nodded. "I never thought about having kids, at least not until I saw you with Henry when you came back to town."

"Neither did I," Bryce said. "But I have one now. And you know what? I'm not sure how I ever got along without the little guy. Kids change things, Joe. I can't say how much I look forward to his little smile. And my parents are having a blast. I'm no spring rooster. I wasn't sure I'd ever have a kid, but I'm sure glad I do."

My parents hadn't lived to see any grandchildren, but I felt certain there would be some. Jade and Talon would probably have a child at some point. Would I? I'd have liked to think I would.

Melanie Carmichael's face popped into my head. She had gotten to me the first time I saw her, and now, after that kiss... I wasn't sure how to deal with it. There wouldn't be any need to deal with it, because she had called it off. She didn't want to have a relationship with me, so I had no other choice. If I wanted to see her, I had to make another appointment for therapy.

Whether she would take my appointment was up in the air.

CHAPTER SIX

Melanie

Gina's parents had never contacted me.

I sat in my bedroom in my loft in downtown Grand Junction, reading over Gina's file. Yes, it was self-torture, but after I had inadvertently come across her letter earlier, I couldn't help myself. This was far from the first time I had pored through the file, wondering where I had gone wrong. I'd taken copious notes after each session, just like I did with all my patients. I never took notes during the session. I liked to concentrate on the patient. But I was very detailed in my notes once the session was over.

At no time during the six months I treated her had she given me any reason to indicate that she was suicidal. What had I missed? Had I not asked the right questions? Had I not read between the lines as I should have? And how could I have not realized she had feelings of love for me? How had I missed that?

Developing feelings for one's therapist was very normal. I'd had it happen before in my career. It had been with a man, and I had nipped it in the bud right away and sent him to another therapist—just like I was going to do with Jonah Steel. Was it because Gina was a woman that I hadn't seen it coming? And did the fact that she'd fallen in love with me have anything to do with how she presented herself? Perhaps she'd wanted to look good for me, and she put on an act so I wouldn't realize she was suicidal.

I sighed. Gina had been through hell. But so had Talon Steel, and he wasn't suicidal. So had most of my patients, and very few were suicidal. But Gina had been, and I hadn't seen it.

A good therapist should have been able to tell. Frantically I searched the file, looking for something—anything—I had missed.

I eyed the cordless phone on my night table. So many times I'd been tempted to pick it up and call Gina's parents, to offer my apology. I'd tried a few days after her death, but her mother had refused to take my call, and I'd been advised by counsel not to contact them again.

I had never been sued before, and I had no reason to believe I would be now.

Of its own accord, my hand reached for the phone. It was eight p.m., not too late to call. Without thinking, I dialed the number of Gina's parents in Denver.

"Hello?" a masculine voice said.

I quickly ended the call.

What had I been thinking? I stuffed the papers back into Gina's file. I got up. Maybe a nice warm bath would help. I stripped off my clothes, put on a robe, and was heading toward my bathroom door when my phone rang.

A quick look at the caller ID, and my heart sank. The number I'd just called. Shit. What had I done? I couldn't ignore the call. Well, I could, but they could easily find out who the number belonged to. No, best to deal with the consequences now.

I picked up the cordless. "Hello?"

"Yes." A throat cleared. "We just got a call from this number?"

"Is this Mr. Cates?"

"Dr. Cates, yes."

Right. He had a Ph.D. in linguistics. "I'm sorry to disturb you. This is Melanie Carmichael. I was your daughter Gina's therapist. Yes, I did try calling earlier, but the call didn't go through. I thought I would try again in the morning." I bit my lip, hoping he'd buy the lie.

"What is it that you want, Dr. Carmichael?"

I cleared my throat this time. "I just wanted to check in with you and your wife. See if there was anything I could do for you."

"We are doing as well as can be expected. The loss of our daughter has been hard to bear."

"I'm sure it has been. It's been weighing heavily on my mind as well. I'm so very sorry for your loss."

"Yes, I'm sure you are."

What was that supposed to mean? I had no idea. This call had been a mistake. I knew better than to let my emotions get the better of me. "Gina was a very special person." I bit my lip. I wanted to say that she was in a better place, that she was happier now, free of the burdens of this life, but I didn't know what his beliefs were, and I wasn't sure I believed that stuff myself. Instead I said, "If there's anything I can do for you, please don't hesitate to let me know. I apologize for intruding on your evening. Good night."

Dr. Cates said nothing, so I ended the call.

Gina hadn't left a suicide note other than the letter she sent to me. I hadn't shared that with her parents, and they hadn't asked for anything from me. Should I have told them about the letter? It was personal, not part of the record, and I was not obligated to divulge it to them. Plus, I wasn't sure how they would feel about their daughter falling in love with her female therapist. She told me herself she had only dated men, so they probably had no idea she was gay or bisexual.

If only I could go back—go back and do something differently—Gina might be alive today.

But there was no going back. Like Jonah Steel, I was filled with guilt. Filled with a case of the "what ifs." How many times had I told my patients not to play the "what if" game? It was damned good advice, too. Still, I couldn't help playing the game myself. What if I had done something differently? What if I had seen that she was harboring feelings for me? What if I had seen something to indicate she was suicidal?

But I hadn't.

And I couldn't go back in time, as much as I wished to.

★ ★ ★ ★

A couple of days later, when Randi gave me my schedule for the day, I widened my eyes.

"Jonah Steel?"

"Yeah. He called yesterday, and you had an opening because Macy Andrews canceled at the last minute. So I slipped him in."

"Okay." I had neglected to tell Randi not to schedule him again. Honestly, I hadn't thought about it. I figured he wouldn't call after the last time. "I won't be seeing him as a patient anymore, but there was no reason for you to know that. I'll call him myself and cancel."

"I'm happy to do that for you, Dr. Carmichael."

"No, I need to do this. Thanks, though."

I closed my door behind me and headed to my desk. I grabbed Jonah's file and found his number. And of course I got voice mail.

"This is Jonah Steel. Please leave a message."

Short and sweet. Very Jonah-like. "Hello. This is Melanie Carmichael. I see you scheduled an appointment for this afternoon at three. I'm afraid I have to cancel. As you know, given what happened the other day, I can't see you professionally anymore. I'm happy to recommend another therapist. I wish you the best."

Good. That was that. Hopefully he'd get the message.

And then suddenly I knew he wouldn't. So I got online and looked up the number for Steel Acres ranch. I tapped in the number.

"Steel Acres, may I help you?"

"Yes, please, I'd like to speak to Jonah Steel."

"I'm sorry. Mr. Steel isn't in the office. He's in the pastures, and he's going to the city this afternoon for an appointment."

Of course. An appointment. With me.

"May I take a message?"

"Yes, this is Dr. Melanie Carmichael. I have to cancel his appointment for this afternoon. Please let him know."

"Did you try his cell phone? He won't be back in the office today."

"I did, but I would appreciate if you could also try to get the message to him."

"Of course. I'll do my best."

But it wouldn't happen. Jonah would not get my message, or if he did, it wouldn't matter. He would show up in my office at three o'clock today.

★ ★ ★ ★

"Sorry, I didn't get a message." His eyes glinted with mischief.

He had gotten my message, all right.

It wouldn't do any good to fight him on it. He was here, so I'd say my piece in person.

"Mr. Steel."

"Jonah."

"Fine, Jonah. You cannot be here. You know why— because of my unprofessional behavior the last time you were here. I should not have kissed you. That effectively destroyed any doctor-patient relationship we had."

"Well, you're the only therapist I want. If I can't talk to you, I don't want to talk to anyone."

"Jonah, you're putting me between a rock and a hard place. I want you to have therapy."

"Then give me therapy. Here I am."

I sighed. "Look, I have this hour available. Let's talk if you want to talk. But it will be like two friends talking. This won't be therapy. I won't charge you for it."

"That doesn't seem very fair."

I shook my head. "I feel very strongly about this. I won't charge you. Just two friends talking."

He smiled. "What if I want to be more than friends?"

"Oh my God, you're not making this easy."

"Good things never come easy, Melanie."

"Just sit down," I said. "Since you're determined to be here, let's at least talk about something."

"Okay. Last time you asked me to think about what I was truly responsible for."

Had I? Normally I reviewed the patient's file prior to a session, but because I didn't have any intention of having a session with Jonah, I hadn't. "That's right. So let's start there."

"I am responsible for the beef ranch."

"And?"

"That's it."

"All right. So you're responsible for the beef ranch. Technically, that's all you're responsible for."

"Yes."

"Now, what do you *feel* responsible for?"

He sighed. "Everything. I feel responsible for everything, Melanie."

CHAPTER SEVEN

Jonah

Her beautiful emerald eyes focused intently on me. Melanie Carmichael was an old soul. Until now, I had never believed in any of that crap. But those eyes... They had seen things. Things I couldn't even begin to imagine.

"You know what I mean, don't you, Melanie?"

She chewed on her bottom lip.

She knew.

"Yes, I do know what you mean. For people in your situation, it's very common."

I shook my head. "No, that's not what I mean. I mean you *know*. You, personally, know."

She said nothing, just looked down at her hands folded in her lap.

"You gnaw on that lower lip of yours any more, and you're liable to draw blood."

"We're not here to talk about me."

"Why not? This is just a friend talking to a friend, remember? This isn't therapy. Those are your rules. Not mine."

She looked at me, her green eyes glaring. "What makes you think I'm your friend?"

"Isn't that what you said? It would be like a friend talking to a friend? I think you're the one who said we were friends,

Mel."

"No one calls me Mel."

"It's a spunky name." I smiled. "I feel like you need a little spunk in your life."

"You don't know me well enough to know what I need."

"Melanie it is, then. I'd like to get to know you. *Melanie.*"

She gnawed on that lower lip again. Damn, she was sexy. Her lips were already red as currants, but when she nibbled on them like that, they turned a deeper burgundy. Melanie Carmichael had great lips.

"So why do you think you're responsible for everything?" she asked.

Back to that, were we? Well, I could play this game. "I don't really know. Why do you think you're responsible for everything?"

There went the teeth on the lip again. "I don't."

Maybe she didn't. Maybe I was misreading her. But I was pretty sure little miss therapist had her own baggage. And I was going to find out what it was.

"Let me answer your question. I don't really know why I feel responsible. I am the oldest, and my father told me to protect my younger brothers. Marjorie too, when she came along. Although at that point, I had already failed miserably protecting my brother."

"And you never got over that."

"No, I didn't. And there's something you never got over as well, isn't there?"

"I don't want to talk about me."

"All right. That's fair. Tell me how I can help myself, then. Tell me how I can leave all this fucking guilt at the door and have a good life. Because that's what I want, Melanie. I want a good life, a life of happiness and wonder. A life filled with love. How do I find that?"

Her green eyes misted over. Hell, I hadn't meant to make her cry. It looked like the waterworks were coming. I wanted to go to her, force her out of the chair, and hold her, tell her everything was all right.

But I didn't know if everything *was* all right.

I sure as hell didn't know how to get away from my own guilt. How could I help her with hers? She was the therapist, not me. I stayed seated, willing my body to relax. This was her office. She hadn't come to me like she had the last time. When she'd rushed toward me and launched herself at my heart, I hadn't known what to do. So I'd done nothing, just held her, and then she pulled me down for that kiss—that amazing kiss.

I had never experienced a kiss like that. Never. Not even in my younger days.

"Melanie? Are you going to answer me?"

"I..."

"What?"

"I just can't. I can't tell you how to get over the guilt, Jonah, because I just don't know how to do it for myself."

"I don't believe that for a minute. You're the best of the best."

"I specialize in childhood trauma. Not adult guilt."

"Then why did you agree to see me?"

She shrugged, looking away. "Talon asked me to. He was worried about you after you were found nearly beaten to death. And I also didn't realize..."

"What?"

"That we would..." She sighed.

"That we would be so attracted to each other?"

She nodded.

"Well, I'm about as attracted to you as I've ever been to anyone. You're beautiful. I can see everything in those gorgeous green eyes of yours. You've felt things, experienced things. And physically, your damn near perfect. Your blond hair is like silk flowing over your shoulders, and your body—"

She looked away. "There's nothing special about my body. Nothing special at all."

"While I haven't had the pleasure of seeing it—unclothed, that is—I think you're probably wrong about that."

"I'm not curvy enough. I'm too tall."

"You don't look too tall from where I'm standing."

"Most men aren't as tall as you."

"My sister stands near six feet tall. I'm used to tall women. I like tall women."

She said nothing, just chewed on her bottom lip.

"Listen, I'm attracted to you, and I know you're attracted to me. Okay, so we both have issues. Maybe we both need some therapy. But can't we get to know each other? It's been a long time since I met a woman who I want to get to know, Melanie."

"I'm not who you think I am."

"I know you're brilliant. I know how far you brought my brother in just a few months. And I know you've done that for others as well. So you're feeling a little inadequate right now. Don't we all feel like that from time to time? I've felt inadequate for the last twenty-five years of my life."

"I have no business being in a relationship with you or anyone."

Fine. "Who said anything about a relationship? Why don't we just go to bed?"

She blushed from her forehead down to the tips of her

fingers. My guess was she was pink all the way to her toes, though she was wearing pumps and I couldn't see them.

"So I've embarrassed you?"

"I'm not used to men being so forward."

"Hey, you started this. You kissed me the other day, remember?"

She blushed even rosier.

"Melanie, I'm not asking for your hand in marriage. I'm not even asking for anything beyond tomorrow. But why not? I fucking want you so much I can't see straight. Let me take you to a hotel. Let me take you into my bed. I promise you that you won't regret it."

CHAPTER EIGHT

Melanie

I was too weak to resist him. He wanted me, and I wanted him. No reason to look beyond tomorrow.

In a pink haze, I somehow ended up in a suite at the Carlton with Jonah removing my clothes. I hadn't said more than a few mumbled words since we'd left my office.

He brushed my blouse off my shoulders, and his breath caught on an audible inhale. "I don't know why you said there is nothing special about your body. You're beautiful."

I warmed all over. With my pale skin, I easily colored like a raspberry.

He unhooked my bra, and my perfectly average breasts tumbled free.

Again I heard his breath.

"My God." He sighed. "So fucking beautiful."

He set me down on the bed. Then he lifted my hips and pulled my stretch pants and beige panties over them, down my legs, and off.

I sat there, naked, forcing myself not to cover my chest with my arms. Thankfully, I had shaved my legs yesterday, but my dark-blond bush was in full glory. I didn't shave down there. What would he think about that?

I ceased worrying when he began to take off his clothes.

He unbuttoned his paisley western shirt, and I bit my lip. With each new inch of bronze that was exposed, my heart beat faster. And then a little faster. A smattering of black and silver chest hair grew around his coppery nipples. He removed his shirt and slung it over the back of a chair. He sat down next to me, and I sneaked a look at his crotch. Sure enough—the bulge.

I squirmed. I knew I was wet. I knew what he'd find when he looked between my legs.

He stood again, unbuckled his belt, unsnapped his jeans, each tiny zing of the teeth on his zipper growing louder. He pushed his jeans and boxers down and stepped out of them. And then he turned to face me.

I gasped.

He had the biggest dick I'd ever seen. For a minute, I wasn't sure it would fit inside my thin body. As wet as I was at this moment, though, there probably wouldn't be any trouble.

He smiled at my gasp. "See anything you like now?"

I warmed again. Was I capable of getting any redder?

He pulled me up to him and clasped my naked body to his. He kissed my neck, nibbling on it lightly, and then tugged on my earlobe.

"I'm going to fuck you every way possible this afternoon, Melanie. I'm going to have you up against the wall, on the bed, cowgirl, missionary, doggy—every position there is. We're going to do it on the table over there. I'm going to fuck your brains out in every corner of this room."

My knees buckled. Luckily he held me steady.

"I wanted to do this when I first laid eyes on you in that hotel bar. I wanted to take you back to my room. Everything I wanted to do to you that night, I'm going to do to you now, Melanie. Believe it."

I had no reason not to believe it. I saw it in his eyes. Eyes never lied. I'd learned that through my business. Right now, Jonah Steel's eyes said that he wanted me, and he was going to have me.

And I wouldn't resist.

He took my lips with his. I opened for him immediately, and he swept his tongue into my mouth. Our lips were fused together, our tongues engaged in a duel. My God, I couldn't get close enough to him. *More. I want more.*

He kissed me hard. This was no sweet kiss. This was the kiss of two people denied human contact for far too long. It wasn't a kiss of passion. It was a kiss of need. Of urgency.

This was physical, purely physical. We didn't know each other well enough for it to be anything else. As a professional, I knew that. This was chemical and nothing more.

But that didn't stop me from melting into his kiss. My nipples hardened, poking into his chest. I swore I could feel the juices dripping down my thighs.

He cupped my breasts, thumbing my erect nipples. God, it felt so good. No one had touched me intimately for so long.

I moaned into his mouth.

He groaned back, and I felt the vibration of his voice all the way to my toes. When he finally broke the kiss, we were both panting.

"I want you," he said. "I swear to God I've never wanted a woman so much."

I opened my mouth, but no words emerged. Didn't matter anyway, because he sealed his lips to mine again, and his tongue filled my mouth, taking me, spiraling me beyond control.

We kissed again—kissed and kissed and kissed—and he moved his hand down from my breasts to between my legs.

He broke the kiss and sucked in a breath. "God, do you have any idea how wet you are? You're soaked, Melanie. You're soaked for me."

I didn't doubt it. His huge erection was poking into my belly. Yes, physical chemistry. We certainly did have that.

He turned me around and pushed me against the wall. "Don't move," he said in my ear.

From my position, I heard the rip of a condom wrapper. In about three seconds, he was behind me, his front to my back, his cock nudging the crease of my ass.

"I told you I'd fuck you up against this wall. Get ready, baby."

I gasped as he thrust himself into me. "God, you're so big."

"Shh," he said against my neck. "You'll get used to it."

I was used to it already. I felt complete in a way I never had before. No one had ever felt like this inside me, and I knew no one ever would again. So I was going to savor this afternoon. I was going to let him do whatever he wanted.

He pulled out and thrust back in. I gasped again.

"You like that? You like my big hard cock inside you?"

I wasn't used to such language, but I liked it. God, I liked it very much.

I wept a shaky "yes."

He continued pumping into me, and with each stroke, I spiraled higher and higher.

"Reach down and touch yourself, sweetheart. I want you to come."

He didn't need to tell me twice. After a few seconds of playing with myself, I was flying, the orgasm taking me with a force I had never experienced.

"That's it, sweetheart. Come for me. Come all over my big

dick."

When my spasms finally cleared, he pulled out and turned me around. Then he lifted me in his arms and set me down upon his hard cock. This man was strong. He held me, lifted me up and down upon him, and oh my God, it felt good. Within minutes, without any clitoral simulation, I was coming again. Coming all over him.

"Oh my God, Jonah. Oh my God, so good." I cried out, screamed, words left my lips without thought. I loved every minute of it.

"That's it, baby. Show me how much you want me. Show me how much you like it. I want you to come. I want you to come all over me."

He carried me to the bed and laid me down, not gently. Then he plunged inside me again, my legs over his shoulders.

Something about that angle... God, I was exploding again all over the place. The orgasms kept coming one after the other, wave after wave after wave of surging pleasure.

His cock hit the perfect place inside me, making me melt around him again and again and again.

"You're so responsive. I've never had a woman stay this wet for so long. My God, you are something else. So gorgeous. So perfect."

I bit my lip to keep from crying out again.

Then I thought to myself, why bother? I opened my mouth and screamed. It was freeing and wonderful.

He clamped his lips to mine and continued pumping into me. Our tongues swirled together. And with every new ounce of pleasure he forced from me, I only wanted more.

He pulled out, quickly broke the kiss, and flipped me over so I was on my hands and knees. He gave my ass cheek a quick slap.

I gasped. No one had ever done that to me.

Before I could decide if I liked it, he slapped me again, and then he thrust back into me.

"My God, so good. You're so tight." He continued to pound into me, and then he pulled out and lay down. His cock was still standing, huge and erect. "Get on top of me, Melanie. Ride me."

It never occurred to me not to do what he asked. I scrambled on top of him and groaned as I sank onto his hardness.

He reached toward me and grabbed both of my breasts. "Gorgeous. Such beautiful breasts. They're perfect in every way."

They were average, but I wasn't going to contradict him in the middle of sex.

"Your nipples are the same ruby-red color as your lips. So beautiful. So perfect." He thumbed each hard bud.

I was riding high, right on the edge of yet another orgasm. When I writhed around him, he started thrusting upward, faster than normal.

"I'm going to come with you this time, sweetheart. I want to come all over that hot little pussy of yours."

And then he rammed up into me so hard, I thought he might have touched my heart.

He squeezed his eyes shut. "Melanie, fuck."

When my spasms finally stopped, I fell forward onto him, both of our chests slick. I closed my eyes, my breath coming rapidly.

"My God," he said. "That was amazing."

As soon as I could catch my breath, I would agree with

him. For now, I'd clamp myself against him, my hair sticking to my back and shoulders, his stubbly cheek scratching my own.

After a few moments, he rolled me over. "Sorry, sweetheart. I have to take care of the condom."

The loss of his warmth against me made me whimper, but I moved over on my back, a drift of air from the ceiling fan above us feeling heavenly against my moist skin. I closed my eyes.

A few minutes later, the bed sank with his weight.

"That's right, baby. Take a little nap. Because we're not done. Not by a long shot."

CHAPTER NINE

Jonah

Melanie's breathing became shallow, and I knew she had fallen asleep. It was nearing five o'clock, but I was not yet sated. My need for her had been so great I'd gone straight for the gold. I hadn't yet tasted her ruby-red nipples, her beautiful pussy. I hadn't yet felt her gorgeous lips around my cock. What must she think of me? Other than a bit of kissing, we'd had no foreplay. It wasn't like me to be so selfish, but my need for her had been that intense.

My dick stirred and hardened again. Just being near her affected me. But she looked so peaceful and serene in her slumber—a peace I didn't see when she was awake. Something was eating her up inside. Maybe one day she'd tell me what it was. I had the distinct feeling that she understood my guilt better than she let on.

While I longed to wake her up and get started again, I decided to let her sleep.

She appeared to need it so much.

So I rolled to the other side of the bed and closed my eyes as well.

Big mistake.

When I woke up, she was gone.

★ ★ ★ ★

I left several messages for Melanie after we'd been together, but she hadn't returned any of my calls. I couldn't think about it today though, because I sat with Bryce, waiting for the prison guard to bring Larry Wade out to talk to us.

We weren't separated by glass, since we had come during regular visiting hours and there were two of us. We sat at a round table in the visiting area. The guard watched Larry closely.

Larry sat down. "Jonah Steel," he said. "To what do I owe this pleasure?"

"Hello, *Uncle*," I said with sarcasm. I was hardly in the mood to be cordial, but I had to introduce Bryce. "This is my friend Bryce Simpson. Tom Simpson's son."

"The mayor. Sure. Good man."

I wasn't sure what to make of his sardonic tone. It had been Mayor Simpson, after all, who had appointed Larry as city attorney when he came back to town a few years ago. I'd always known he was a shady character, and from what I'd heard from Jade, the man was about as unethical an attorney as there was. People like him gave lawyers a bad name.

Of course, bending ethics as an attorney was the least of Larry Wade's crimes.

"Hello, Mr. Wade," Bryce said.

Larry groaned. "So what do you two want?"

"Answers," I said.

"Ask away. I'm pretty sure I don't have any."

"You can start by telling me why you left a red rose on Jade's pillow a few months ago."

He rolled his eyes. "I don't know what you're talking

about."

"Quit playing dumb, Uncle Larry. We all know what kind of man you are. The kind of man that kidnaps and fucks little boys. Pretty sick. Also, you killed Colin Morse."

"Hey, I had nothing to do with that."

"Whatever. So if you're that kind of guy already, breaking and entering and leaving an ominous rose on a woman's pillow would be nothing to you."

"I *said* I don't know what you're talking about."

I couldn't read him. Jade had said he had a champion poker face. She was right.

Larry turned to Bryce. "To what do I owe the pleasure of the mayor's son's company?"

"My cousin Luke was one of the other kids who was taken twenty-five years ago," Bryce said. "So I'm as involved in this as Joe is."

"Great." Larry rolled his eyes yet again.

"You might want to try being a little less of an asshat," I said. "You know we can make or break you."

"Are you kidding me? My fate is sealed. Don't try to work some deal with me, Steel. I'm headed up the river, and we all know that."

"Well, you should be. But we have some business to discuss. You're going to tell us who the other two men are who took Talon."

"Nope." Larry crossed his arms over his chest. "I ain't talkin'. Period."

"You need to change your tune. The prosecution will be a lot easier on you if you cooperate."

"I know my rights. And I know what the prosecution will and won't do. But I will not talk. I can't."

"Why can't you?" Bryce asked.

"Because they'll fucking kill me."

"You're in prison, for God's sake. No one from the outside can get to you in here. Why not do yourself a favor and make your life a little bit easier?" I said. "I'll make it worth your while."

"Are you offering me money, Steel? What good would money do me now?"

"Well...you can hire yourself a decent lawyer rather than the public defender you've got right now."

Larry licked his lips. God, he was a snake. Was he considering my offer? I couldn't tell.

"That's interesting. How much are you offering?"

"I'd say two hundred grand could buy you some decent representation."

"That's it? Everyone knows you're worth way more than that, Steel."

"It may come as a surprise to you, Uncle, but my main business isn't paying off criminals. I'm offering you more than enough to pay a decent attorney."

Larry shook his head, laughing. "It's still pennies to you."

I tensed.

Bryce nudged my arm. "Don't let him get to you, Joe."

I had no intention of anything "getting" to me. If he wasn't talking, I'd take the money off the table.

"Forget the money, then. Do what's right for once in your life. Do it for your nephew, whose life you made hell. Do for your sister, my mother."

"No can do." Larry looked at the guard. "I'm done with these people."

"Wait," Bryce said, standing. "You can't leave yet."

"Oh, yeah? You have money you want to throw my way?"

"I don't have any money. Not that I'd give it to you if I had it. But I do need some information."

"I told you. I'm not naming the others."

Bryce shook his head. "I get that. But I want to know something else. I want you to tell me what happened to my cousin. Luke Walker."

My heart thrummed against my sternum. If Larry told Bryce... I should have seen this coming. I had to be the one to tell Bryce about Luke, not this degenerate. I should have told him before we came. Instead, I'd taken the easy way out, putting off the unpleasant—hell, unpleasant was stating it mildly—until later. One thing was for sure. I couldn't let Larry tell him. I opened my mouth to put an end to Bryce's question, but Larry spoke first, his eyes wide.

"Come again?"

"You heard what I said. What happened to my cousin?"

Larry erupted in laughter. Evil laughter. "Steel, you haven't told him?"

Bryce, still standing, turned and looked down at me. "What's he talking about, Joe?"

Why hadn't it occurred to me that Bryce might ask Larry about Luke? It should have. Definitely not my finest moment. I'd been desperate for someone to accompany me, and I hadn't been able to ask either of my brothers for obvious reasons. And Bryce had offered...

I opened my mouth to speak, but Larry beat me to it.

"I don't have any firsthand knowledge of what happened to your cousin," he said. "And neither does Jonah here. There's only one person you know who can tell you for sure what happened." He cocked his head. "Actually, there are two people."

One was Talon. Who was the other he was talking about? Who else would be able to tell Bryce? The only other people who knew were—

The other two abductors.

Was Larry insinuating that Bryce might know one of them?

I stood and addressed the guard. "Get this piece of shit out of my sight."

"What was he talking about, Joe?" Bryce asked after the guard had led Larry away. "What happened to Luke?"

I didn't relish this moment. How exactly was I supposed to tell my oldest friend in the world that his cousin had been killed, chopped into pieces, and stuffed inside a garbage bag?

"Let's find a bar and get a drink," I said, nearly choking. "And I'll tell you everything."

★ ★ ★ ★

"How could you keep this from me?" Bryce took a long drink of his beer. "I thought we were friends, Joe."

"We *are* friends. I only just found out about this a couple weeks ago myself. What would you have done in my place? I haven't seen you in years, and first thing I tell you is that your cousin was chopped up while my brother was forced to watch?"

"Why did you want me to go see Larry with you? Surely you knew I'd ask about Luke."

I sighed. "I probably did know in the back of my mind. I just wanted the company. And you do have a stake in this as well. Luke was your cousin."

Bryce shook his head. "Damn," he said. "Twenty-five

years. I haven't given this a thought in...over a decade at least. So now, all of a sudden, why is it so damned raw?"

I didn't know how to answer my friend. Yes, twenty-five years had passed, and it had been raw for me the whole time. Bryce didn't know how lucky he was. "It's raw because it's heinous. It's unthinkable. Inhumane. Unbelievable that people like those three exist in the world. I wish I knew what to tell you. But just remember that it was twenty-five years ago. Luke is long gone. He was dead before they took Talon."

Bryce finished his beer and signaled the waitress. "You want another?" he asked me.

"No." Beer wasn't my drink, and I was nursing the martini I'd ordered. "Look, I was going to tell you. I just didn't know how."

He nodded. "I understand, man. Not exactly news anyone wants to reveal."

He was taking this better than I expected, and for that I was very grateful.

"I'm really sorry I didn't tell you before we saw Larry. That was an idiot move on my part."

"I won't disagree, but I get where you're coming from. I know you didn't want to see the guy alone, and you couldn't ask your brothers to go with you."

I took a long drink from my gin infusion. Good stuff. I still felt like shit, though. "There's one more thing we have to think about, Bryce."

"What's that?"

"Larry said something that stuck with me. He said there were only two people that you knew who had firsthand knowledge of what happened to Luke."

"Yeah, the other two kidnappers, I guess."

I shook my head. "That's not what he meant. He said specifically that they were people *you* knew. One of the people he was talking about was Talon. I'm sure of it. I think he gave us a clue about who one of the other kidnappers is."

"What clue?"

"That you *know* him, Bryce. You know one of the other men who took Talon."

CHAPTER TEN

Melanie

Sitting across from Talon Steel in a session wasn't easy. I had the eerie feeling that he could tell what I had just done with his brother a few days prior. But I was still Talon's therapist, and he had made much progress, so I needed to continue his sessions. Knowing that I was helping Talon and my other patients was the only way I felt a little bit better about what had happened to Gina.

He hadn't asked Jade to marry him yet.

"So what's stopping you?" I asked.

"Well, Jade's mom, Brooke Bailey, moved in with us. She's going to stay while she continues to recover from her accident. She and Jade are trying to rebuild their relationship. This is really important to Jade, so I don't want to interfere."

"And you think proposing marriage would interfere?"

He chuckled. "Not interfere so much. I just don't want Jade having to think about other things while she's rebuilding a relationship with her mom. She's also the city attorney now, so she's always swamped at work, thanks to my esteemed half-uncle." Talon visibly tensed.

"What's going on with that?"

"He's sitting in prison, waiting for his trial."

"Has Jade been up to see him again?"

"No, but my brother Joe went up to see him."

I widened my eyes, hoping Talon didn't notice. "Jonah? Why would he go up?"

"For the same reason Jade did. He wanted to try to talk Larry into naming the two guys so we can get them put away."

"And how did that go?"

"It didn't. The asshole won't budge."

I wasn't surprised. Talon probably wasn't either. "Did Jonah manage to get anything out of him at all?"

Talon shook his head. "Because of something Larry said, Joe is now convinced that his friend Bryce Simpson might know one of the attackers personally. But I doubt it. I still think one of them is that boyfriend of Jade's mother, Nico Kostas. Pretty strange that he just disappeared. And in all likelihood, he tried to kill Jade's mom."

I had heard the whole story of the insurance policy and accident. "There's no way to know for sure."

"I know, Doc. But it all makes so much sense."

I couldn't fault him there. Either this was a huge coincidence, or the man wanted to collect on insurance money. But I didn't know.

"What about Jade's ex-boyfriend, Colin?"

"The cops are looking into that right now. Since they found his belongings on Larry, they figure they got the right guy. They just don't have a body, and Larry's maintaining his innocence. But Larry's such a liar, so I have no idea."

"Do you think Larry was set up?"

"It's possible. If he *was* set up, it was probably by the other two sickos who took me."

What Talon said did make sense, but there was no way to be certain, unless we found out who the other two were.

"Okay, Talon, so we have one who has a phoenix on his left forearm, and the other has a birthmark on his arm that looks kind of like the state of Texas."

"Yeah."

"And you're still determined to find them."

"I *will* find them, Doc. I swear."

I had talked to Talon before about not mistaking vengeance for healing, that he needed to heal whether he found the others or not. I thought he understood, but it wouldn't do any harm to say it again. "You need to continue your healing, whether the others are caught or not."

"Yeah, I know that. You've told me."

"I don't mean to repeat myself, but sometimes I think you get so caught up in finding the others that you put that goal over your own healing. You've come so far already, and I'd hate to see you slide backward. Revenge is not healing."

Talon leaned forward. "I do hear what you're saying. I really do. I know you think I'm looking for a needle in a haystack. And maybe I am. I promise, I am healing. I'm sleeping in the same bed with Jade every night now, and I don't fear I'm going to hurt her. I know I would never hurt her. And my dreams, well, they haven't disappeared altogether, but they are lessening."

I nodded. It had been a while since Talon had told me about a dream. "When was the last time you had a dream?"

He shook his head. "Wow, I think it's been about a week at least."

"That's good. Do you remember what you dreamed about?"

"No. I normally don't. Unless I wake up right in the middle of it. Usually what happens is I wake up agitated and know I had one, but I don't remember the content. Then I look next to me, and I see Jade sleeping peacefully. I caress her soft shoulder, maybe give her a kiss on the cheek. And I go back to sleep."

"That's great. Really."

"Thanks."

"So how are things going at home? I mean with Jade's mom being there."

He rolled his eyes. "I don't like to say this, but she's kind of a diva. She keeps Felicia running. And Jade, when she's there. She doesn't ask me for much of anything. I gave Felicia a significant raise for dealing with her."

I smiled. "That's generous of you."

"No, not generous. Believe me, Felicia earns it."

"I don't doubt it. What do you think of Jade's mother? Other than that she's a diva."

"I only really know what Jade and her father have said. She does seem to want to make amends with Jade, and I appreciate that. I don't want Jade to have any bad feelings in her life."

"And Jade? How is she doing?"

"There are days when she wants to strangle her mother. I try to talk her down from it, and I'm usually successful. But it's important to her that Brooke be there and that we help her. A nurse comes in once a day for a few hours to check on her, do some PT, give her meds, and the nurse also takes her into the city overnight for more therapy once a week. It's great for Jade to get that time off from Brooke."

"And what will happen when Brooke is ready to live on her own?"

Talon sighed. "Jade and I haven't had that talk yet, so I

don't know. I can set her up somewhere on the ranch, but I really don't want to."

"I understand. You can figure that out later."

"Yeah. She's getting better. Although I wouldn't put it past her to hold on to being taken care of for as long as she can."

I smiled. "Some people are like that."

"I'll tell you, Doc. Jade and her mom both have those gorgeous steely blue eyes, but other than that, I can't imagine how this woman gave birth to Jade. They're nothing alike. Not just in looks but in personality and demeanor. So completely different."

"From what you told me, Jade is more like her father."

He nodded. "Yeah, he's a great guy. She looks more like him too."

I glanced at the clock on the table. My time with Talon was nearly up. I appreciated his need to talk about Jade's mom staying at the house, but that wasn't really what we were here for. So I got ready to change the subject.

I was startled by a knock on the door. Randi knew better than to interrupt me when I was in session.

"I'm very sorry, Talon. Would you excuse me for a moment?" I went to the door. Instead of letting Randi in, I walked out into the reception area. A man I didn't recognize sat on a chair, leafing through a magazine.

"What's going on?" I asked Randi.

"I'm so sorry, Dr. Carmichael," Randi said, "but he insists upon seeing you right now. I tried to explain that I couldn't interrupt a session, but he threatened to make a scene."

I looked over to the man. "Sir, I have no idea who you are, but this is entirely inappropriate."

He stood, staring at me with intense blue eyes. He

didn't look happy. "I don't rightly care about the rules, Dr. Carmichael. I came to talk to you, and I aim to do so."

"Who are you?"

"I'm Rodney Cates, Gina's father."

★ ★ ★ ★

Talon had been very gracious when I cut his session short. Now I sat in my office across from Gina Cates's father. He was a tall, muscular man, average-looking, with sandy-brown hair and blue eyes. He wore a tweed jacket and jeans. He was a professor at the University of Colorado. Gina had told me all about him. I probably knew more about him than he would be comfortable with.

"Dr. Cates, I would be happy to talk to you anytime. You know that. But it's not appropriate for you to come storming into my office and interrupt a session with one of my patients."

"As I see it, the patient who left here is still very much alive. So I think I take precedence."

Clearly there was going to be no reasoning with him. I mentally berated myself. He was no doubt here because of the stupid phone call I'd made the other night.

"I am so very sorry for your loss, and I am happy to discuss anything you would like to discuss. You'll have to make an appointment. I have another patient coming in fifteen minutes."

"Cancel."

"Why would I do that?"

"Because again, that patient happens to be alive. He or she can reschedule."

"Need I remind you, Dr. Cates, that you are also alive?

Therefore, you can call my office and schedule a time to talk to me." I stood, hoping I was pulling off an image of control when inside I was shaking. "Make sure you leave your number with Randi."

He stood as well, towering over me. "I don't think you're understanding me. I came to talk to you now, and that is what I'm going to do."

My pulse started racing. I wasn't exactly frightened. After all, Randi was right outside, and my cell phone sat on the table next to me. However, I did not like this man or his tone, and I was experiencing discomfort. No. Definitely more than that. Goosebumps prickled my flesh. I *was* frightened. But showing my fear would only give him what he wanted.

I picked up my cell, my knuckles white with tension, and stood. "You will make an appointment."

He came toward me, closing in on my space. I sat back down in my chair.

Now my heart started thumping. "I'm going to have to ask you to back off," I said.

"I did not come here to harm you. I am not a violent man. But I lost my daughter, Dr. Carmichael, and you *will* hear me out."

Anxiety coursed through me. "Fine," I relented. "You have ten minutes. After that, I have a patient who booked this time in advance. I will be happy to speak to you further, but we will have to decide on a time that is mutually agreeable."

He sat down, and I breathed a sigh of relief. I gave myself a mental pat on the back for not losing it. Hopefully he could say what he wanted to say in ten minutes.

"All right."

"Now, what was so important that you barged into my

office and interrupted my session?"

He sighed. "I had to take my wife to the hospital today."

"I'm very sorry. Is she ill?"

He shook his head. "No. At least not in the way you mean. I had to admit her to the mental wing here at Valleycrest."

"I'm very sorry to hear that."

"What did you expect? The woman lost her child. She hasn't been able to cope. We've tried therapy. We've tried medication. First the psychiatrist thought she had situational depression and that it would run its course. That she was grieving. Well, of course she was grieving, but it didn't get any better."

"Again, I'm sorry." I didn't know what else to say.

"Anyway, yesterday morning, I got out of bed to get myself off to work. She hasn't been getting out of bed until noon, not since Gina died. So I didn't think anything of it. But then I came home for lunch, and she wasn't there. The car was there, but no sign of her. I found her still in bed, nearly catatonic."

"I'm sorry."

"All she would say was 'Dr. Car, Dr. Car.' I assumed she was trying to say Carmichael, and that she wanted to see you, so I packed her up and drove here. We stayed at a hotel last night. Then, this morning, I woke up, and she wasn't in bed next to me. I found her in the bathroom. She was cutting herself."

I sucked in a breath. "Cutting can be a normal reaction when one is in a lot of emotional pain. It's good that you took her to the hospital. She'll get the help she needs."

"You don't understand, Dr. Carmichael. She wasn't just cutting herself to alleviate emotional pain. She was slitting her wrists."

CHAPTER ELEVEN

Jonah

Walking alone at night. Again.

My ribs were still a little sore from my last encounter, but here I was again. Nights were growing cooler now that autumn was turning, and not as many vagrants were out in the dark alleyways. So I headed to the main street. I continued walking until I came to a bar. I walked in and sat down.

The barkeep sidled up to me. "What'll it be?"

"A CapRock martini."

"What the hell is a CapRock martini?"

"A martini made with CapRock gin."

"Never heard of it."

"It's organic gin, made here in Colorado."

The barkeep let out a guffaw. "Organic? You gotta be kidding me. We've got our basic well stuff. And no vermouth. I can give you well gin in a martini glass." He smiled. He was missing one of his cuspids.

"Sure. What the hell?"

The old guy a couple seats away was eyeing me.

I turned to him. "You got a problem?"

He shook his head, smiling. "Nope, no problems. You just look a little familiar to me." He stood and closed the gap between us, sitting on the stool next to me. He held out his hand. "Name is Mike."

"Jonah Steel."

"Met another Steel in here a while back. Funny name, too."

Funny name... "Talon Steel?"

"Yep, that's the one. Guy was dressed a lot like you, expensive boots and all."

"He's my brother."

"Nice guy. Had a big chip on his shoulder. Something was eating him but good."

The geezer had no idea.

"Good man, though. He sent me a case of this great bourbon called Peach Street."

This guy must be something else if Talon had sent him a case of his favorite whiskey. "If you've got a case of that at home, what are you doing in this dump?"

"Oh, this place gets to be home when you come in enough. You never know who you'll meet in here. I come in about once a week and let Lucky over there pour me a glass of rotgut, and I watch the people coming in and out of this place. You'd be surprised who ducks through that door."

"Someone like me, you mean?"

He nodded. "I haven't seen boots like those in here since your brother. But believe it or not, we get a wide variety of different people in this little dive. It's nice to have someone to talk to. I've been widowed now for a while."

"I'm sorry to hear that. Here, let me buy you another drink."

"I'd be obliged." He signaled to Lucky. "I'll have another."

Lucky sent a drink sliding across the bar. Then he set my "martini" in front of me. "Take it slow," he said. "Shit's a little rough around the edges."

I took a sip. Stung my throat. Smooth this was not.

"So if my brother sent you a case of Peach Street, you must have done something pretty amazing to earn it."

Mike shook his head, laughing. "Nope. Just talked to him. He was going through a rough patch."

Rough patch. Seemed to belittle what my brother had been through. But I didn't know exactly what he'd told Mike, and I sure as hell wasn't going to elaborate.

"He's doing better now," I said.

"Good to hear. Ever hook up with the girl he talked about?"

"If you mean Jade, then yes, he did."

"I'm not sure he gave me her name. Good for him. A good woman is a man's better half, I've always said. I sure do miss my Melanie."

My heart thumped. "Melanie?"

"Yup. My wife's name was Melanie. Melanie Rose Mitchell, before she met me. The prettiest thing around. I sure do miss her."

"Melanie," I said again.

"Yep, that was her name."

"Beautiful name."

"For a beautiful woman. Never met a woman with a bigger heart either. We never had much. I wish I'd been able to provide for her better. But even with as little as we had, she was always ready to lend a hand, always willing to give to someone who had less. Woman was a saint."

"She sounds wonderful."

"Yeah, she was."

"I know a woman named Melanie."

"Do you now?"

"She sounds a lot like your Melanie. She helps people."

"Is she yours?"

How I wished she were, but that wouldn't happen. "No, I'm not that lucky. I don't have a woman right now."

"So why'd you walk in here...Jonah, did you say?"

"Yeah. You can call me Joe."

"So why'd you walk in here, Joe?"

Should I tell him I'd been skulking around, trying to find someone to kick my ass? All the times I'd been down here, and never once had I stopped in this little bar. What had led me here tonight?

I took a drink of my gin—not CapRock by a long shot—and looked Mike in his rheumy eyes. "If I could tell you, I would, but I don't have a fucking clue why I'm here."

Mike chuckled. "You sure do remind me of your brother."

"How can you say that? You only met him once."

"Well, you probably heard this before, but you look a lot like him. The two of you could be—well—brothers."

That got a smile out of me. This guy was all right. "Yeah, we do look alike. We have a younger brother too, and he looks a lot like both of us. We all favor our dad."

"He must be a good-looking man."

"He was. He passed away a while ago."

"I'm sure sorry to hear that."

Mike had no idea. If my dad were still alive, we might be able to get some real answers about what had happened to Talon. Like why the hell our father had swept it under the rug for so long. But nope, we were stuck figuring it out on our own. And I was stuck trying to figure myself out on my own. I had effectively screwed up the doctor-patient relationship with

Melanie. Not that I regretted sleeping with her. I hadn't had anyone like her for a long time. I wasn't sure if I ever had.

That was bullshit. I had never had a woman like her, and I never would again.

"Hey, people die." I took another sip of rotgut gin.

Mike sighed. "That they do. I sure miss my Melanie."

"You ever think of dating again?"

He laughed so hard I thought he might choke. "An old goat like me? Who would be interested?"

I couldn't help a smile. "A woman your age maybe? You seem like a nice enough guy."

"No, I'm good by myself these days. No one could ever replace Melanie. I'm not looking for advice on my life. I'd rather go about giving advice to people who need it. Like you."

"What do you think I need advice about?"

"Well, when I said you reminded me of your brother, I didn't just mean in looks—although you do look just like him. He ended up here one day not too long ago, and I asked him point-blank what the hell he was doing hanging out down here when he could obviously afford a better place. And now here you are. What the hell are you doing out here, son?"

"Just came in for a drink."

"There are plenty of other places in the city where you could get that first-class gin you're looking for."

I looked down at the martini glass in front of me. I downed the rest of it and stood, pulling my wallet out of my pocket and throwing a twenty on the counter.

I looked over at Mike again and threw another twenty down. "Buy Mike here a couple more drinks if he wants them," I said to Lucky.

"Didn't mean to chase you out of here," Mike said.

"You didn't. I just have no business being here. See, I didn't come down here to stop in the bar."

"Yeah, I was pretty sure you hadn't. Why *did* you come here?"

I wasn't going to tell Mike about my penchant for getting my ass whooped. And hey, didn't the fact that I stopped this time count for something? An empty alley wouldn't have stopped me before. I'd have just kept walking until I found someone to pick a fight with.

I needed to see Melanie. I wanted to discuss this with her. Maybe she couldn't be my therapist anymore, but I felt an overwhelming urge to open up to her. I didn't relish telling her that I got my ass beaten on purpose, but she was a trained professional. She would understand. Even when I didn't quite understand myself.

But even then, no matter how much I yearned to open up, I knew I wouldn't tell her. At least not yet.

"I don't know, Mike. I really don't know."

"Sit back down for a while. Maybe I can help."

"No one can help me. I've tried." I gave him a pat on the back and walked out.

CHAPTER TWELVE

Melanie

My phone buzzed once again while I was waiting to be taken in to see Erica Cates, Gina's mother. It was Jonah again. He'd called several times during my walk to Valleycrest Hospital, but I hadn't picked up. I sighed. Sooner or later I'd have to deal with Jonah Steel, but right now, all I could think about was Gina's mother, here in the mental wing of Valleycrest. I wasn't sure coming to see her was a good idea, but I had to know that she was okay. That she would live.

I had privileges at Valleycrest, so I figured it wouldn't be any problem to get in to see Mrs. Cates. Because of the nature of the situation, though, I had to jump through a few hoops. Dr. Cates had said his wife had been repeating my name, or what he thought was my name. Did that mean she wanted to see me, or did it mean something else?

One of my favorite nurses, Beth, walked toward me. "Dr. Carmichael, she does agree to see you, but I need to stay with you while you visit with her."

"That's fine, Beth. I understand. I really just want to make sure she's all right."

My words sounded foolish. Of course she wasn't all right. She'd tried to end her life, and she had lost her only daughter less than a year before. How the hell was she supposed to be all right?

"Her life hasn't been in danger," Beth said.

"I'm thankful for that. Who is the doctor working with her?"

"Dr. Bennett."

Miles Bennett was a decent physician, but his bedside manner wasn't the best. I'd always wondered why he chose psychiatry as a specialty. In psychiatry, a doctor who didn't have a good bedside manner usually didn't get very far. Miles worked exclusively with hospitalized psychiatric patients instead of taking patients for psychotherapy as I did. Rarely had I had to hospitalize any of my patients, though there had been a few over the years. I was familiar with the mental health staff here at Valleycrest.

"When was the last time Dr. Bennett was in to see Mrs. Cates?" I asked.

"This morning, during rounds."

Beth led me into a private room. A dark-haired woman, brown eyes sad and sunken, lay on the bed, her head propped up with several pillows.

"Mrs. Cates?" Beth said. "This is Dr. Carmichael."

"Hello, Mrs. Cates," I said.

The woman did not turn toward me. "Hello," she replied.

"Thank you for allowing me to see you."

"It doesn't matter."

I sat down in the chair next to her bed. "I understand you're seeing Dr. Bennett. He's excellent."

This time she turned toward me. "What would you know about excellent? You couldn't save my daughter."

A dagger sliced into my gut. I opened my mouth, but no words came out.

"Dr. Bennett is a very good doctor," Beth said, "and so is Dr. Carmichael."

I appreciated Beth's confidence in me, but I wasn't sure now was the right time for her to voice it.

"Mrs. Cates, I'm so very sorry about what happened to Gina."

"Not sorry enough."

What could I say to that? She had experienced an unbearable loss, and in her mind, I was to blame. She could never know how sorry I was. She had refused to take my call after Gina's death, and after that, I'd sought advice from an attorney. He advised me not to communicate with Gina's parents. If I hadn't called the other night, would Mrs. Cates be lying here now? Had my calling brought her pain back somehow? God, that call had been a mistake. It had been pure self-indulgence, only to ease my own guilt. I'd berated myself over and over again since then. I *knew* better, and I hadn't given a thought to how it might affect Gina's parents. Ironically, it hadn't done a thing for my guilt anyway.

Tears emerged in the corner of my eyes. *Hold it together, Melanie. You can't cry in front of this woman.* I inhaled and stood. "I'll leave you to get your rest now, Mrs. Cates. Thank you for seeing me. I'm so glad you're okay."

I turned and walked out. Beth's soft padded footsteps followed me.

"Dr. Carmichael," Beth said, "I want you to know that none of us here on staff think any of this is your fault."

I wiped my eyes. "I know that. Thank you."

"Dr. Bennett doesn't think it's your fault either."

"I appreciate that, Beth. I really do. However, I feel like complete shit."

She nodded. "It's never easy to lose a patient. I've lost my share of them."

I was sure she had, but it was different for a nurse. Granted, nurses cared for patients on a daily basis and sometimes got to know them as well or better than their physicians did. But it wasn't the nurse who was charged with primary care. It wasn't the same thing at all.

"I know." I didn't know what else to say. I couldn't tell her that I thought it was different for her, even though I knew nurses felt the loss of a patient deeply. Maybe it wasn't so different. "Thanks for getting me in to see her. Please take good care of her."

Beth smiled. "You know I will, and so will Dr. Bennett."

I nodded, unable to speak past the lump in my throat. I gave her a small smile and walked toward the elevator.

The elevator doors opened, and I gasped. Standing in front of me was none other than Jonah Steel.

I froze in my tracks. What to do now? What else could I do? I got on the elevator.

"Hello, Jonah," I said rather formally.

"Hello, Melanie," he said in a similar tone.

"Aren't you getting off the elevator?"

"Why would I?"

"I just assumed maybe you were visiting someone on the floor?"

"Nope."

"Then you're coming from another floor?"

"No."

"Then what are you doing on this elevator?"

He smiled, and my heart nearly leaped out of my chest.

"I'm looking for you."

"How did you know I was here?"

"I called your office. Randi said you were over at Valleycrest doing rounds. So here I am."

I'd have to have a little chat with Randi. Normally I never made it a secret that I was doing rounds, and I had told her that was where I'd be this afternoon, so really she hadn't done anything wrong. "Well, you're here, and I'm here now. What can I do for you?"

"I thought we could talk."

"About what?"

"You know, kind of help each other. Since you can't be my therapist. As friends. Like we tried to do the other day."

Was he serious? The other day had effectively ended any friendship between us before it could have ever begun. "Given our...history, I'm not sure that would be appropriate."

"What history?"

Uh...the fact that you screwed my brains out? I warmed from my forehead to my toes. "You know..."

"Of course. Our afternoon together. That afternoon when I fell asleep and you disappeared. Interesting that you would bring that up."

I was getting a little miffed. Emotion from seeing Gina's mother whirled through me, and I wasn't in any shape to deal with Jonah's and my mutual attraction. "What the hell is interesting about it? I'm..."

"You're what?"

I looked away. "Embarrassed."

He grabbed my arm and forced me against the elevator wall. "Embarrassed?" he said through clenched teeth. "You're embarrassed that we had amazing, mind-blowing sex for an hour?"

I cleared my throat. "I don't regret it or anything."

"You don't *regret* it?" Fire laced his dark eyes.

I shook my head, biting my lip hard. He let go of me and quickly pushed the emergency stop button on the elevator.

I gasped. "What are you doing?"

"This." He smashed his lips to mine.

I opened for him without thinking, as if it were a reflex. And perhaps it was. Perhaps I would always open for him. For Jonah Steel—a man so strong, yet holding on to so much guilt. I understood him better than he knew. My God, the man could kiss. I had never been kissed like this, never been kissed the way he kissed me. He had elevated it to an art.

Again, my emotions overwhelmed me. I'd just seen my dead patient's mother... Gina... Gone... And Jonah... Here...

And very much alive.

My nipples tightened, and my pussy began to pulsate.

I ground into his mouth, swirling my tongue with his and loving every minute of it.

When he finally paused to take a breath, I inhaled deeply.

"Jonah, no. I work here. Everyone knows me at the hospital."

He smiled. "Fine. I'll let you go. If we continue this. At your place."

I gulped and nodded. I'd have been happy to continue here, if it were any other building. Finally, he let go of me and pushed the button on the elevator so we resumed our downward ride.

What must I look like? I walked out of the elevator, nodding to a few people. And then there was the monstrously handsome man with his arm on my back. What would everyone think?

"Where's your place?" he asked.

"A couple blocks from here, a downtown loft."

"You have a car?"

I shook my head. "I walked."

"We'll take mine."

★ ★ ★ ★

Jonah kissed me breathless in the car at my building. He kissed me breathless in the elevator rising to the fourth floor where my loft was located. He kissed me breathless against my door, stopping only for me to unlock it.

He grabbed me and pushed me against the wall after kicking the door shut, kissing me breathless one more time.

He broke the kiss and inhaled. "Bedroom?"

I pointed toward the open door on the other side of the living area.

He lifted me in his arms as if I weighed no more than a child and swiftly carried me across the living area into the bedroom. I hadn't made my bed that morning, but he didn't seem to notice.

He dropped me on the bed and then sat down, his lips next to my ear. "I need to be inside you. I can't wait. But I promise you I will not leave you hanging. After we rest, I want to take it slow. I want to taste every inch of you, Melanie. I want to sample those sweet nipples. I want to make you scream as I eat your pussy. I want to lick your ass. I won't stop until I've tasted every fucking millimeter of your gorgeous body."

My breath caught.

"Get undressed," he growled.

It never occurred to me not to obey him. I shed my clothes as he shed his, baring his beautiful body to me.

He grabbed his wallet out of his jeans pocket, quickly opened and put on a condom, and then forced me back down on the bed. Instantly, he was inside me.

He groaned—a groan I had heard before. From my patients who were drug addicts. They groaned like that when they got their fix. Could I be Jonah's fix? The thought made me melt. I wanted to be his fix.

He held himself inside me for a moment, letting me get used to his size.

Little did he know, I was already used to him. Again, as had happened the first time, when he entered me, I felt like I had come home.

"God," he said. "You feel so good around me."

He pulled out and thrust back in. I gasped against his shoulder.

"You all right?"

I sighed. "Yes. All right." I bit my lip.

"Thank God." He thrust back in.

I let out a soft moan every time he slid back into me, and before I knew it, a climax was primed and ready to go. Just as I was about to start coming, he pulled out.

"You are beautiful right now. Glowing. Just gorgeous." He stuck his dick back into my heat.

I grasped the comforter, balling my hands into fists around the fabric.

He fucked me hard and fast. The orgasm on the edge teetered over into full force.

I cried out. With passion and power, he fucked me, groaning my name.

"God, sweetheart, I'm going to come." One last thrust, and he groaned, allowing his weight upon me.

I flattened on the bed, his weight too much for me to bear, but I didn't care. I wanted him on top of me, close to me. I welcomed it.

Within a few seconds, he had rolled over onto his side. "Sorry about that. I know how heavy I am."

I turned to face him. "No reason to be sorry. I wasn't complaining."

"Let me rest for a minute, and then I'm going to take my time. I'm going to savor every inch of skin and every drop of juice you have to offer."

I swallowed audibly. I couldn't think of anything to say. I didn't have to, because he gently brushed his lips over mine.

"I hope I make you feel half as incredible as you make me feel," he said. "My God, you're amazing." He rolled onto his back and closed his eyes.

Soon his shallow breathing indicated he had fallen asleep. I looked at the clock. It was nearly six. I got up, went to the bathroom, put on a robe, and headed out to the kitchen. He'd be hungry when he woke up, probably for food. I smiled at my own joke. I looked through the cupboards and the refrigerator. Not a lot to work with, so I made a quick call to my favorite Thai place and pulled a bottle of lusty red Zinfandel off my wine rack. When he woke up, dinner would be waiting.

CHAPTER THIRTEEN

Jonah

I opened my eyes and took in my surroundings. Melanie's bedroom was decorated in burgundy and ivory, with dark wood accents—just feminine enough without being too froufrou for a man's taste. Her bathroom was off to the left, so I went in to take care of business. I looked in the mirror and couldn't help a chuckle. I looked well and thoroughly fucked. And damn, I felt good.

Back in the bedroom, the zesty aroma of chicken and peppers wafted toward me. I pulled on my jeans and walked out, my feet and chest bare.

Melanie was standing in the kitchen wearing a short, silky green robe. God, she had great legs—long, lean, and shapely.

I gave her a whistle.

She turned. "Are you hungry?"

"I am now. Something smells great."

"Thai basil chicken," she said. "But don't get too used to it. It's takeout."

Don't get too used to it. Did that mean I wouldn't be here for meals? Or did it mean it was takeout, so don't get used to it, because normally she would be cooking? Hell, it could mean either. Right now, all I cared about was doing a little carbo-loading so I could get her back in the sack.

"Whatever it is, it smells great." I inhaled.

Her small table was set for two, and takeout containers sat on what appeared to be fine linen. She had class, this one. She'd poured two glasses of wine and set two goblets of water by two plain white china plates. Elegant and feminine without being overstated. I liked this woman.

A lot.

"Go ahead and sit down. Help yourself."

"I'll wait for you," I said.

"I'm right behind you." She turned off the faucet, drying her hands quickly on a kitchen towel, walked a few strides, and sat down across from me at the table.

"I have no idea what you like. I hope Thai is okay."

"I like anything. We're big eaters in my family."

"I'm sure you probably prefer beef, since you're a beef rancher."

"I eat beef all the time, Melanie. Chicken is great. I love Thai."

"Well"—she cleared her throat—"don't be shy. Please, help yourself."

"Ladies first. Give me your plate."

She looked at me oddly as she handed it to me. Was she not used to chivalry? There was a lot I didn't know about Melanie Carmichael. I aimed to find it all out.

I gave her a healthy portion of chicken, brown rice, and a spring roll and handed the plate back to her.

"Thank you," she said, flushing.

Oh, how I loved to make this one blush. Those raspberry cheeks bloomed as fresh as a pink rose.

I quickly served myself and then picked up my glass of wine. "To us."

She blushed again, more red than pink this time. "Us?"

"Sure, why not? I'm here, you're here, we just had some amazing sex, and now we're sitting down to a nice dinner. To us."

She timidly raised her glass and murmured, "To us," not quite looking me in the eye.

I took a sip of the wine. "Zinfandel?" I asked.

"Well, yeah." She smiled. "It's sitting right there on the table."

"I haven't looked at the bottle yet." I pulled it toward me and turned it to read the label. "So I got it right. Ryan would be proud of me."

"Yes, he's the wine connoisseur in your family."

I chuckled. "You have me at a severe disadvantage, don't you? You know a lot about my family and a lot about me from your sessions with Talon. I have a lot of catching up to do to find out as much about you."

"Me? I'm an open book."

I couldn't help a loud laugh that time. "Melanie, an open book you're not. You are so closed off, you're not just a closed book. You're shrink-wrapped. Tell me, what's eating at you?"

She cast her gaze downward.

Knife in gut. I felt really bad. "I'm sorry. I didn't mean to put you on the spot. After you made me dinner and everything."

"Let's eat. You don't want your food to get cold, do you?"

Wow, she really was timid. And I thought *I* was closed off. I decided to leave it for now and just enjoy her company.

"This is good wine. I like a good Zin. I'll bring you a bottle of Ryan's Zin sometime. It's great. He's a master winemaker."

She raised her eyes and met my gaze. Then she gave me a small smile. "I do enjoy a good bottle of wine."

"Anything to get a smile out of you." I smiled back. "You're very beautiful when you smile."

She closed her eyes, her long brown lashes lying against her creamy skin, and then opened them. Demurely.

My groin tightened again. She truly had no idea what she did to me, probably what she did to all men.

I took a bite of my chicken and decided to stop talking. Maybe then she would talk. But she seemed comfortable in silence. And the funny thing was, I was comfortable as well. Just being with her was comfortable. I didn't feel like I had to make small talk. I loved that about her, because God, I hated small talk.

The food was good for takeout. I cleaned my plate in no time and helped myself to a second serving, first asking Melanie if she wanted any. She shook her head.

I topped off her wine glass and refilled mine. "You say you like a good bottle of wine. What's your favorite?"

"I like all of it. Red and white. I guess I prefer red over white if I have to choose, but I like it all. My favorite of all is a good aged Cabernet Sauvignon."

I nodded. "Yeah, Cab is great. I like wine too, but my drink of choice is a martini."

She widened her eyes. Surely a martini couldn't be that surprising. I cocked my head at her.

"That's my drink of choice too. A martini. I mean, a real martini made with gin."

I smiled. A woman after my own heart. "A vodka martini isn't a martini."

A broad grin split her face. "That's exactly what I always say."

"Well, Dr. Carmichael, I think we finally found something

we have in common. Other than amazing sex."

She blushed again. God, she was adorable.

"You know what I think?" I said.

"What?"

"I'm willing to bet we have even more in common, and I'm going to ferret everything out of you until I know you like the back of my hand and I can read you like a book."

She cast her green gaze downward once more. She was so easy to embarrass. It had almost become a game with me. What could I do to embarrass her more?

She fidgeted with her napkin. "Are you still hungry? I have some chocolate ice cream in the freezer."

I rose and stalked toward her, took her hand, and pulled her up. "I'm still hungry. But not for food." I clasped her lithe body to mine and took her lips.

She sighed beneath me. I broke the kiss and gazed into her emerald eyes.

"Do you like kissing me, Melanie? Because I sure as hell like kissing you."

Her answer was a moan, and I took her lips again. She tasted of the spicy wine and the zesty food we had just eaten. And she tasted of Melanie, sweet and succulent.

Without breaking the kiss, I backed her toward her bedroom door, into the room, and to the bed. Again without breaking the kiss, I spread the sides of her robe, brushing the satin fabric over her shoulders. My dick was hard against the denim of my jeans. I wanted her again. I had promised to go slow the next time, to savor every inch of her. I hadn't yet tasted her most secret places.

But I couldn't wait. I needed her now. Needed to be inside that hot little cunt. I reached into my pocket for my wallet.

Thank God I normally carried two condoms and that I had resupplied after our first encounter at the hotel.

She looked into my eyes. "I... I'm on the pill. I have been forever. And I'm clean. I swear it."

I flashed back to my conversation with Bryce earlier, how his Vegas showgirl had assured him he was on the pill. But Melanie didn't strike me as the lying type. "You don't want me to wear a condom?"

"I'm saying you don't need to. If you're clean."

My heart nearly burst. To actually feel her silkiness with no barrier would be nirvana. "I swear, Melanie. I'm clean too."

That was for sure. I hadn't had a woman in so long, I was surprised sex hadn't changed.

I shed my jeans quickly, and my cock stood straight out. I knew I was large, even larger than what was normally considered large. She'd been able to take me. She fit me perfectly. I couldn't wait to feel every tiny ridge inside her sweet channel.

I pushed her onto the bed and touched her between her legs.

Wet and silky. She was ready for me.

I sank into her.

Fuck. She felt amazing. I thrust into her again.

Bliss. Had I ever used that word before in my life? Now was a good time to start. I had just had her an hour ago, and already I was prepared to spill. This time, without the restriction of the latex barrier between us, I felt every crevice, ridge, every bit of soft suction. And I couldn't help myself. My balls bunched up, and the tiny seizures started low.

"I'm so sorry, baby. I wish I could last longer, but oh my God." I thrust into her with one powerful plunge, spilling into her deepest recess.

She exhaled beneath me, her forehead beaded with sweat. She hadn't had an orgasm. I'd been so selfish. Again.

"Sweetheart, thank you for indulging me. And now"—I licked my lips—"I'm going to make it up to you."

CHAPTER FOURTEEN

Melanie

Jonah's cock was soft against my thigh. He moved toward me and kissed me—a gentle kiss this time, not the frantic, ferocious kiss he usually gave me. Now that he'd taken his sexual edge off, maybe he truly did want to see to my pleasure.

And I would let him.

He broke the kiss and inhaled, looking down at me. His eyes were nearly black and full of fire. "My God, you're beautiful, Melanie. You look like an angel."

An angel I was not, but I didn't want to ruin this moment.

"And you look like the devil," I said.

He raised his eyebrows.

"I mean that in a good way. There's a darkness in you, Jonah, a darkness I seem to be drawn to, that I can't say no to."

He smiled then. "As long as you can't say no." He trailed kisses across my cheek to my earlobe, where he nibbled, and then he thrust his tongue into my ear canal.

I shivered all over, oozing between my legs.

Then he trailed his tongue down my neck and inhaled. "Mmm, you always smell like lavender."

Lavender was my favorite fragrance and flower. Perhaps he hadn't noticed the lavender plant on my night table. He was probably getting a good whiff from that as well.

He inhaled again. "I'll never get tired of your scent."

He continued to trail his lips down, over my shoulders, down my arms. He kissed each fingertip of my left hand and then went back up my arm. He kissed my chest and then stopped for a moment and cupped my breasts.

I'd always felt woefully inadequate in that area, but he eyed them lasciviously, licking his lips.

"I can't tell you how long I've wanted to taste those red nipples." He gave my left breast a slap.

I gasped. It didn't hurt, actually. It just felt...different. And I was very afraid of different. Melanie Carmichael was a good girl. I grabbed his hand. "I..."

"What?"

"I'd rather you not do that. No one's ever...done that to me during sex."

"You don't like it?"

I couldn't say I disliked it. I just wasn't sure how I felt about it. Mostly just uncomfortable. But how could I explain that to him? "I just would rather you not slap me. Period. On my breasts, my butt, anywhere."

"All right, Melanie."

Now I felt terrible. "I know a lot of women like it. But for now, please. Just don't."

He rolled over onto his back. Shit, now I'd done it. He wouldn't want me anymore. Well, if he couldn't have sex without a slap, maybe we weren't meant to be together. We hardly knew each other, after all.

I looked over at him. "Are you all right?"

"I'm fine. I just...like that. That's all."

"I know. That's obvious. I just don't have any experience with that kind of...sex. And I'd rather not do it. At least not right now."

"You want me to leave?" he asked.

"Of course not. I want you to stay. I want you to do what you promised me but without slapping me."

His eyes were laced with something I couldn't read. He turned on his side and propped his head in his hand. This was the darkness I knew resided within him. Darkness that I was both drawn to and afraid of. The darkness that called to me. One day, I knew I would succumb to it. But I had to be ready.

He still hadn't said anything.

"You don't have to do anything," I said. "I'm sorry if I spoiled the moment."

"You didn't spoil it." He rolled onto his back and closed his eyes.

At least he wasn't leaving. He was a better person than I was. I had sneaked out after that first time. It had been a coward's way out, and I'd felt like shit for doing it. I had to do something to lighten up the mood here. I gazed at his tense body, so perfect. From his angled masculine jawline, his rugged silvery stubble, his long wavy dark hair, his broad shoulders, just the right amount of chest hairs scattered over his flat nipples, and his gorgeous rippled abs. His nest of black curls, and his flaccid cock, looking ever so normal, a far cry from how massive he was erect. His thighs were big and strong too, leading down to sleek calves and oddly smooth feet for such a rugged man.

What could I do to make this situation better?

And then I knew.

I crawled down to his waist, nestled between his legs, and took his soft cock between my lips, watching his face.

His eyes shot open. I let his cock drop, and I smiled

without saying anything.

I sucked it between my lips, swirled my tongue around the head, and soon he began to grow within my mouth.

He was large, and a blow job would be difficult, but I was determined. He continued to grow. There wouldn't be any deep-throating, but I could still give him a blow job, and that was exactly what I intended to do. I licked up and down his large shaft, pausing at his balls and sucking each one into my mouth.

He groaned above me.

I worked back up to the glans and gave it tiny little sucks, tightening my tongue and forcing it into the tiny slit. Then I thrust down, taking him as far as I could, ignoring the gag reflex.

I was impressed with myself. I made it farther than halfway down before I had to come back up. I gave him more soft sucks of the top of his cockhead and then went back to tiny kisses, pointing my tongue and fucking his tiny opening. He tasted of salt and clove, of male musk and leather. Delicious.

"God, Melanie, you give fucking great head."

I'd never considered fellatio among my talents, but if he liked it, all the better. I was aching for him to return the favor. Years had passed since a man had gone down on me, and I knew on instinct that Jonah would be great at it.

To make up for my inability to take it down my throat, I lubed him up good with saliva and then added my hand so I could get all the way down to the base. Once I started that, he stopped me.

"No, I can't come again until you do." He sat up, grabbed me by the shoulders, and pushed me down on the bed so I was lying flat on my back.

"Where did I leave off? Yes, these gorgeous nipples." He lowered his head and kissed one of them. Instantly it hardened even further. He cupped both breasts, swirling his tongue around my nipple. I sucked in a breath. He continued kissing my nipple, and when he started sucking, I nearly lost it.

"That feels so good," I said.

"Beautiful," he murmured against my chest. Then he moved to the other nipple and sucked while thumbing the first. He sucked me gently, though a little harder as time went on, but I wanted more.

"Harder," I said.

He obeyed, still not to the point where I wanted though. Had I done myself a disservice? Perhaps he was afraid to get a little firmer with my nipples, given that I didn't want him smacking me. So I grabbed his head, and he dropped my nipple with a soft pop.

"Look at me, Jonah. I'm not fragile. I won't break. I want you to suck on my nipples, bite, even pinch a little. I like it."

He didn't smile, but he did get back to work. He sucked a little harder, even nibbled a bit. Well, we'd work on it. Right now another part of me was craving his attention.

"My p-pussy, Jonah. I want you to eat my pussy."

Never in my life had I said those words to a man, and I was no doubt seventy different shades of crimson, saying them now. He left my nipples and kissed his way down to my patch of blond curls.

"You're beautiful. Au naturel, just the way I like it." He fingered my blond hair. "Oh, baby, I want this pussy. I'm going to eat all of that cream out of you and make you come and come and come, until you plead with me to stop."

I wasn't used to his blunt language, but I found it turned

me on. He started slowly, sliding his tongue up and down my wet slit. Then he swirled his tongue around my clit, and I nearly lost it right there. It had been so long since anyone had licked me between my legs. So very long. Too long.

"You taste so good, sweetheart."

"Works for me," I murmured.

I began moving my hips, rubbing myself against his lips, his stubble. My God, it felt so good. I shuddered, and goosebumps erupted all over me. My nipples were tight, my nerves on edge. So good, so good, so good, and then he sucked on my clit and slid two fingers into my channel.

I lost it.

The orgasm hit me with such force, I nearly couldn't take it. I climaxed around him, trembling, and as he pumped into me with his fingers, nudging my G-spot, I went crazy.

"That's it. Come for me. Keep coming. Keep coming."

When I started to come down from the euphoria, he began licking my lips again. He pulled my labia into his mouth and tugged. And then he sucked my clit. It was sensitive from my orgasm, but it still felt good. He slurped as he ate me, and everything from his head bobbing between my legs to the sucking sounds he made with his mouth against my flesh made my skin sizzle. He flicked his tongue in and out of me, and then he moved my legs farther forward and licked my ass.

This was new, and I wasn't wholly comfortable, but I didn't want to stop him. Last time I had stopped him from doing something, he'd frozen for a bit.

So I let him lick my puckered hole, and I found, oddly, that I enjoyed it.

"It's a gorgeous little ass you have," he said. "And God, this pussy, as ruby red as your other lips." He sank into me again, tickling me, sucking at me. "I could eat you all day. You taste so fucking good."

Soon I was starting on my second orgasm, and when he thrust his fingers into me again, I soared. My nipples tightened, and all my energy came from the outside in, centering in my pussy, helping me fly.

And then I started to come again.

This man had made me multi-orgasmic—something I'd never thought could happen to me—and my God, it was thrilling.

He continued sucking me, biting my labia, swirling his tongue around my butthole, all the while finger-fucking me in and out and in and out and then pushing up against my G-spot. So, so good.

"You like this, baby? You like how I eat your pussy?"

Again his blunt, graphic words drove me insane, and I started on yet one more climax.

"That's it, baby. You just keep on coming. Come for me. Only for me. God, you're so hot. That's right, sweetheart. That's it."

I screamed this time, clutching at the comforter. My hips were moving wildly, and I was grinding against his face.

He continued eating me, and the orgasms kept coming, coming, coming...

Until I couldn't take it anymore.

"God, Jonah, stop."

I raised my head a bit to look up, and he was smiling between my legs, his fingers still pumping in and out of me.

"I told you I'd eat you until you pleaded for me to stop."

I giggled. "Yes, you did say that."

"I'm hard as a rock right now, Melanie. I need you. Soon."

"My legs are spread, and I know I'm wet as hell. What's stopping you?"

He lunged forward and pressed into my heat.

I was so sensitive, even a slight nudge of his cock against my clit and I was close to coming again.

He slid right in, absolutely no resistance. I was so slick that I could take that large cock with no trouble at all.

He pumped above me, looking into my eyes, his own blazing with flames. "God, Melanie, you feel so good."

"So do you," I said. "God, so do you."

He thrust in and out, hard, and with each thrust, I grew more and more certain of three things.

I had never had sex like this.

I had never known a man like Jonah Steel.

And I would never know a man like him again.

CHAPTER FIFTEEN

Jonah

Although I'd had two orgasms previously this day, this last one was unlike anything I'd ever known.

As I thrust into Melanie's body, as she shivered and shuddered beneath me, crying out my name, I let go, and my whole body—not just my cock, not just my balls, but my whole fucking body—convulsed.

It was fucking amazing. I'd had no idea an orgasm could be so all-consuming.

Regular orgasm was a release.

This had been a deliverance.

From what, I wasn't sure. But I felt renewed.

I collapsed on top of her for just a moment, our bodies melded together, but then I moved over to the side, not wanting to crush her.

She crawled upward into a pillow, curling up her body. She patted the other side. I moved there and watched her fall into slumber.

And then I left.

★ ★ ★ ★

It was late when I got back to the ranch. The lights were on in the main house, so I figured I'd stop and see if Talon wanted to have a drink. I let myself in and gave his mutt, Roger, a pat on the head. No one was in the living area or the kitchen, but light was coming from under the door of Talon's office. I walked toward the room and knocked.

"Yeah, come in."

Talon sat at his desk, typing on the computer. He looked up. "Oh, hey, Joe. What are you doing over here at this hour?"

"I just got back from the city. I saw your light and thought I'd stop by and see if you want to have a drink or something."

Talon raked his fingers through his hair. "Yeah, sure. I could use one."

"What are you working on?"

"Well, I started going over some of the orchard accounts, but I ended up looking for information on Jade's ex, Colin Morse."

"Why are you looking for information on him? He's dead."

"I'm not so sure he is. He's mixed up in all this somehow. I can feel it." He stood and walked around his desk.

I followed him out into the family room. I sat down on a leather couch while Talon played bartender.

"I ran into a guy the other day," I said. "Said he knew you."

"Yeah?" Talon raised his eyebrows. "Who?"

"An old guy named Mike. Met him in an old dive bar around skid row in Grand Junction."

"What the hell were you doing down there?"

"I could ask you the same thing."

"I asked you first."

"I'm the older brother. You need to answer me first."

Talon shook his head. "Oh, hell, no. You're not going to pull rank on me. Those days are long gone."

True, they were. I had lost the right to pull rank on Talon

one fateful day when I was nearly thirteen.

"What the hell does it matter why either of us was there?" I asked.

"Doesn't matter a damn to me. You brought it up." Talon took a sip of his whiskey and handed me a martini.

I accepted the drink gladly and took a long sip. Mother's milk.

Definitely time to change the subject. "Why are you researching Colin?"

"Jade says Larry is claiming his innocence regarding Colin. Not that I take Larry's word for anything but the shit it is, but remember a few weeks ago, when Jade got a call from Colin's phone?"

"Yeah."

"It just doesn't sit right with me. Larry had disappeared. And if he had Colin's phone, why the hell would he call Jade with it?"

"I don't know. She was his assistant city attorney. Maybe he was calling to check up on things."

"Then why didn't he say something? And if he cared about how things were going at the city attorney's office, why did he disappear in the first place?"

"I don't know, Talon. None of this makes any sense at all. Why is Colin even an issue? He certainly wasn't one of your abductors. He would have been about a year old, at most."

Talon rubbed his jawline. "He hates me. One, for taking Jade from him, although he dumped her first, and two, for kicking the shit out of him. He is involved in this somehow. How else would his phone and wallet get into Larry's possession?"

"Easy. Larry offs him, and he takes his phone and wallet. It makes perfect sense to me."

"Come on, Joe, you're smarter than that. Dig a little deeper."

"Talon, did it ever occur to you that maybe you weren't meant to figure this all out? Maybe you should just concentrate on healing."

"God, you sound like Dr. Carmichael."

I stiffened, hoping Talon didn't notice. "What makes you say that?"

"She says I should concentrate on healing, because whether these guys are ever caught won't help me either way."

"She's a smart lady. You should probably listen to her."

"By the way, how's it going with you and her?"

My cheeks warmed. "What do you mean?"

"I mean your therapy, dumbass. What did you think I meant?"

Of course he meant my therapy. He didn't know about the other...stuff. I sure as hell couldn't tell him about the sex. I also couldn't tell him that I was no longer seeing her for therapy, because then he would ask why, and I would have to tell him something, anything, and I hadn't a clue what that would be.

I had no idea what was going on with Melanie. It was the best sex I'd ever had, and I couldn't deny the attraction between us. But we wanted different things. She'd freaked out when I slapped her. I would never hurt her, of course, but I liked to play rough during sex. I was a natural Dominant, and I'd never had anyone complain about it before. Then again, she'd given me the best blow job of my life, and she had the sweetest little pussy I'd ever tasted...

"Therapy is going fine."

"She's good, isn't she?"

"Oh, yeah. She's good." Of course, I wasn't talking about

therapy.

"Are you figuring things out?"

"Sure." I wasn't convinced I was telling the truth to my brother. But the last time I'd skulked around in the alleyways, I stopped before finding someone to pummel me. That had to say something. I sure as hell wasn't ready to tell Talon about my secret pastime.

Funny thing was, I hadn't done it for several years—until Talon started healing through therapy. That had brought the whole thing back to the front of my mind, reviving the guilt. It clutched at me like sharp hooks, refusing to let me go.

I wasn't going to do it again—no more trips to skid row for me. I was going to figure this out. I'd prefer to do it with Melanie, but if she couldn't help me, I would do it alone.

Hell, I did everything else alone.

No, that wasn't fair. I didn't run this ranch alone. My brothers and all the other employees helped.

So why did I always feel responsible for everything? Logically, I knew I wasn't.

I had to figure that out.

I took another sip of my martini. Good stuff. Then I turned the tables on my brother. "So how's *your* therapy going?"

"It's going well. Dr. Carmichael thinks I'm making great progress."

I didn't need my brother to tell me that. Just looking at him, I could see what a changed man he was. Was it from therapy? Jade? Himself? Probably a combination of all three, but Jade had no doubt been the catalyst.

I had never believed a woman could change anything. I still didn't. But I couldn't lessen what Talon and Jade shared. It was beautiful to watch them together.

"Anything new on the rose on the pillow?"

"I had Steve Dugan come over to dust for prints around Jade's room, where the rose was left. He didn't get anything, and we didn't get anything off the rose itself."

"Well, it was a while ago," I said.

"I changed all the locks on the doors, of course, and changed the security system too. Who the hell could have gotten in here?"

I shook my head. "I sure don't know. Makes me cringe, thinking about it."

"You're telling me. I was here. I was *in* the fucking house. Jade was in her shower, not fifteen feet away from the bed, when this happened." He rubbed his eyes. "I can't let myself think about it too much or I get crazy. Makes me want to pound somebody."

"Keep your temper in check."

"Oh, I'm fine. Who would I pound anyway? Larry Wade is in prison, and Colin is God knows where. That nutty boyfriend of Jade's mother's is God knows where. And I don't even know who the third one is. Six months ago I would've found someone to pound, but not now."

I lifted an eyebrow. "What are you talking about?"

"Didn't Dr. Carmichael tell you?"

"Dr. Carmichael and I don't discuss you."

"I gave her permission to."

"I know that. She told me. But I'm not comfortable with that. So what the hell are you talking about, Talon?"

Talon cleared his throat. "I'm not exactly proud of this, but before I started therapy, there were times when I'd go to the city on the weekends."

"Yes, I know that."

"Sometimes I'd find a girl and have meaningless sex. Other times I..."

"Yeah?"

"Other times I'd walk down a dark alley on skid row, find someone to mug me so I could beat the crap out of him."

I shot my eyes open.

"God, don't look at me like that."

"I'm sorry."

"I never beat someone up for the hell of it. I waited for him to try something on me."

"Sounds like you put yourself in danger." I was one to talk. To think, my brother hung around those sleazy alleyways for the exact opposite reason I did. Him to feel more in control, me to punish myself.

God...that was how we'd both ended up in that bar. What if we had run into each other?

"You don't do that anymore, I hope."

"Of course not. I don't feel like I need to. I look back, and I wonder why I ever did it. It didn't change anything. Kicking the shit out of Colin didn't change anything either. I'm lucky I didn't get locked up. And none of it mattered anyway. It didn't change the fact that I was kidnapped and raped by three men."

"I know. I'm sorry."

"Oh, Christ. I didn't tell you this for you to feel bad. None of this is your fault. You know that, and I know that."

I gulped. I did know. I knew it as a sane, logical person. But it wasn't my logical side that had the issue. Still, that last time I went to skid row myself, I hadn't done anything. That had to be a good sign. At least that's what I kept telling myself.

I wasn't ready to tell any of this to Talon. "I'm glad you don't feel you have to do that anymore. You could've gotten yourself into big trouble."

"I know. Believe me, I was careful. I never did any lasting damage, and I was long gone before a cop could have gotten there. But none of that makes it right. I was wrong to do those things. Like I said, it didn't end up making me feel better anyway. The only way it would have made me feel better is if I'd met one of my abductors in a fucking alleyway. But I never found a guy with a missing toe, or a guy with a phoenix tattoo, or a guy with a birthmark the shape of Texas."

My heart dropped to my stomach. "What are you talking about? A birthmark shaped like Texas?" Jesus, Bryce had said his father had a birthmark with that shape. Of course, he hadn't said where the birthmark was. "I thought you only remembered something about two of the guys."

"I'm sorry. I should've told you. My mind has been focused on that damned rose that was left on Jade's pillow. I've spent the last several weeks trying to figure that out. But yeah, Dr. Carmichael did a guided hypnosis with me several weeks ago. She took me back to that time and that place." He visibly shuddered.

"You don't have to go on. I can tell this is bothering you."

"I'm okay." He twisted his lips, his features grim. "Anyway, she took me back...there. Back when they were...doing it to me. It was freaky, Joe. I was there. I really was there. Anyway, I was able to look around. The guys, sometimes they wore black wife-beaters. And I noticed, on the one I remember having a low voice, that he had a birthmark on his right arm. On the underside, right under his armpit hair. It was a weird shape, and I didn't realize at the time what it was shaped like, only that I knew I'd seen the shape before. As an adult, I figured it out. It reminded me of the shape of the state of Texas."

My blood ran cold.

★ ★ ★ ★

It was after midnight, and instead of going home, I drove into town, to the mayor's house, where Bryce was staying with his parents. I had tried calling his cell phone, but he didn't answer. He was probably in bed, and most likely so were his parents. I didn't righteously care. I had to know.

I drove up to the mayor's house and skidded my car into park. I ran up to the door and rang the doorbell, my pulse racing. I waited. No response. I rang the doorbell again.

Again, no response. So I started pounding on the door, pounding as if my life depended on it. *Damn it, Bryce. I have to talk to you.*

No one answered. There were no lights on in the house, but the dog was barking behind the front door. Certainly they could hear me. I continued pounding on the door, until finally the elderly neighbor lady looked outside the front door.

"What's going on over there?" she yelled.

"Nothing, Mrs. Norris," I said. "It's just me, Jonah Steel. I need to talk to Bryce."

The woman walked forward in her bathrobe and slippers. "For goodness' sake, Jonah, stop all that racket. The Simpsons aren't home."

"Where the hell are they?"

"They drove to Grand Junction to the hospital. Something was wrong with the baby."

Bryce's son? Shit. "Is he okay?"

Mrs. Norris shrugged. "I don't know, but he was making a lot of noise. Sounded horrible. Bryce and his parents were frantic."

"My God." No wonder Bryce hadn't answered my phone calls.

"I'm really sorry to disturb you," I said.

I was tempted to drive to the hospital, but I didn't know which hospital they'd gone to. And Bryce wasn't answering his phone. I called him one more time and left a voice mail, asking him to call me when he had news about Henry. Then I drove home.

Damn.

CHAPTER SIXTEEN

Melanie

It had served me right. After all, I'd left him the first time we were together. Still, Jonah leaving me stuck in my craw. It hurt. And I wasn't exactly sure why.

I also didn't know why I went back to the lingerie shop the next morning before my first appointment. I was fingering the silken material of the Midnight Reverie collection when the same blond salesgirl came up to me.

"That would be a great color on you," she said.

"I've heard that before."

"I'm not surprised. With your opalescent skin tone, purple is a no-brainer."

I chuckled. "No, I meant I've heard it from *you* before. I was in here a while back."

She blushed a little but at least had the courtesy not to stammer. "Well, I was right then, and I'm right now." She let out a nervous giggle.

"I don't wear purple," I said. "My eyes are green. It would clash."

"Don't be silly. You'd be great in purple. What's your size? You can try one of the bras on."

"No, thank you."

"What colors do you like to wear? I'm sure we have

something that would look lovely on you."

"Green, beige, teal, blue," I answered automatically. Oh crap, now she would want to sell me something.

"Oh, I must show you our Oceane collection. Colors of the ocean. Blue, teal, emerald. They'd be lovely on you. We just got in some beautiful satin nightgowns." She grabbed my arm and pulled me. "I can't wait for you to see them."

I had no choice but to follow her until we came to a display on the other side of the store. The collection was indeed lovely, and instead of skimpy bras and panties, these were long gowns, very pretty.

"Look," she said, holding up a bright-green gown. "This nearly matches the color of your eyes. And with that beautiful blond hair of yours—goodness, you'll be gorgeous."

I sighed. The gown was stunning. It was simple, spaghetti straps and a sheath style, cinched in slightly at the waist and then fanning out over the butt and into a skirt that hit halfway down the calf.

"What's your size, hon?" she asked.

Hon? She had to be half my age.

"Medium, usually. Sometimes a large."

She looked me up and down. "Let's try a medium. You're not too busty."

Sure, rub it in.

She grabbed the medium and handed it to me. "Dressing rooms are over there." She pointed. "Please, try it on."

What the heck? After all, I had come back to the shop. I ambled into the dressing room and shed all my clothing down to my panties. I put the beautiful gown over my head and let it fall onto my body.

I gasped when I looked in the mirror.

The gown was made for me. It accentuated every part of my body, gave me curves where I had none—a swell of my breasts, a tiny swell of my belly, swell of my hips. And then the silk fell around and softly over my knees.

Wow. I looked hot. I laughed out loud. When was the last time I'd thought I looked hot? Probably around the fifth of never. I knew I was pretty enough, and I had a decent enough body. There just wasn't anything extraordinary about me whatsoever. Definitely not hot.

This gown made me hot.

I made a decision then. I would buy it. I might never wear it, but I hardly ever indulged in anything purely frivolous. Maybe Jonah would like it.

The thought made me turn red. I quickly looked away from the mirror and changed back into my clothes.

I hurried toward the register before I changed my mind. Then I saw the price tag poking out of the fabric. I hadn't bothered to check the cost, so I pulled the tag toward me now.

Six hundred and seventy-five dollars?

I threw the gown on the nearest shelf and hurried out of the store.

★ ★ ★ ★

I didn't have a session until eleven, so I headed over to the coffee shop next to my office with my laptop to check e-mails, quickly texting Randi to let her know where I'd be. I ordered a vanilla latte and then sat down and opened my computer. I was midway through my e-mails when a masculine voice startled me.

"Melanie? Melanie Carmichael?"

I looked up, and in the doorway to the coffee shop stood... I did a double take.

"Oliver?"

The auburn-haired man smiled. "Yeah, wow. How long has it been?"

"Since med school," I said.

"Melanie!" the barista called.

I stood.

"I'll grab that for you." Oliver took my latte from the barista and handed it to me. "Mind if I join you for a few minutes?"

"Not at all. You want to get a coffee?"

"Yeah," he chuckled. "Kind of why I'm here, I guess. Sorry, seeing you kind of derailed me for a minute." He walked over to the line where a few people stood already.

I stared at my laptop screen and caught my breath. Oliver Nichols. Wow. I hadn't seen him in over a decade. We'd gone to med school together, and right after graduation, we had a little one-nighter. Then he went off to California for his internship and residency, and I came here to Grand Junction to do mine.

I warmed from my head to my toes. He was so gorgeous, no silver yet in his auburn hair. He still had those twinkling blue eyes. He had been the best-looking male student in our class. Also had the best personality. Always jovial, always smiling. I had never thought he would look my way, but after a few drinks in the hot tub at a friend's graduation party, things had gotten...friendly.

I pretended to go through e-mails, but I couldn't concentrate. I could feel his gaze upon me. We'd never vowed to stay in touch or anything. After all, he went to California and I stayed here. I had looked him up on the Internet from time to time. He specialized in pediatric nephrology and had ended up doing several fellowships. With all that education, he hadn't been in practice very long at this point.

He had also authored several very well-respected papers. Of course nothing I would read, since I knew absolutely nothing about pediatric nephrology beyond the basic anatomy.

My lips suddenly felt dry. I grabbed my purse from where it was hanging on the back of my chair, pulled out some lip balm, and smoothed it over my lips.

Why in the world was I so freaked out? Oliver and I had never had a relationship. He had never even looked my way most of med school. I hadn't dated anyone during those times, at least not seriously. I hadn't had the time, and once I started internship and residency, I'd had even less time.

He sat back down across from me, holding a large coffee cup. "I can't believe it. How are you, Melanie?"

"I'm fine. What are you doing here? Have you left California?"

He nodded. "I'm spearheading some research over at Valleycrest Hospital. They're setting up a pediatric nephrology unit."

Impressive. Though everything Oliver Nichols did was impressive. "How long will you be in town?"

"A few months, at least. It's possible they may want me to stay on, in which case I'll open a practice here."

I nodded. "What an incredible opportunity. You'll love it here."

"So what have you been up to?"

"I'm in private practice as a psychotherapist here in town. In fact, my building is right next door. I don't live too far from here either. I have a downtown loft."

"So you never left here after your residency?"

"No. The city grew on me. And I've got to tell you, the Western slope of Colorado has the best peaches and apples you'll ever taste." I smiled shyly. "They're in season right now, but not for much longer. Be sure to sample them while you're here."

"I absolutely will." He eyed my laptop. "I'm not interrupting your work, am I?"

"No, I just felt like sitting over here instead of my office this morning. I don't have a session until eleven." I looked at my watch. Ten twenty.

"Yeah, sometimes it's nice to get out of the office."

I nodded. Silence for a few moments. Normally, silence didn't bother me much. I was a natural introvert. But right now, with dashing Oliver Nichols sitting across me, the silence felt like tension in the air. Funny how it hadn't felt that way with Jonah Steel…

"I'll be looking for a place to stay. Where did you say you live?"

"A couple blocks away. Bainbridge Lofts."

"Have any rentals in there?"

"Honestly, I don't know. I own."

"Maybe I'll take a look over there. I'm meeting a realtor later today to help me find something for the next six months. And as I said, it may turn into a longer situation."

I nodded again. No wonder Oliver and I had only had one night. We clearly didn't have much to say to each other.

"So fill me in on the last fifteen years or so of your life, Melanie. Are you married? Have any kids?"

"Never been married. No kids. How about you?"

He took a sip of his coffee. "Divorced. For two years now. I have a couple kids. Two boys. Ages six and eight."

"Are they still in California?"

"Yeah. This was a tough decision, coming here. But they offered me a lot of money, and the more money I make, the better college funds I can set up for Josh and Corey. I'll miss them, but I'll be flying out every other weekend to hang out with them. It'll be like a big event for them."

"That's nice." Inside I was dying a little bit. Here he had two kids, and I hadn't had a significant relationship in God knew how long.

He smiled at me as he drank. "I have to tell you, Melanie, you haven't changed a bit. You look the same as you did the first year of med school, bright-eyed and ready to learn. The only difference is your hair should be flowing over your shoulders."

I'd worn my hair up, as I often did for work. My cheeks warmed. Something about this felt all wrong.

"You look great yourself. Not a gray hair on that head of yours."

"Good genes. This red hair comes from my mother's side. She's Irish. She's sixty-five and still only has a few strands of gray."

"Well, you look great." I had no idea what else to say.

He regarded his watch. "I have to go." He took another sip of his coffee and then placed the lid on it. "I'm thrilled I ran into you. It will be nice to know someone around town. Would you like to have dinner with me tonight?"

I bit my lip. Dinner? Was he proposing a date? I wasn't sure.

"We can talk about Grand Junction, Valleycrest, and anything else interesting around here."

What would be the harm in that? "Sure, I'd like that. I'm

done tonight by six. You want to meet somewhere?"

"Do you have your card handy with an address on it? I'll just pick you up there."

I pulled the card out of my laptop case and handed it to him. "Okay, if you're sure you don't mind. See you at six."

He smiled, his eyes twinkling. "I'm looking forward to it."

CHAPTER SEVENTEEN

Jonah

I finally got a text from Bryce the next morning before lunch. It said only, "We're home."

I called. No answer.

So I drove over. Half an hour later, I arrived at the mayor's house in Snow Creek. I knocked on the door.

Bryce's mom, Evelyn Simpson, answered the door. "Oh, hello, Joe."

"Hi, Evelyn. I came to see Bryce. Is Henry okay?"

Evelyn looked pale and fatigued. "He's fine. Evidently he had a chill. Last night he was crying and crying, and his lips started to turn blue. We were worried that he was suffering from lack of oxygen, and it was after hours so we ran to Grand Junction to the emergency room. I've never been so scared in my life."

"So he's okay?"

"By the time we got to the hospital, he was starting to look better. His temperature was below normal. Nobody seemed to know what caused it. The ER doctor said it was probably a virus. But that confuses me. I always thought viruses were supposed to make your temperature go up, not down."

"I certainly don't know."

"He seems to be fine now. We stayed there a while, ended

up being gone all night. Just got back a little while ago."

"Where's Bryce?"

Evelyn held the door open for me. "He and his dad are in with the baby. Come on in."

His dad. My skin tightened around me. I wasn't sure I wanted to see Tom Simpson.

I walked into the house, following the sound of the baby's cries. "Bryce?" I said, standing in the door of what appeared to be a makeshift nursery.

Tom Simpson was holding little Henry, rocking him in a recliner. Bryce was putting medicine into a syringe.

"Hey, Joe."

I cleared my throat, trying not to look at Tom. "I hear you guys had quite a night."

"Yeah. I'm sorry I didn't answer your calls or texts. I was freaked."

"No problem, man. I understand. How's Henry?"

"He's got a fever now. It was the strangest thing. I seriously thought he was dying."

"Wow."

"I can't even describe how scared I was. You don't have kids, so I'm not sure you'd understand anyway."

I thought I'd understand just fine, but I didn't want to upset Bryce. "What happened?"

"Last night his lips and nail beds turned blue, and every book on raising a kid says that's a big danger sign. My mom and I totally freaked. Only Dad remained calm." He looked over at Tom. "You'll never know how much I appreciate that, Dad. You sure know how to keep your head in a crisis."

Tom smiled slightly. An eerie feeling swept through me. Remaining calm in a crisis would be a great characteristic...for a criminal. A psychopath.

Bryce handed the filled syringe to Tom.

"Here you go, buddy," Tom said, putting the syringe to Henry's lips. "Come on. Take your medicine."

Tom finally got the medicine in Henry's mouth, although some of it dribbled down his chin. He wiped it up with a towel and handed Henry back to Bryce. "I ought to get into the office. I haven't had any sleep, but there are a few things that can't wait." He turned to me and held out his hand. "Always good to see you, Joe."

I flinched a little. I had to shake his hand. Hell, I'd shaken it hundreds of times before. I'd grown up with this guy. He was the father of my best friend. So I forced my arm out and took his hand.

Again, a strange sensation surged through me, like ice-cold water trickling over my neck and chest. My stomach churned.

He conveyed something to me in that handshake, whether he knew it or not, and whatever it was, I didn't like it.

I felt one million times better when Tom left the room. I cringed, thinking of him holding Henry, taking care of him. I had to find out where Tom's birthmark was. And I had to find some way to tell Bryce about my suspicions.

How the hell did I tell my friend that I thought his father was a child molester? A sick criminal? It was as bad as finding out my own uncle had taken part. In fact, worse. From what I knew, Larry hadn't been the one who chopped up and disposed of the bodies. If what I suspected was true, Tom Simpson had not only abused and disposed of random kids, he also did it to his own nephew, Luke Walker.

Again, the icy trickles of water...

Calm down, Joe. You don't even know he had anything to do with the abduction.

Right now, I had to be there for Bryce. He was clearly distraught over his son.

"He's always been such a healthy kid, Joe," Bryce said. "I wouldn't have freaked out so much over a fever, but when those little nail beds turned blue... Man, I've never been so scared in my life."

"Your mom said he had a chill?"

"Yeah, that's what the ER guys said. Said it was a normal thing. I'd never heard of it. They checked his pulse ox and he was fine, so the blue nail beds and lips were caused by the chill, not lack of oxygen. He's got some kind of virus. Now he's running a fever."

He set Henry, who had finally calmed down, into his crib.

"So what did you need last night?"

"What do you mean?"

"Well, you texted me several times. And Mrs. Norris came by this morning and said you were pounding on our door last night at midnight."

Shit. I shouldn't have done that. I'd been going crazy after what Talon said. Had I really thought I could barge into this house and demand to see a guy's birthmark?

I said nothing.

"Seriously, Joe. What were you doing here at midnight?"

I had to think of something and think of it quick. "I was... in town at Murphy's, and I'd had a few drinks. I guess I thought something was more important than it actually was."

"What?"

"Something about Talon and Luke Walker. I thought I had a lead, but I found out this morning that it was nothing."

"So what was it?"

"I... I can't say." *Yeah, good save, Joe.* No way was Bryce going to buy this.

"What do you mean you can't say? You were pounding on my door last night to tell me."

"Yeah, I know. I'm sorry about that." I cleared my throat. "I found out this morning that what I thought was a lead wasn't, and the people involved asked me to keep the information in confidence."

"Seriously? You can't tell me? You know my word is as good as gold, Joe."

"Yeah, I know. You know I trust you implicitly. But I just can't. I'm sorry."

He sighed. "No matter anyway. Right now, I'm so relieved that Henry is okay that I don't really care about anything else."

Thank God. He'd bought it. I'd have to find out about his father's birthmark on my own. Why would I drag my old friend into this when he had a son to worry about? At least I'd have to wait until Henry had gotten over this virus or whatever it was.

Bryce leaned over the crib and put his hand on Henry's forehead. "He's so warm. God, Joe, I never knew I could be this scared."

"He's a great kid," I said. "He's going to be all right. Kids get sick."

"I know. But he's so little."

"I remember when Marj came home from the hospital when she was born. Talk about little. She'd gained weight by the time she came home, but she was still under six pounds. The most fragile little thing. But she was a trouper and she survived. Look at Henry. He's ten months old, good and chubby, the picture of health. He's going to be fine."

Bryce nodded.

"You want something? I can go out to the kitchen and get you some coffee."

He smiled—sort of. "That'd be great. I think my mom has a fresh pot brewed."

"No problem." I left the nursery and went to the kitchen. Sure enough, a fresh pot of coffee sat on the burner. I'd been to this house so many times when I was a kid, and I knew where they kept everything. I opened the cupboard door, got out a mug, and poured a cup of coffee. I poured another for myself.

"Anything I can help you with, Joe?"

I nearly spilled the coffee when Tom's deep voice met my ears. Talon remembered the man with the birthmark as having a low voice. Tom's voice *was* low. Was it lower than Larry's?

Hell, I didn't know. They were completely different voices, and my own voice was deeper than either of theirs. Talon was remembering as a prepubescent ten-year-old. All grown men's voices were low to a ten-year-old.

I turned, willing myself not to wince. "Just getting some coffee for Bryce and myself."

"Sounds good." He took a mug out of the cupboard. "Tell Bryce to come out here to the kitchen. I'll join you."

So much for Tom going into the office for a few things that couldn't wait.

"I don't think he wants to leave Henry."

"Nonsense. Henry's fine. Do you know how many viruses Bryce had when he was a kid? Hell, I remember when he and Luke both had the chicken pox. What a mess."

Luke. Why did he have to bring up Luke? Did they still talk about Luke?

I drew in a breath and let it out slowly. "Wow," I said, "I

haven't thought about Luke in a long time. I assume you're talking about Bryce's cousin, Luke Walker."

Tom nodded. "Yup."

He sounded so matter of fact. So unaffected. It creeped me out.

"That was a tough time. Talon took that particularly hard."

"I had no idea that Talon was even involved. I can't believe your father covered that up. And now Larry Wade has been arrested. Just odd all around."

His tone didn't indicate that he thought it was odd at all. The vibes coming from him felt sinister.

"Well, Bryce is waiting for his coffee."

"Right. Go ahead."

Evidently he'd given up the notion of the two of us joining him in the kitchen for coffee. Just as well. I didn't want to be in the same room with Tom Simpson a minute longer than necessary.

On the other hand, he could be a source of information. Maybe I could get him to slip up. Get him to admit something he didn't want to admit. But as I stared into his cold blue eyes, I knew the truth. Tom Simpson would not be tripped up. Nothing fazed him.

I took the coffee back to Bryce in the nursery.

"He's nodding off now," Bryce said, gesturing to Henry.

Bryce sat back down in the rocking chair, and I looked at the sleeping baby for a few moments, his blond peach fuzz hair plastered to his head with sweat from his fever. Thank God he was okay. Then I sat down in another chair. I took a sip of my coffee.

"So what's going on with you?" Bryce asked. "I need to get my mind off this crap."

"Not much, really." I thought about telling him about Melanie, but I wasn't sure I could do that without telling him I was in therapy—or rather, no longer in therapy—with Talon's therapist. I wasn't sure Talon wanted anyone to know he was in therapy, and I was damned sure I didn't want anyone to know I was.

"Well, something's going on. You must be doing some research into the situation with Talon, since you were pounding on my door at midnight last night."

He had me there. "Talon and I are working on it, but we haven't found much."

"What about Ryan? I haven't seen him around town in a while."

I swallowed the sip of coffee I had just taken. "This is Ryan's busy time of the year. He's harvesting the grapes and having a great time making new batches of wine. Pretty soon it'll be bottling time for the wines that are ready." I shook my head. "Don't ask me to explain it to you. I have no idea what he does. Ryan's freaking brilliant."

"He does make a good wine," Bryce agreed.

"Yeah, neither Tal nor I know where he got that artistic streak. We sure didn't get any of it."

"Maybe from your mother?"

"Maybe."

Sadness hit me. I had been around fifteen years old when my mother committed suicide, and even though I had lots of memories of her, I still didn't know much about her. Talon, Ryan, and I had spent most of our time with our father on the ranch when we weren't at school. My father was a man's man and would have been considered a sexist by today's standards. He felt that outdoor work was men's work, and my mom seemed fine with that. I smiled. Once Marj hit eight or nine years old, she would have none of that. She helped with the "men's work." Of course, Mom was gone by then.

"And speaking of moms," Bryce said, giving me a shit-eating grin. "How's Brooke Bailey?"

I chuckled. Sometimes I still couldn't believe Brooke Bailey was living at the main ranch house.

Bryce continued, "Do you still have that poster? You know, the one in the blue spandex one-piece?" He grinned again. "I believe you built an altar around it."

While I was happy Bryce was in a better mood after Henry and the virus, I didn't really want to talk about Jade's mother. Yeah, I had nursed a massive crush on her when I was a horny teen, but I was hardly the only one. That had been decades ago.

"You know, she's not that much older than you, Joe."

Okay, this had to stop. "Bryce, shut the fuck up, will you?"

He laughed. "Did you ever in your life think, while you were jacking off to that poster, that she'd be living in your house someday?"

I hadn't given Brooke Bailey a thought in twenty years. This conversation had to end. "Bryce, that was years ago. I have no interest in Brooke Bailey."

"Well, a forty-three-year-old supermodel probably doesn't look the way you remember her."

Actually, she still looked great. "The long blond hair is now cut in a pixie, and one of her eyes is a little misshapen from the accident. She has a few scars on her face, but she's still a great-looking woman."

"And the body?" Bryce said.

"Yeah, she still has the body. She's not quite as tall as I expected. I thought she would be taller."

"Well, you know, people shrink with age."

"Not everything shrinks."

Bryce let out another guffaw of laughter.

"Well, where do you think Jade got them from? Certainly not her dad."

"So what's stopping you? She's living in one of your houses, and her boyfriend has flown the coop. Why not give it a shot?"

Because she wasn't Melanie. But of course I couldn't say that. Melanie Carmichael had me twisted up in so many knots, I wasn't sure where anything began.

"Because she's Jade's mom, for God's sake. And also, she's five years older than I am, and I'm not interested."

"Then maybe I'll have to come by and say hi."

"You're welcome to come by anytime, but I wouldn't get involved with Brooke Bailey."

"Why the hell not?"

"Because something isn't right there. To hear Jade talk, she was a terrible mother. Basically abandoned her kid. And I would think you wouldn't want to get involved with another woman who abandons her kid." I glanced at Henry, now sleeping soundly in his crib.

"Oh, hitting below the belt." Bryce held up his hand in mock surrender. "I'm not looking for a relationship, man. But I wouldn't mind a roll in the hay with Brooke Bailey."

"Why?"

"Why else? So I could say I had a roll in the hay with Brooke Bailey." He laughed.

I picked up one of Henry's stuffed animals sitting next to me and threw it at Bryce.

"Oh, you're such a girl. Pillow fight?" Bryce laughed.

I stood. I knew he was joking, but Bryce calling me a girl

rubbed me the wrong way, and I suddenly wanted to escape this house. "Listen, I'm really glad Henry is okay. I'll check in with you tonight or tomorrow. Right now I've got to get back to the ranch."

"Hey, I didn't mean to freak you out. Stay. Stay for dinner, even. My mom's making meat loaf."

Meat loaf? When I could stop by the main house and eat whatever Felicia and Marj had cooked up? Not a chance. "I would, but I can't."

"Why?"

Oh, because I don't want to be in the same house as your father, who I think might be a child molester and murderer. "Just got things to do. Thanks for the invite. Stop by anytime if you want to meet Brooke. Bring Henry along."

"I will. And I was just kidding about the roll in the hay. I wouldn't do that to you or to Jade."

I nodded. "I know. See you around."

I walked out of the nursery and past the kitchen. Tom was still sitting at the table. This time he had a laptop open in front of him. Evidently he'd decided to do his work from home.

I walked briskly past the entry to the kitchen, not saying a word.

"Joe?"

Shit. Now I had to talk to him. I poked my head in the kitchen. "Yeah?"

"Leaving so soon?"

Yeah, I have a ranch to run. Why did people seem to forget that? Steel money didn't grow on trees. Well, it did, and also in pastures and vineyards. But a hell of a lot of work went into it too.

"Yeah. Lots of work at the ranch."

"Understood. It was good to see you. Stop by more often. Evelyn and I miss seeing you around here."

I turned and lifted my foot to walk toward the front door, when something made me hesitate.

"Tom?"

"Yeah?"

"Could I bother you for another cup of coffee?"

"Sure, no problem. Help yourself. Sit on down here with me. We can talk."

Talk.

And I had just the person to talk about.

CHAPTER EIGHTEEN

Melanie

My five o'clock session rescheduled earlier in the afternoon, so after my four o'clock, I was left with an hour to kill before Oliver met me at the office.

I didn't have long to wait, though, because I had a visitor. Rodney Cates. At least he hadn't barged in on a session this time. Randi had left for the day, so he knocked on the open door to my office.

"Dr. Cates?" I cleared my throat, my nerves jumping. "What can I do for you?"

"I just wanted to let you know that Erica seems to be doing a little bit better."

A heavy sigh of relief left me before I could stop it. "Thank you. You don't know how glad I am to hear you say that."

"I don't know how glad *you* are? I lost my daughter, and then I almost lost my wife. And you think I don't know how glad *you* are that my wife is doing better?"

I hadn't meant to hit a nerve. He was right. My remark had been selfish and unfeeling. This man was hurting, so I resolved to deal with him as I would with anyone else who was hurting. "I didn't mean to upset you. I am absolutely sure you're glad that your wife is doing better."

"May I come in?"

I couldn't very well say no, no matter how much I wanted to. "Of course." I was sitting at my desk, but I stood and walked over to my session area and sat down in my chair. I gestured to the couch and the other recliner. "Please, have a seat."

He plopped down on the couch and turned to face me. Yet he said nothing.

"What can I help you with, Dr. Cates?"

"There's something I wanted to ask you. About Gina."

I wasn't about to reveal anything from my session notes, but I didn't need to tell him that. "Of course. What do you want to know?"

"Did Gina say anything to you about falling in love?"

My throat thickened. She hadn't, at least not until the letter I got after she died.

So I shook my head. "Not during our sessions, no." Technically, that wasn't a lie. "Is there a reason why you're asking me this?"

"Yes." He cleared his throat. "One of her friends told Erica and me that Gina had been in love."

"I see."

"Wouldn't this be something she would discuss with her therapist?"

I fidgeted with my hands in my lap. "Not necessarily."

"This friend of hers, Marie, swears that she told her she was in love. Why would someone who was in love want to kill herself?"

"Dr. Cates, I wish I could help you. But honestly, there was nothing in my sessions that indicated Gina was suicidal."

"Marie said Gina knew the person she was in love with would never love her back."

"Like I said, it wasn't anything we discussed."

Dr. Cates stood and paced around my small session area. "I don't understand it. If she was in love and upset that her love might be unrequited, why wouldn't she discuss that with you?"

Because I was the one she was in love with. But I couldn't say that. I hadn't yet dealt with the fallout from Gina's feelings myself.

"Who wouldn't have wanted Gina? She was brilliant and beautiful."

"And she was also very troubled, obviously," I said.

Dr. Cates's face twisted into...not rage, exactly, but not anything good. Clearly those words had not been the right ones.

"How did you not see this? What kind of a therapist are you?"

How did you not see that her uncle—your brother-in-law—was abusing your daughter all those years? I desperately wanted to say the words, but that would only make things worse. I stood. "Dr. Cates, I think it would be best if you left now."

"No. You tell me." He inched toward me.

Chills ran up my neck.

"How could you not have seen this happening? How could you not know she was in love?"

My blood ran cold. He was between me and the door. Randi was gone. It was after five o'clock, so unless a security guard was walking down the hallway, no one would hear me if I screamed.

I didn't think Dr. Cates would actually hurt me, but I knew enough to see that he wasn't completely in his right mind.

I gritted my teeth. "Dr. Cates, I will tell you one more time. You need to leave. Now."

He took one more step toward me. "Not until I get some answers."

"I don't have any answers."

"If you don't have them, who does? You're the only one. You've got to have answers. Where's your goddamned file?"

My file was locked up, thank God. After the other day when the letter from Gina had slipped out, I realized how stupid I had been leaving it on my desk. How was I supposed to move on if that file stared at me from my desk like a vulture? It was safely locked in my file cabinet at home with my other files of patients who were no longer active.

I wasn't an attorney, but I knew better than to give my files to this man anyway. After Gina died, I had spoken with an attorney and with another therapist who was a respected colleague, both of whom went through my files. They both concluded that I had not committed any malpractice and that there had been no reason to believe Gina Cates was suicidal.

Of course, I hadn't told them about the letter.

That letter was between Gina and me.

And damn it, I was taking it to the grave.

CHAPTER NINETEEN

Jonah

I tried to read Tom Simpson's eyes. They were blue, and looking into them felt oddly like looking at my best friend. Bryce did resemble his father, and so did Henry. My nerves raced and I felt uneasy, seeing the resemblance. His mother, Evelyn, was mostly gray now, but she'd had light-brown hair when we were kids. But Tom was blond like Bryce and his son, even though he was silvery white now. He sat, typing something into his computer.

"Damn," he said.

"What?"

"Just a typo." He held up his right hand. "This damned bandage." He had a Band-Aid on the tip of his right index finger.

"You okay?"

He nodded. "Just a paper cut. I get them a lot. So much paperwork for this tiny city."

My nerves were on edge, but damn it, I was ready to discover some answers. I opened with, "I'm really glad Henry is okay." I wasn't lying, but I also hadn't been able to think of anything else.

"He's a great kid, isn't he?"

I took another sip of coffee. "He sure is. Bryce seems crazy about him."

"Oh, yeah, he's a great father. I was always surprised that he didn't marry sooner. Speaking of that, it's nice to see that one of you boys will be settling down. I assume Talon and Jade are serious?"

"As serious as Talon has ever been."

"What about you and Ryan? You're not getting any younger, you know."

I certainly wasn't here to talk about my brothers and me settling down. I needed to get back to Larry. But then something occurred to me. Henry had that little birthmark on his arm, and it was clearly visible as he was lying in his crib wearing just a onesie and a diaper.

"I noticed that Henry has a birthmark."

"Yes, he does."

I cleared my throat. "Bryce said he might have gotten it from you."

"I'm not sure why he said that."

"Oh? You mean you don't have any birthmarks?"

"No, that's not what I meant. I do have one, but it looks totally different from Henry's."

"Maybe he did get it from you, then, because Bryce said neither he nor Henry's mother have one."

"I suppose that's possible. But Evelyn has one too. Cutest little thing right on the cheek of her ass."

I squirmed uncomfortably. I really didn't want to talk about anything a sixty-five-year-old woman had on her ass. I couldn't force him to remove his shirt and show me the inside of his right arm. Time to ditch the birthmark investigation.

"I've been meaning to talk to you, Tom," I said.

He raised his eyebrows. "Oh?"

I cleared my throat. "About Larry Wade. Did you know he was my half-uncle?"

"Nope. That was as big of a surprise to me as it was to the rest of you."

I didn't believe him for a minute, but I was willing to play along. "Yeah, it was pretty crazy. Anyway, when he came back to town a few years ago, you hired him on as the city attorney. How did that happen?"

"As you may know, George Stanford retired in the middle of his term, so the position was vacant. Until Larry moved back a month later, we'd been using contract attorneys to do our work because Snow Creek is such a small town. But that was no longer cost-efficient. Talon's girlfriend, Jade, is doing an excellent job, by the way."

His lips twitched subtly. Just a bit, but I noticed. He was trying to sidetrack me off of Larry by mentioning Jade.

"Yes, she's a very smart and driven young lady. But back to Larry. Why wasn't he elected city attorney?"

"Since it would be a while before we had a regular election, I decided to make an appointment."

"But why Larry? He turned out to be very unethical."

Tom twisted his lips again, this time not so subtly. "I've known Larry a long time. Believe me, if I had known what kind of man he was, I would never have appointed him. But we knew each other back in the day, went to high school together in Grand Junction, and he was a licensed attorney and needed a job. None of the other attorneys here in Snow Creek wanted the job. They preferred to stay in their own private practices. So what choice did I have?"

I saw through his game again. He was trying to put me on the defensive. "Why not hold a special election?"

"This is Snow Creek, Joe, not Denver. Who the hell would turn out for a special election?"

"My brothers and I would have."

"That's three people. Plus Evelyn and me. Maybe Bryce if he was in town. It wasn't a feasible solution. We needed to wait until a presidential election year. That's the only time you see any results in a small town. I hope Jade will run next year. She'll be a shoo-in, and we couldn't ask for a better city attorney."

Trying to distract me again. Jade was Talon's girlfriend, not mine, and I wasn't going to be sidetracked. Before I could say anything else though, Tom spoke again.

"Why all the questions about Larry? He's locked up where he deserves to be. Case closed."

"Why *not* all the questions about Larry? Aren't you as upset about this as I am? My brother was one of his victims, and so was your nephew."

"He was Evelyn's nephew. Victoria Walker is her sister."

I forced myself not to widen my eyes. Had I heard him correctly? Was he denying feeling remorse because he wasn't Luke's uncle by blood? What a coldhearted bastard.

I knew then that if I stood and forced this man out of his shirt, I would see that birthmark Talon had described.

I had been right in my original assessment.

Larry Wade might be a psychopath, but Tom Simpson was far worse.

He was an iceman.

CHAPTER TWENTY

Melanie

Dr. Cates continued toward me, his right hand balled into a fist. "I'm going to see that file today, Dr. Carmichael, before I leave this office."

I bit my lip. "The file is not here. It's in storage."

"What the hell kind of therapist are you?"

I shivered nervously. "The kind who doesn't clutter up her office with obsolete records. I have followed the guidelines for storage of records for patients who are no longer active. And I couldn't let you see it even if it was here. Those records are confidential."

"The death of the patient ends doctor-patient confidentiality. Everyone knows that."

"I'm afraid you're wrong. Psychotherapy notes have special protection under HIPAA."

"That's ridiculous."

"I didn't write the Health Insurance Portability and Accountability Act, but I can assure you that I'm correct. I can't give you the file, even if it was here."

"I'm not interested in your medical and legal jargon."

He was so close to me now that only about a foot separated us. My pulse beat hard, and nausea churned in my throat. His breath stank of alcohol. So that was it. He had been drinking.

"I'm going to have to ask you to leave now, Dr. Cates."

His blue eyes glazed over with rage and fire. "I'm not sure I made myself clear. I'm not leaving without that file."

"And I told you"—I swallowed—"it's not here."

He grabbed my arm, and I instinctively jerked backward, hitting the wall.

"Don't you dare touch me," I said.

"Then give me the file."

"I do not have it here."

"Listen, bitch." He grabbed me by the throat. "You're going t—"

"Melanie?" A soft rap on the door.

Oliver! Thank God.

Dr. Cates removed his hand from my neck, and I gasped in some air. The gasp was more from fear. He hadn't obstructed my breathing, but damn it, I was scared to death.

"Oliver, am I glad to see you." I smoothed out my blouse.

"This isn't over, Dr. Carmichael," Dr. Cates said. "I will get the information one way or another."

Without acknowledging Oliver, Dr. Cates stomped out of my office. I could still hear his footsteps after he left the reception area and traveled down the hall to the elevator.

"Are you all right?" Oliver asked. "What was that about?"

I lost my footing, and he rushed toward me, catching me. He helped me to my couch and sat down next to me.

"Melanie?"

And the tears came. Whether they were tears for Gina or tears for the fear that had just coursed through me, I didn't know.

Oliver put his arm around me. "God, what happened? Who was that guy?"

I sniffled into his shirt and then looked up at him, grabbing a tissue from the box on the coffee table. I wiped my eyes and blew my nose quickly.

"He was the father of a former patient of mine."

"Should we call the cops? For a second I thought he was choking you."

Normally I would have said yes, but I shook my head. "I'm all right. The man has been through enough."

"Are you kidding me? He just tried to strangle you."

"He wouldn't have done me any harm." And in my heart, I did believe that. "He's distraught. His daughter was a patient of mine, and she ended up killing herself." I bit my lip to force back tears. "I've been over her file time after time after time, Oliver, and I cannot find anything that indicated she was suicidal. What did I miss?"

"He has no right to blame you."

"But I must've missed something." And I had. Gina had fallen in love with me, and I'd had no idea. "And there's more," I continued. "His wife just attempted suicide a few days ago. She's over at Valleycrest in the mental ward. So he's not in his right mind."

"That's still no excuse for him treating you that way."

In theory, I agreed. But the way I was feeling right now—so woefully inadequate, wishing I could go back in time and see what I had missed, to pay better attention—I couldn't concur.

That letter haunted me. I should have given it to the attorney. I should've put it in the file. I should've let my colleague and attorney review it. But I hadn't. I'd kept it. And now it was too late. I couldn't bring it up now.

"Really, I'm fine. Just drop it, okay?"

"Are you still up for dinner?"

Dinner. Hell. Well, a girl had to eat. I blew my nose again and stood. "Sure, let's go to dinner."

Oliver stood and then reached for me and wiped away an errant tear rivering down my cheek. "I'm sorry you're going through this," he said. "As you can imagine, in pediatric nephrology, I've lost a few patients too."

"And they were children. That's got to be a lot worse. I'm sorry, Oliver."

He pursed his lips. "I wish I could tell you that you get used to it." He shook his head. "I certainly never have."

"Any physician who gets used to it probably shouldn't be practicing medicine," I said. "And I'm the one who decided to practice psychotherapy. I could've been a more routine psychiatrist, just dispensing meds and referring patients to psychologists and counselors. I knew ahead of time there would be people I just couldn't help."

"You have such a caring nature. I can't imagine you just dispensing meds." He cupped my cheek. "You've always been that way. Always thinking of others. You know, Melanie, I've thought about contacting you many times over the past decade. I read your book on overcoming childhood trauma. It was brilliant."

My cheeks warmed. "Why in the world would a pediatric nephrologist read a book on psychotherapy for overcoming childhood trauma?"

"Because I knew the author. And I knew she was brilliant."

I chuckled. "You were the one who was always at the top of all of our classes."

"And you were always right behind me." Oliver smiled.

"You have no idea how annoying that was," I said. "My main goal in life was to pass you up, and I never could."

"Ha! The reason you were never able to do it is because I forced myself to work that much harder to stay ahead of you."

I warmed again. "You're saying I was an incentive for you?"

"Yes, totally. You don't know how close you came to beating me. There's a reason I didn't socialize."

Oliver hadn't had a social life? He was always so jovial and good-looking, always had two or three women clinging to his every word. I was the one who'd had no social life. Of course, since I hadn't had one, I wouldn't have known whether he had.

"I don't think any of us did much socializing in med school, and that was nothing compared to internship and residency."

"You're telling me. Those hours were brutal." He caressed my cheek with his fingers.

I was getting uncomfortable. I cleared my throat. "What are you in the mood for? There are some great restaurants around here. There's a nice sushi place about a block over and a couple Italian places."

"Sushi sounds great. Let's try that."

"All right. Let me grab my purse out of my desk."

Warmth came up behind me as I was bending to pick up my purse out of the locked drawer where I kept it. I grabbed the bag and turned around. Oliver was right behind me, and he quickly brushed his lips over mine. I jolted backward, falling into my desk chair, my ass plunking on the leather. I bit my lip.

"I'm sorry," he said. "I just couldn't get that out of my mind."

I stood nervously. I wasn't sure how I felt about the kiss. Granted, Oliver and I had been intimate long ago, but only once, and it was certainly not part of any kind of relationship.

He grabbed my elbow and pulled me toward him. "Let's

try that again," he said.

And before I could pull away, his lips were on mine once more.

He ran his tongue over the seam of my lips, and although I wasn't sure, I opened to him. He slipped his tongue into my mouth. I closed my eyes, trying to concentrate on the kiss, trying to melt into him the way I had melted into—

"What the fuck is going on here?"

CHAPTER TWENTY-ONE

Jonah

My body went rigid, and my hands clenched into fists. Another man had his lips on Melanie.

My Melanie.

But she wasn't my Melanie. Until that moment, I hadn't known how much I wanted her to be.

Instincts took over, and my hackles rose. I stepped toward her, feeling feral, primal. I grabbed the man's suit coat by the back of his neck and pulled him off of her. He landed on the floor on his ass.

"Hey! Who are you?" he said. "What the hell do you think you're doing?"

I ignored him. He wasn't the problem. The woman kissing him was.

Melanie inched backward slightly, rubbing at her lips. They were red from another man's lips.

Never again.

"Who the hell is he? And what was he doing kissing you?"

"He... He's a friend of mine from medical school."

"Is that how you say hello to all of your friends?"

"Look, Jonah, this isn't any of your—"

"The hell it's not."

The other guy had gotten up, and he touched the sleeve of

my shirt. "Look, I think we have a big misunderstanding here. It's like Melanie said. I'm Oliver Nichols, a friend of hers from medical school."

I shrugged away from him and pushed him down to the floor again.

"For God's sake, Jonah, would you stop that?" Melanie knelt down to the other guy. "Oliver, are you all right?"

Oliver stood and brushed off his pants. "Yeah, I'm fine. Look, maybe we should have this date another time."

"You have a date with him?" I spat out.

Melanie stood. "He's a friend, Jonah."

"I'm going to excuse myself now," Oliver said. "Melanie, I'll call you."

"Don't bother," I said over my shoulder.

He walked out the door.

"What do you think you're doing?" Melanie demanded. "He and I had dinner plans."

"Yes, dinner plans with your *friend*. A friend who had his tongue shoved down your throat."

She reddened. That beautiful raspberry flush... But no, I was not going to fall prey to her feminine wiles. I was angry—livid, actually—and she was going to answer to me.

"Why was he kissing you?"

"I don't know. I was as surprised by it as you were."

"You didn't look surprised from where I was standing."

"You came in at the exact wrong time. He had just started to kiss me, and I was about ready to end it."

"Oh, you were? And I'm supposed to believe that?"

"It doesn't really matter what you believe, Jonah. You and I are not together."

"Seems to me we've been together a couple of times now."

"It was sex. Really good sex, but we don't even know anything about each other."

Right. She knew all about me from her sessions with my brother. "I'd say you know a hell of a lot about me."

"Fine." She sighed. "*You* don't know anything about *me*."

I pulled her to me, molding her breasts against my chest. "I know more than you think." I inhaled. "I know you always smell like fresh lavender. I know exactly how your ruby-red lips feel under my own. I know your nipples are almost the same color, and I know you like them sucked. Hard. I know every little crevice of your hot pussy and how it tastes like sweet peaches and earthy musk. I know how many times you come when I suck your hard clit and put my fingers inside you." I lowered my voice to a whisper and grabbed her ass, not gently. "I know you don't like your ass slapped during sex. And I also know that will change."

She gasped against me.

"Yes, that will change. I guarantee it, Melanie. I want to slap that sweet little ass of yours. Slap those peachy breasts of yours. Tie you to a bed and fuck you silly. And in the end, I *always* get what I want."

She shuddered, falling into her chair. She bit her lip, trembling all over. "And what do you want right now?"

My dick was so hard I thought it might pop out of my jeans. I had to have her, had to mark her, had to make her mine. Another male was stalking her, and that wasn't going to happen under my watch.

"You. Here. Now."

"This is my office. My door is open."

"Don't care."

"But...I work here. People *know* me."

"Still don't care." I unbuckled my belt and unsnapped my jeans.

She sucked in a breath. I pulled her up from her chair. She was wearing a cream-colored silk blouse and a black sheath skirt. No pantyhose from what I could tell.

I bent her over her desk and lifted her skirt. God, basic beige cotton panties. And for some reason, they were the hottest thing I'd ever seen. I ripped them off her.

"Tell me now, Melanie. Tell me now if you don't want this, because if you don't say no right this minute, I'm going to take you."

"I want this," she said softly. "Take me, Jonah. I want this."

I plunged into her wet heat.

God, what sensation. I groaned. The sweet suction of her musky pussy completely enveloped my cock. I thrust in again and again, her beautiful ass spread out like a smorgasbord. I pumped into her, taking her. Below me, her breathing came rapidly, and soft moans escaped her lips, wafting their way to my ears, making my blood boil. I wanted to last, but before I knew it, I was nearing the edge.

"I'm going to come now, Melanie. Come hard and come into you. This is me, coming into you."

"Yes," she sobbed, her voice muffled by the blotter on the desk.

I pulled out, thrust once more, and emptied into her, my whole body shuddering.

I collapsed on top of her back, regretting that I hadn't taken the time to remove all of our clothing.

There would be time for that later.

I inhaled and let out a deep breath. Finally, I withdrew.

I pulled up my jeans, snapped them, and buckled my belt.

I helped Melanie up, straightening her skirt over that beautiful ass.

"I'm sorry you didn't come. I'm sorry I couldn't wait."

She bit her lip. "It's okay."

"And I'm sorry if..."

"What?"

"If I was a little...*forceful.*"

She shook her head. "You asked me before you did anything. I said I wanted it."

What if she had said no? I had been so filled with wanting. What if I hadn't been able to stop?

Thank God she hadn't wanted me to.

"I don't think I've ever wanted a woman as much as I want you. Seeing that scumbag kissing you..."

"Oliver."

"Yes, I know it has a name."

She sighed. "He's not an 'it.' He's a friend of mine from medical school. We were just going to have dinner."

"It didn't look like dinner."

She moved away from her desk and sat down on the couch. "I don't need to explain Oliver or anything else to you. But I would like to know why you showed up here tonight."

I'd nearly forgotten. I did need to talk to her. "I had a talk with Tom Simpson today."

"The mayor, right? Your friend's father?"

"Yeah."

She fidgeted, pulled her hands together, clasping and then unclasping them. Something was clearly bothering her, and I began to feel like an asshole. I hoped it didn't have anything to do with Oliver Twist or whatever the hell his name was.

"Melanie? Are you okay?"

She closed her eyes and sighed. When she opened them, they were glazed over with unshed tears.

I reached toward her and cupped her cheek. "What's going on?"

She shook her head. "It's nothing."

"It's not nothing. Give me a break. Is it...that other guy? Is he someone you wanted to be with? Is he..." I couldn't bring myself to finish that sentence. Melanie Carmichael with another man wasn't a thought I could form in my head.

"I'm fine. It's not anything I can talk about."

"You can tell me. My word is as good as gold." I drew in a breath and let it out slowly. "Do you want to be with him?" It shouldn't matter to me, but it did. I had gone batshit crazy when I saw them together.

"No, believe me. It's not Oliver. I was telling the truth when I told you he was just a friend."

"Why the kiss, then?" I felt like shit as soon as I'd said it. "Never mind. You don't have to answer that. If that's not the problem, what's bothering you? Let me help."

I truly did want to help. The thought of Melanie being in any kind of pain or distress bothered me. Disturbed me. Made me want to crush whoever was making her feel this way.

"I know that. But I really can't talk about it."

"At least tell me how I can help you."

She rubbed her arms. "You can't. I wish you could."

"Oliver? Your...friend? Was he going to help you?"

"No. He's a friend from med school, but he's not a psychiatrist. He's a pediatric nephrologist."

"Nephrologist? That's kidneys, right?"

"Yes. He just came in to town to do some work here on a temporary basis. We ran into each other at the coffee shop downstairs, and he invited me to dinner. It was all very innocent."

Then why the kissing? The question sat on the edge of my vocal cords, but I refrained from asking it again. She was clearly upset about something, and now that I knew it didn't have anything to do with this guy, I truly did want to help her. But she was being a closed book, as usual.

"Since you won't talk to me, how about this? I ruined your dinner date, so can I take you to dinner?"

She smiled. Oh, what a beautiful smile it was. "You know? I'd like that."

"Where were you going to go?"

"The sushi place a block away."

Sushi? Really not my thing. I was a rancher, for God's sake. A meat and potatoes kind of guy. But for Melanie Carmichael, I'd eat raw fish. "Sounds good," I said, hoping I was pulling it off. "Sushi it is."

She gave me another smile. And then her phone beeped. "Excuse me, I just need to take care of this." She walked outside to the reception area to take the call. Within a few minutes, she was back. Her eyes were rimmed again with sadness—or was it fear?

"Melanie? What is it?"

"Nothing. But I'm afraid I can't—"

"Oh, hell, no," I said. "We're having dinner. And then we're going back to your place, and you're going to tell me every little thing that you're keeping from me. In your business, you know it helps to talk to someone."

I just hoped I could be there to listen and not get so crazy that I had to fuck her brains out first.

CHAPTER TWENTY-TWO

Melanie

I could tell that sushi wasn't Jonah's favorite meal. But he was a trouper, and he tried everything I ordered. He actually liked the *unagi*—freshwater eel—quite a bit. I almost felt bad having to tell him it was cooked. We talked mainly about the food. One thing that was great about Jonah—I didn't feel like I had to keep talking. I hated small talk, and I sucked at it as well. So we finished up, shared a dessert of green tea ice cream, and then walked back to my place.

"Do you want a drink?" I asked. "I can open a bottle of wine."

"No, I have to drive home later, and I already had that sake at the restaurant. But I'd love a cup of coffee if you have it."

"Sure. I'll start a pot. Make yourself at home." I walked to the kitchen, fiddled with the coffee maker, and ground some beans.

Then I went into the living room. Jonah was leafing through a copy of my book.

He looked up when he saw me. "That first time I met you, when you were at the psychology conference and I was at the agricultural conference, you told me you were working on a book. Is this the one?"

"Yes, although the book was done by then. I just said I was

working on it because it hadn't been published yet. It came out a month ago."

"You said it was about overcoming childhood trauma. That caught my interest. Obviously, it's a topic I'm familiar with."

"Of course. Talon."

He nodded. "I kept your card. That's how he came to you."

"I know. He told me."

"I told him you came highly recommended. But I have to be honest with you. I really didn't know much about you, other than that you had written a book and you were presenting at the conference, so I figured you were an expert."

"That's how a lot of people get referrals. By doing conferences."

"You turned out to be a great fit for him, Melanie. He's a changed man. He really is. I mean, he told me he still has dreams sometimes and that he knows there are parts of this that will never leave him, but he's dealing with it now, and he's living his life."

Warm happiness dribbled through me. I did have successes—far more successes than failures. But that one failure really hurt. I didn't want to go there. I couldn't go there with Jonah.

"You know," I said, the sake from dinner giving me the courage, "Talon told me something at one of his sessions. Something about you."

He quirked his eyebrow. "Oh? I hope it was good."

I gave him a half smile. "He said you had the hots for me."

His cheeks went ruddy. Difficult to discern on his nicely bronzed face, but I could tell.

"I hope I haven't embarrassed you."

"Why should I be embarrassed? I think it's clear from my behavior up to this point that what he said is true."

I couldn't help a little laugh.

"Look, now, there's nothing I'd like better than to take you to the bedroom, but I want you to tell me what's going on. Something scared you earlier today, and then you got that phone call. Maybe this is none of my business—in fact, I'm sure it's not—but you can tell me anything. My word is as good as gold."

The second time he had used those words. I knew I could trust him. I never doubted it. And oh, how wonderful it would be to unburden myself to someone. I had opened up a little bit to Oliver about it, as another physician. But to tell Jonah? To him, I was the brilliant therapist who'd saved his brother. What would he think of me? I couldn't bear it if he thought less of me. And at this point, I didn't think much of myself. I just couldn't tell him.

"I can't."

"You can. It will help. You know it will."

From the kitchen, the coffee maker dinged, telling me my pot of coffee was ready. I ignored it. There was only one way to get Jonah's mind off of what was bothering me. And I knew what that was.

I sat down on him, pulling my spandex skirt up my thighs and straddling him, cupped his cheeks, and lowered my mouth onto his.

It didn't take long for him to respond. His cock hardened beneath me. I ground against it, my clit tickling from the roughness of the denim enclosing him. Oh, how good it felt.

He broke the kiss. "My God, you're driving me fucking insane."

I took his lips again. Good, insane. Exactly what I wanted. I wanted to be driven insane too. I wanted to escape from the emotions overwhelming me. Escape from my patient who had taken her own life, from the love she'd hidden from me, from her father who'd threatened me.

Just escape.

And even though I knew it couldn't last—escape never did—what better way to escape than in the arms of the most beautiful man on the planet? For that's what Jonah Steel was. He was darker and even more rugged than his brother Talon. The silvery flecks in his stubble and in his beautiful black hair made me swoon. I unbuttoned his shirt quickly and pushed it over his shoulders. A gorgeous chest, too, adorned with just the perfect amount of black and silver chest hair. He let go of me long enough to pull his arms out and then grabbed me, cupping my breasts. He found my nipples through my blouse and bra, and they hardened, pushing through both layers of fabric.

I gasped into his mouth.

He pushed me off of him and laid me on the couch, touching me between my legs.

"Oh my God. You're so wet. So wet for me." He pushed my skirt the rest of the way up to my waist and spread my legs. "The lips of your pussy are engorged, Melanie. I'm going to eat you raw. And then I'm going to stuff my cock into you and fuck you. Fuck you all night long."

I closed my eyes as he lowered his beautiful mouth to take my most secret place. When he swiped his tongue across my clit, I nearly unraveled.

"God, you taste so good." He nibbled on my thigh, sucking, biting. "I could suck you all night long."

"I won't stop you," I said, my eyes still shut.

"Open your eyes, Melanie. Open your eyes. Watch me as I lick you."

My head was propped up slightly by a pillow on the couch, and I opened my eyes. His own brown ones were blazing as he licked between my legs.

"Don't stop looking at me, Melanie. I want you to look as I suck this pussy. Tell me you want that. Tell me you want me to eat your pussy."

"Yes. I... I w-want you to eat my pussy."

He dived back in, shoving his tongue into my wet channel. Frantically, I unbuttoned my blouse and then lifted my bra over my chest to expose my breasts. I grabbed them both, flicking my fingers over my hard nipples.

Jonah dropped my labia out of his mouth. "So hot, sweetheart. Beautiful. God, I'm so hard right now."

I continued twirling my nipples with my fingers, and he went back to my pussy, nibbling on my labia. I was going crazy, still playing with my nipples.

I closed my eyes.

He dropped my lips again. "I told you to leave those eyes open."

I opened them once again, and he was staring at me, his eyes alight with fire.

"Don't close those eyes again, Melanie, or I'll stop eating you."

I panted. "Oh my God, no. Don't stop. Don't ever fucking stop."

He smiled. "I like it when you talk like that. I like it when you talk dirty."

I was sure my cheeks were turning red, though I was already so warm I couldn't tell. I was so hot, on fire, flames reeling all around my body.

When he forced two fingers inside my heat, I splintered around him. The orgasm came up on me fast, starting in my clit and then radiating up into my abdomen, my chest, throughout my limbs. I trembled, shouting, squeezing my nipples harder.

"Yes, Jonah, yes. I'm coming. So good. So good. So fucking, fucking good."

In a flash, Jonah had unbuckled his jeans, unzipped them, and pushed them and his boxers over his hips, his cock springing forward. He climbed atop me and thrust inside.

"Oh, God," he moaned.

"Yes, yes, you feel so good inside me." I was still on the edge of my orgasm, and I could feel my walls spasming around him. "You feel that? You feel me? I'm still coming. Still coming."

He groaned. "God, yes, amazing,"

He thrust and he thrust, panting against me, his chest hair abrading my bare breasts. When he finally released inside me, I came again, and together we completed our journey, panting against each other.

He took my lips in a kiss so violent, so fierce, I was sure we would both have bruises. I didn't care. I wanted it. I wanted it all.

Our orgasms finally subsided, and he broke the kiss.

I looked around the room, embarrassment flooding me. My skirt was around my waist, my slingback sandals still on my feet. My bra was up around my breasts but still hooked, and my arms were still in the silky sleeves of my blouse. Jonah's shirt was gone, but his jeans and boxers were midway down his thighs.

For the second time tonight, we'd screwed each other nearly fully clothed.

There was something hot about that.

I cleared my throat and pulled my bra down over my breasts.

"It's a shame to cover those," Jonah said.

I gently eased my skirt back down over my butt and thighs. "The coffee's ready."

He smiled, his beautiful lips and chin still glistening with my juices. "Yeah, let's have a cup of coffee because, Melanie, neither one of us is going to sleep anytime soon."

CHAPTER TWENTY-THREE

Jonah

Melanie's coffee was a lighter roast, like a breakfast blend. I preferred a dark roast. French roast was my favorite, but no matter. Coffee making could be taught. As could many other things. I planned to teach Melanie a lot. She would eventually surrender to me.

But the essentials I didn't have to teach her—like how to kiss me like a fucking siren, how to give me head as if she were sucking a golf ball through a garden hose, how to clamp my cock in her pussy so sweetly.

No. The essentials she had down.

The rest I could teach her. I *would* teach her. For I wasn't giving her up anytime soon.

I took a sip of my coffee and felt the buzz of my cell phone through the pocket of my jeans. "Excuse me," I said to Melanie. I pulled out the phone. Talon.

As much as I wanted to take Melanie to her bedroom and finish what we'd started, I couldn't ignore Talon. Not after I'd failed him. I would always come whenever he called.

"I need to take this. It's Talon."

She nodded. "I understand."

I stood and walked from the kitchen into the living area. "Hey, Tal."

"Joe, thank God. Where are you?"

"In the city. What's wrong?"

"I need you to come home. I hired some high-priced detectives to go through Jade's old room at the house to figure out where the rose might have come from. You won't believe what they found."

★ ★ ★ ★

Talon hadn't told me what they'd found, just told me to get home right away. It was late, but Melanie understood. I rushed home.

When I got to the main house, Talon and Jade, along with Ryan, Marj, and two guys I didn't recognize, were sitting at the kitchen table.

"What's going on?" I asked. It had better be good since it interrupted my night with Melanie.

"A huge clue, Joe," Talon said, rising to greet me.

"What is it?"

One of the guys I didn't recognize held out a business card in gloved hands. I reached for it.

"No, don't touch it," he said.

"Then why the hell did you hand it to me?"

"So you could see it."

"This is Trevor Mills and his partner, Johnny Johnson," Talon said. "I hired them to go through Jade's old room and also to try to figure out how someone got into this house. Guess whose business card this is?"

"Well, if you let me see it, I'll tell you."

I moved forward and took a hard look at the glossy card the man named Mills held. Colin Morse. Jade's ex-fiancé.

"So you think Colin left the rose?" I asked.

"Not necessarily." Jade shook her head. "He never gave me a card either of the two times he was here. The guys found this wedged under the carpeting."

"It was planted," Talon said. "If someone had dropped it, we would've found it. But no one could drop it so that it ended up wedged under wall-to-wall carpet."

"Still, it's pretty good evidence that Colin left the rose," I said.

"We could go with that"—Talon sat back down at the table—"if Colin's fingerprints were the only ones on the card."

I raised my eyebrows.

Mills spoke up. "Johnny and I have dusted the card, and there are three distinct sets of prints on this card."

"See, Joe?" Talon rubbed his temple. "Even if we assume that one set of prints belongs to Colin, there are still two others who touched this card."

I turned to Jade. "Are you sure he never gave you a card? Maybe those are your fingerprints."

"No. I've never seen this card. He never gave me one. Even if he had, why would I hide it under the carpeting in my room?"

I had no answer for her.

"We need to get all of you guys fingerprinted," Johnny Johnson said. "Just to rule out anyone with access to the house. Your housekeeper too."

"Of course, whatever you need," Ryan said. "Though I'm pretty sure you won't find any of our prints on that card."

"I'm sure we won't," Johnson said. "But we need to rule out everyone in the house first."

"Why would anyone leave Colin's card lodged in your room, Jade?" I asked.

She sighed. "Beats me."

Mills shook his head. "We can't assume it was Colin, based on the fact that there are three distinct sets of prints on the card."

"Is there any way Colin's prints might be on file somewhere? You have access to the state databases at work, don't you, Jade?" I asked.

"Yes, I do. But I doubt Colin's prints are available. I don't think he's ever been arrested or charged with any crime."

"What about Larry Wade?" Marj piped in. "Since he's been arrested, his prints will be on file somewhere."

Jade raised her eyebrows. "They've been on file for a while. Every person who takes the Colorado bar exam has to be fingerprinted. I was."

"Well then, eureka," Ryan said, standing. "Let's get that checked out."

Mills nodded. "Will do, first thing in the morning. But even if Wade's fingerprints are positive, there are still two other unidentified sets on the card."

"And I know just whose they are," Talon said. "I bet you anything they belong to Colin and that idiot boyfriend of your mother's, Jade. Nico Kostas."

Jade shushed him. "For God's sake, Talon, don't mention him. My mother's asleep, but if she hears his name, she'll wake up in a second. She's still convinced he's coming back to her."

"Besides, you're jumping the gun," I said to Talon. "We still have no proof that Nico Kostas is even involved."

Talon gritted his teeth. "I have all the goddamned proof I need."

I wasn't so sure. I wanted to believe we were on the path to one of the other criminals as much as Talon did. But we had no idea where this Nico character was, and even if we found him, we had no proof he was guilty.

Then something occurred to me. Talon was sure. I recognized that look in his eyes.

It was the same look he would have seen in my own eyes when I became convinced of Tom Simpson's involvement.

I had to tell Talon sooner or later of my suspicion, but now was certainly not the time. I wanted him to heal, and as long as he was hell-bent on catching these guys, he wasn't paying attention to the things that really mattered—his healing, his relationship with Jade, his relationship with the rest of us.

I looked over at Jade. She was smiling up at him adoringly. Maybe their relationship was okay after all.

"So tell me exactly where you found this card," I said to the two detectives.

"We can do better than that," Mills said. "We can show you."

I followed them down the hallway, Jade at my heels, toward the guestroom Jade had used when she first came to the ranch. The room was vacant, and the carpeting had been pulled up, rolled into a cylinder, and was standing against one wall.

"We went through all the furniture with a fine tooth comb." Mills said. "Then we moved it to another spare room so we could take a look in all the crevices."

He showed me the spot where he'd found the card, right against the wall, where the foot of the bed had been.

"Whoever did this got in and out quickly," Jade said. "I couldn't have been in the shower for more than about fifteen minutes."

"It wouldn't take long for someone to slide this card into

the carpeting and put a rose on the pillow," Mills said.

"Yeah, but how the hell did he get in this house?" I asked.

"We're still working on that," he said. "We'll figure out what happened. Don't you worry. There's not a case in the world Johnny and I can't solve."

"I hope you're right. Where did Talon find you guys?"

"We found him."

I widened my eyes. "What the hell do you mean?"

"We're friendly with the police departments around the state of Colorado. When there's a case they can't figure out, they pull us in sometimes. The city of Snow Creek has never used us before. Small towns can't usually afford our services. But they figured your brother might be able to."

"Okay. That still doesn't tell me who you are. You have any references?"

"Sure. Call any police department in any big city in Colorado. They'll vouch for us."

I swallowed. I had no reason to think the guys weren't on the level, but the Steel money was well-known. They could have crawled out of the woodwork.

"We're on the up-and-up, Mr. Steel," Mills continued. "We wouldn't stay in business if we weren't."

I had no idea whether I believed him. What kind of detectives worked at midnight? They could've easily sniffed out our money and come calling, assuming we wouldn't call the police and check them out.

I was going to call. Absolutely. I'd call the Grand Junction Police Department and the Denver Police Department. If both of them had heard of these guys, I'd let it go.

"Anything else in this room that looked suspicious?" I asked.

"Not that we've seen so far, but we'll figure this out. I guarantee it."

"If it's all the same to you," I said, "I'd like to call a police officer I know and trust to handle the evidence. I want him to keep it in his custody."

"But we're the ones who'll be running the tests."

"How in the hell can you find fingerprints?"

"We can't reveal our sources," Johnson said. "Could lead to—"

"Shut up, Johnny," Mills said.

Right. On the up-and-up all right. But they left their scruples at the front door.

"Would you excuse me for a moment?" I said.

I was going to call Steve Dugan, a Snow Creek police officer. If he had heard of these guys, I'd let it go for now, but I was still going to call Grand Junction and Denver tomorrow.

I walked down the hall into Talon's study and closed the door. I dialed Steve Dugan's cell number.

"Dugan."

"Hey, Steve. Jonah Steel."

"Joe? Why are you calling at this hour?"

"Talon's got these two high-priced detectives in the house. I wanted to know if you knew anything about them."

"Mills and Johnson?"

"Yeah, I think that's their last names."

"They've come around a few times, offering services. They seem to be legitimate. I mean, legit in that you pay for their services and they deliver. I don't know whether everything they do is legal. I think they're probably hackers, and I imagine they do their share of breaking and entering. How else could they solve crimes that we can't?"

"Have you talked to any of the larger police forces about them?"

"I haven't personally," he said. "But the sarge has. He seems to think they're okay."

"All right. Thanks. I'm going to call the police in the city tomorrow. Sorry to bother you, Steve. Good night."

I heard him yawn into the phone. "No problem, Joe. Anytime."

I ended the call, went back to Jade's old room, and found it empty. The two men had gone back to the kitchen and were talking to my brothers and sister and Jade.

Johnson had sat back down at the table and was examining the card with his gloved hands through what appeared to be a jeweler's loupe.

"A-ha," he said.

"What did you find, Johnny?" Mills asked.

"There's a tiny brown smudge on the edge of this card. I didn't see it before because it's only on the edge, not on the card itself. Someone wiped the card clean. But the glossy finish doesn't extend to the edge."

"What is it?" Talon asked.

"My best guess?" Johnny twisted his lips. "Blood. Looks like whoever had the card got a nasty paper cut."

"Well, that doesn't help," Talon said. "This was weeks ago. Any paper cut would have healed by now."

"Yeah, but we can get DNA from the blood."

And it hit me. The Band-Aid on Tom Simpson's right index finger. I hadn't thought anything of it, but he said he got paper cuts a lot.

My God. I was jumping to conclusions, just as Talon was with Nico Kostas.

But I knew it in my soul as much as I knew the sun would rise tomorrow.

Tom Simpson's blood was on that card.

Mills and Johnson would check the fingerprints. Larry's would be on file, and his fingerprints would be on that card. The second set would belong to Colin himself. And the third set...

The third set would match the blood.

The blood of Tom Simpson.

My best friend's father. The fucking mayor of Snow Creek. That blood was his.

I just had to figure out how to prove it.

CHAPTER TWENTY-FOUR

Melanie

I sat, biting my lip, in the conference room on the mental health wing of Valleycrest Hospital. The phone call I had received before I left for dinner with Jonah had been from the Chief of the Psychiatric Staff at Valleycrest, who also happened to be my colleague and Erica Cates's physician, Dr. Miles Bennett. I'd tried to put this meeting at the back of my mind while I had been with Jonah, and I had actually succeeded. But after Jonah got the call from Talon and left so abruptly, I had turned back into a pumpkin. This phone call and meeting had gotten into my mind and wouldn't let go. I tossed and turned all night, getting only an hour or two of sleep. I had to have Randi reschedule two therapy sessions to make room for the meeting this morning. I hated canceling on my patients. Regular therapy was so important to the work I did, and when I had to cancel, patients got off schedule. But I couldn't miss this meeting.

Miles sat across from me, and next to him sat a young woman who I knew as Dr. Eva Wilson, the chief psychiatry resident this year at Valleycrest.

"I hope you don't mind, Melanie. I've asked Eva to join us."

"Normally I wouldn't, Miles, but I don't even know

why you've summoned me here. Until I know the reason for this meeting, I'm not very comfortable having anyone else attending."

"Dr. Carmichael—" Eva began.

"It's all right, Eva," Miles said. "Melanie, everything in this meeting will be held within the strictest confidence. Eva can be trusted."

I nodded. "Fine." I didn't have the energy to protest anymore.

"Erica Cates's husband, Rodney Cates, came to me yesterday. He was a mess. Said he had just been with you. It was nearly six o'clock, and I was getting ready to leave the hospital, but he insisted upon seeing me."

I nodded. What could I say?

"He wants to see your file on his daughter, Melanie."

"The file is in storage," I said.

"I understand that."

"And you probably also understand that my psychotherapy notes are protected under HIPAA."

"I do. But it might serve your interests best to release the file."

I widened my eyes into circles. "Did I hear you right? You want me to disregard the law that protects my patients?"

"Melanie, the patient in question is dead."

"You know the law as well as I do. If he wants to see the file, he needs to go to court, be appointed as the personal representative of his daughter's estate, and then he can demand access to the file. Not before."

"Yes, I know that. But why not show him? Right now, I need to think of my patient, and her husband is driving her slowly crazy."

"I sympathize with you, Miles," I said, "but I have to think of my patient and her rights too."

"May I remind you again, Melanie, that your patient is dead?"

"No, you don't need to remind me of that." I stood, anger getting the best of me. "Don't you know that I think of that girl every day of my life? That I question myself? That I wonder what there was that I didn't see? She haunts me every night, Miles. I did what I thought was best at the time, and I had an attorney and Shelley Barrett, who you yourself have said is one of the best therapists in business today, review my file after Gina's suicide. They both concluded there was nothing in the notes to indicate Gina was suicidal. I believe we're done here."

"Sit down, Melanie."

"I will not. I have nothing more to say on this matter."

"You may not, but I have more to say. Now please, sit."

"I think I'll remain standing. Have your say, Miles."

"This man is wreaking havoc in the hospital," Miles said. "Please understand my position. As a friend and colleague, I'm asking for your cooperation."

"I'm sorry. I can't."

"Then I have no choice but to ask you to take a leave of absence from your practice."

I whipped my neck around. "A leave of absence? On what basis?"

"Pending investigation of the medical review board. Rodney Cates filed a complaint against you early this morning."

I froze, my blood frosting in my veins. "I know my rights. I am able to keep practicing medicine until the medical board tells me I can't."

"You know the procedures as well as I do. Don't make me

suspend your privileges at this hospital."

"Do you hear yourself, Miles? My patients need me. This isn't right, and you know it."

"This is a temporary situation."

"You have no cause to ask this of me. I haven't done anything wrong."

"Believe me, Melanie. It's for your own good."

"So is this the kind of man you are, Miles? Things get a little tough for you, and you roll over and play dead? What are you afraid of? That if you don't kowtow to Cates, he'll file a complaint against *you?*"

Miles reddened. Yes, I'd hit that nail right on the head.

I clenched my hands into fists. "I see how it is. Fine. I'll close up my practice for a few weeks until you're confident this has blown over. I'll let my patients down. But I won't forget this, Miles." I stormed out of the conference room.

The walk back to my office took place in a blur. I was livid. When I reached the fourth floor, I tromped into the office.

"Randi? Take the next three weeks off."

"Excuse me?" Her blond head popped up from her computer.

"You heard me. It seems the universe has decided I need to take a break for a few weeks. I need you to cancel all my appointments for the next three weeks. Don't reschedule anything. We'll call them all when I get back to the office."

"But Dr. Carmichael, this isn't like you—"

"Trust me, it wasn't my idea."

She paled. "All right. I'll call everyone. What about this afternoon's appointments?"

"Cancel them as well." I stepped into my office and shut the door behind me.

What the hell? I hadn't had a vacation in years. I had plenty of money saved up. Why not take a trip? I could use the time to finish writing my book about—

I let out a laugh—but not a laugh because anything was funny. A laugh from the sheer absurdity of it all. My work in progress was a book on preventing suicide in teens.

I hadn't worked on it since Gina's death. Though Gina hadn't been a teen, she was still quite young. I had become numb. I hadn't been able to touch my research and writing since then. I'd forced myself to continue working, but only because my current patients needed me.

And then Talon Steel had walked into my office and fainted dead away after our first session.

I'd found a new purpose in Talon. He had made such amazing progress in such a short time. Even though I had failed Gina, I began to think I still had something to offer, that I could still help people who had a dire need, who had been to hell and had come back kicking.

And even though the guilt from Gina's death had never left me, working with Talon had lifted me out of the depths of sorrow, had given me a new aspiration.

If only I had let that lead me all the way out, all the way back to the light. But I hadn't, and one night I'd made a phone call to Gina's parents.

If only I could go back in time and not make that call.

I laughed again. I always counseled my patients against the "what ifs." They served no purpose. All we could do was handle the situation we found ourselves in currently.

I sat down at my desk, cradling my head in my hands.

Now. This was now. Now was all I had, and I had to figure out how to deal with it.

I breathed in and out, willing the tears not to fall. I had made my bed, and now I had to lie in it. If only...

"God, stop it!" I said aloud. I stood, grabbing my purse, and walked out of my office, shutting the door and locking it behind me.

"Lock up when you're done making the calls," I said to Randi. "I won't be back today."

I needed some fresh air.

And I knew just where I could get it.

CHAPTER TWENTY-FIVE

Jonah

Talon and Ryan sat across from me at my office in the beef ranch buildings. Talon wanted to talk to us about more evidence regarding Nico Kostas. I sat, listening, wanting so much to tell him my suspicions about Tom Simpson. But without solid proof, I couldn't burden him with it. And then there was Bryce. My oldest and best friend in the world, who was a new father.

I owed him honesty too. In fact, since it was his father, I needed to tell him before I told Talon. But I couldn't do either until I had some proof other than my gut feeling.

I'd called the Junction police earlier, and they'd vouched for Mills and Johnson, though they gave me the same caveat Steve had—just don't pay too much attention to how they get things done. But they were good, apparently, as they'd never been caught.

Hell, I didn't mind if they left their scruples at the door. I just wanted justice for my brother and for Bryce's cousin and all those other poor kids who had become nameless in the last twenty-five years.

"Biker Bob found his original records," Talon was saying. "And here they are." He shoved a few papers on the desk toward me.

"Now? I thought you were meeting with him a week or so

ago?"

"I did. He required a little more...incentive."

I rolled my eyes. Talon wanted so much to find these guys, but for all we knew, this Biker Bob guy had fabricated records to get Talon to pay him. I'd go along. This was important to my brother.

I eyed the papers. "This is for the phoenix tattoo?"

"Yeah. He did the tat five times altogether on the left forearm, but only three of these fit the time frame. None of them, unfortunately, are named Nico Kostas."

I scanned the documents. Christopher Headley. Declan Stevens. Milo Sanchez. I wasn't one to say "I told you so," so I didn't. "So what now?" I asked.

"I'm going to track down all of these guys. One of them is him. I know it. He either used another name then, or he's using one now."

"You do realize, don't you," I said, "that this guy doesn't want to be found?"

He nodded. "It's him, though. I know it. Why else would he have disappeared? Clearly he has no conscience. He tried to have Brooke killed, for God's sake."

"You don't have any proof of that either," I reminded him. "And when are you going to find the time to track these guys down? You have an orchard to run, or have you forgotten?"

He raised his eyebrows. "What's with you, Joe? Don't you want to catch this guy?"

More than he knew. "Of course I do. But Tal, we have to be reasonable." I was one to talk. I had Tom Simpson convicted in my mind already. But saying this wouldn't help my brother keep things in perspective.

"Joe's right," Ryan agreed. "Don't get so caught up in this

that you forget to live your life."

Talon let out a breath. "I know, I know." He stood, clearly on edge. "You're right. But why not have Mills and Johnson check these guys out? If anyone can track them down, those two can."

"They can try," I said. "And we can continue to lean on Larry to finger the other two. But that's about all we can do right now. We do have a ranch to run."

Talon reddened a bit. "Yes, we have a fucking ranch to run, Joe. God, you sound just like Dad. Who died and made you responsible for everything?"

"Dad did," I said.

And he had—always drumming into my head that I was the oldest so I had to be responsible for everything.

"You know, Ry and I do our share around here."

"I know."

"So you can drop the big brother routine."

If only it were that easy. I'd dropped the big brother routine one fateful day twenty-five years ago. Unlikely I'd ever drop it again.

Luckily, I was saved by my cell phone vibrating on my desk. I took a quick look and tried to disguise the happiness I felt.

Melanie.

"Sorry, guys, I need to take this," I said.

They both stood and left my office. I knew we'd be revisiting the tattoo guys later, but for now, I wanted to see what Melanie needed.

"Hey," I said into the phone, hoping to sound nonchalant. "What's up, Melanie?"

"Jonah, thank God. I need to see you." Her voice was

scared and timid.

Something was wrong. My nerves skittered under my skin. "Of course. I can get away. Should I come to your office?"

"No. Not my office. I'm near you. I'm somewhere on your ranch. Where are you?"

"You're here?"

"Yeah. I'm sorry. I know it's forward."

"No, don't worry about that. I'm always glad to see you. You know that."

"No, I didn't know that." She let out a tiny nervous laugh. "But I'm glad to hear you say it."

"Tell me where you are."

After figuring out where she was on the ranch, I gave her directions to my house. "Meet me there," I said. "I can get there in about fifteen minutes."

★ ★ ★ ★

Melanie was waiting on my doorstep when I got there. I drove up in my pickup. I'd been out in the pastures earlier this morning, and I was a mess. Definitely needed a shower.

She looked distraught. She was wearing a tan dress and black boots, looking luscious as usual. But those beautiful green eyes were red-rimmed and sunken. She'd been crying.

I walked rapidly to her. "Sweetheart, what's the matter?"

She launched herself into my arms.

"Whoa, baby. Tell me what's wrong."

"Just take me inside, Jonah, please. I need you."

With one hand, I unlocked the door to my place and led her inside. She melded into me, pulled my head to hers, and kissed me, hard.

I broke the kiss quickly. "Baby, I'm a mess. Let me take a shower first."

"I don't care. I need you. Now." She took the Stetson off my head and set it on the table in my entryway. Then she began to unbutton my shirt.

I was grimy with sweat, and I didn't even want to think about what I smelled like. But nothing deterred her. When she had unfastened each button, she parted the fabric and laid her cheek against my chest.

She inhaled. "I love the way you smell."

I chuckled. "I probably smell like sweat and cattle."

"I don't care. It's wonderful." She inhaled again, closing her eyes. She brushed my brown shirt over my shoulders and to the floor and then sprinkled a few kisses on my sweaty skin. "You have the most beautiful chest. You're just so beautiful, Jonah."

I pulled slightly back from her, meeting her emerald gaze. "You're the one who's beautiful. Tell me what's going on, sweetheart. How can I help?"

"You can take me to bed."

I grinned. "There's nothing I'd love more, but I really do need a shower."

"No, you don't. You're so rugged and musky right now. So manly. So very manly." She inhaled again. "You're exactly what I need. All man."

I wasn't sure that being sweaty and dirty made me all man, but I wasn't about to argue with her.

"Please, Jonah, take me to your bedroom."

"All right." I took her hand and began leading her down the hall, but when we got to the entryway kitchen, she stopped.

"I've never done it in the kitchen," she said.

"You haven't?"

She smiled timidly. "I've always been kind of a 'bed only' person. I had never done it in my office or in my living room until you."

I raised my brows without meaning to. Was she really that innocent? Of course she was. She didn't even like the occasional slap and tickle.

But things could change.

Things *would* change.

"You're in luck," I said. "My housekeeper was here this morning, so everything is spic and span and sanitary. What's your pleasure?"

She looked around. "This is a beautiful kitchen. You must be a great cook."

I laughed. "Are you kidding? Marjorie is the cook in the family. I have a personal chef who comes in once a week and prepares and freezes meals for me. I think tonight is beef stroganoff."

"Still, it's a gorgeous kitchen. Nothing like that tiny galley kitchen of mine." She scanned the room, zeroing in on the island. "Your granite countertops are gorgeous."

"You're gorgeous." I backed her up against the island, turned her around, and unzipped her dress. Then I slid it over her shoulders, breasts, and hips. I turned her back to face me.

"Beige cotton bra and panties again, Melanie?" I licked my lips. "Lace and silk certainly has its place, but nobody does cotton like you."

She reddened, biting that gorgeous lower lip of hers. "I guess I've just never been the extravagant type. These do the job, and they're affordable. And quite frankly they're a lot more comfortable than all that lace."

I grinned from ear to ear. "My God, you're adorable." I set her up on the counter.

She squealed when her thighs hit the cold granite.

I relieved her of her boots and spread her legs. "You're wet. I can smell you."

She reddened even further and continued to squirm.

"I could rip the cotton panties off you like the other night. What a shame that would be. Then I would owe you two pairs of panties. And I always pay my debts." I slipped one of her bra straps off her shoulder, inhaling the lavender of her neck. "And Melanie," I whispered in her ear, "I *won't* be buying beige cotton."

Definitely not. Satin and lace for Melanie Carmichael—green or black or—God—purple. She'd be great in purple.

She moaned when I thrust my tongue into her ear canal.

"You like that?" I asked.

She shuddered. "Oh, yes."

I plunged into her ear again, letting her squirm, and then I nibbled on her earlobe, swirled my tongue over the shell of her ear. I blew on the wetness. She shuddered some more.

I pulled back then, looking into her green eyes. "I'm hungry. I'm having you for lunch."

I dived between her legs, finding my wet prize. She smelled and tasted sweeter than cherry wine. "God, you are so hot," I said against her thigh.

I shoved my tongue into her wet heat, slurping on her, eating her cream. Then I nibbled at her clit, and she shivered, her thighs trembling against my cheek.

She was ready. She was ready to come. So I thrust two fingers into her pussy, and she clamped around me. I reveled in her response, taking in every sigh, every moan, every sob.

"You like that, baby?"

She moaned in response and arched her back, her eyes closed.

I continued thrusting, flicking my tongue over her clit, until another orgasm started.

"That's it, sweetheart. Let it go."

As I said those last words, I understood why she was here. She had to let go of something. But I knew all too well that this was only a temporary escape. We would have to talk later.

I thrust one more time, and then I let her come down from her release. I stood, pulling her toward me, and lowered my mouth to hers.

"Kiss me," I said. "Kiss me and taste yourself on my tongue."

She moaned into my mouth, opening for me instantly. Our tongues whirled and swirled together. Her kisses were addictive, raw and addictive. I couldn't wait any longer to have her. I slid one hand down her arm, down her thigh, to my crotch. God, I was hard. I unbuckled my belt and unsnapped my jeans, pushing them down just far enough for my cock to spring free. Still kissing her, I thrust violently into her pussy.

Her soft groan vibrated against the inside of my cheeks and my tongue.

I broke the kiss to take a necessary breath. "You like that, sweetheart? You like my hard cock in your hot pussy?"

"Yes," she whispered, her breath wafting over my cheeks like a cool breeze. "I love it. I love it."

Love. She hadn't said she loved me, but hearing that word from her lips sent warmth right into my heart.

Was I falling in love with Melanie Carmichael? Could she possibly be falling in love with me?

Sex had never been so intense for me, even though she hadn't let me do everything I longed to do to her in the bedroom. But sex wasn't love. Even really good sex wasn't love. Was it?

Hell, I knew nothing about love. Until I worked through the guilt that hung over me like a vulture, I had no business loving anyone.

But God, something about Melanie Carmichael made me crazy. When I had seen that friend of hers, that Oliver, with his mouth on her, I had wanted to grab him with my bare hands and strangle the life right out of him.

I thrust again and again into her. When the tiny convulsions began in my balls and at the base of my dick, I pulled out and thrust one more time into the woman who had come to mean so much to me. I groaned against her, releasing my load, seating myself to the hilt until the spasms finally stopped.

When I withdrew, her head was back, her eyes closed.

"Baby? You okay?"

"Yes." She brought her head up and met my gaze. "Yes, I'm okay."

I grinned. "In that case, I think we *both* need a shower now."

She grinned back.

CHAPTER TWENTY-SIX

Melanie

Jonah led me to his bedroom and through it to a decadent shower and bathroom. Showerheads came from both sides, and when he turned it on, steam rose from faucets on the side of the wall. I was wearing nothing but my bra, and he divested me of it quickly and then took care of his boots, jeans, and boxers.

He opened the door to the shower. "After you."

I walked in and inhaled the fragrant steam. Lavender. "My favorite fragrance," I said. "How did you know?"

"I kind of got the message, since you always smell like lavender and you have a lavender plant on your nightstand."

"You don't seem like the kind of guy who has lavender essential oil lying around."

"You got me." He laughed. "Actually, I have lavender, peppermint, and eucalyptus. They were gifts from Marjorie. She got into essential oils a year or so ago and was convinced that the three of us guys needed their healing properties. I admit this is the first time I've used them."

I smiled. "I'm sure she'll be happy to know they came to good use." I inhaled again. "The next time you have a cold or any kind of congestion, try the eucalyptus and peppermint. They work wonders."

"And what's the lavender for?"

I inhaled again. "Relaxation. Pure, solid relaxation."

God knew I needed that. Lavender had always been a favorite fragrance of mine, but the fact that it had relaxation properties made me love it even more. I hadn't been able to relax much since Gina's death.

Jonah walked under the other shower head and wet his hair down so it was slicked back. "Oh," he groaned. "It feels great."

It did feel great. He pulled a bottle of shampoo off the shelf and squeezed some into his palm, working it into a lather. Then he put it on his head and started soaping up. I reached forward and added my hands to his, massaging his scalp along with him.

"That feels amazing, Melanie."

It felt amazing to me, too, just having my hands in his thick, wet hair. After we had lathered him up thoroughly, he turned around and rinsed his hair.

I grabbed the body wash from the shelf. I began soaping up his back, down to his strong hips, over his finely shaped butt.

He turned. "Time to get my chest."

I lathered my hands once more and skated them over his beautiful chest and rock-hard abs, down into his pubic hair, where I soaped up his cock and balls.

He closed his eyes and then stepped back under the shower head and rinsed off.

"Your turn now," he said.

"I had a shower this morning."

"After that hot sex we had in the kitchen, you're as dirty as I am. I'm going to wash you until you're squeaky clean."

I closed my eyes and smiled. "That sounds like heaven, to

be honest."

Together, we washed my hair as we had washed his, and then he cleansed my body, running his strong hands over every inch of my flesh.

I nearly melted. If I'd been any more relaxed, I would've swirled down the shower drain with the water.

When we were done, he grabbed some towels off the rack, shut off the shower, and we dried each other.

"Would you like a drink?" he asked.

"Maybe just some water or iced tea, if you have it."

He pulled on a pair of boxers. "I do. I'll be right back."

I finished drying off and then wrapped the towel around me. I left the bathroom and looked around his bedroom. It was beautifully decorated but completely masculine. His king-size bed sported a brass headboard and footboard, and upon it sat a dark-brown satin comforter with pillow shams to match.

His chest and dresser were of a dark oak, complete with knots. So rustic. So Jonah. The floor was all hardwood, covered by a burgundy, hunter-green, and brown Oriental rug in an ornate design.

A door led to a giant walk-in closet, and I couldn't help but peek in. A few rumpled shirts were strewn on the floor. He had missed the hamper that was only two feet away. I smiled. Typical man. I quickly deposited the errant shirts into the wooden hamper.

His shirts and pants were hung up neatly, jeans were folded nicely on the shelf, and his shoes were stacked on shelves, including oversize ones for several pairs of cowboy boots.

A throat cleared behind me.

I turned, embarrassed. I had been violating his personal

space. I walked out of the closet. "I'm sorry."

"For what?"

"For...nosing around your closet." I looked around the room again. "This is a gorgeous bedroom."

"It serves its purpose," he said.

"How big is this house?"

"About three thousand square feet."

I gasped.

"It's a lot smaller than the house where Talon and Marj live. That's the main house, where our parents lived. Where we lived when we were growing up."

"So why don't you live there?"

He shrugged. "I just wanted my own place. A place where I could escape. I wanted my own pool, where I could swim whenever I wanted, even in the dead of night, without anyone questioning me."

"That's right. You like your alone time. And you like the water."

He nodded. "In fact, I could go for a swim now. Would you like to join me?"

"Is it warm enough?" Colorado Indian summers were typical, but I wasn't sure whether it was hot enough to be dousing ourselves in water outdoors. We were nearing October.

"The pool's heated, and if you get too cold, we can get into the hot tub instead." He handed me a glass of iced tea.

I took the tea and sipped it—nice, crisp, and tannic under my tongue. I looked down at the towel that was still wrapped around me. "I don't have a suit."

"This is my private home. Who needs suits?" He grinned at me lasciviously.

My cheeks warmed, and I looked down. My chest was

turning ruddy.

"No need to be embarrassed, Melanie. In case you forgot, I've seen you naked a time or two."

I laughed softly. Why on Earth was I embarrassed? "We just took a shower. We'll get all covered in chlorine."

"Are you allergic to chlorine or something?"

"No. But it does dry out my skin."

"Well, you know what the weirdest thing about my shower is?" he said.

"What's that?"

"We can use it more than once a day." He took my hand, squeezing it. "Come on. I want to show you my pool."

"I can't go out in the towel."

He walked to his closet and brought out a silk robe. "You can wear this."

He helped me into the black satiny garment. It was horribly large on me, but the fabric felt cool and soft against my skin. I inhaled. It smelled like Jonah. It smelled like heaven.

"Now what are you going to wear?"

"I've got my boxers on. I'm good."

I laughed. A good hearty laugh, a laugh like I hadn't laughed in a long time. And it felt so good.

"All right, Jonah. Lead me to your pool."

We walked down the carpeted hallway, through the kitchen, to a lovely little family area complete with bar. Two gorgeous French doors opened out onto the redwood patio.

And a huge yard. A panting golden retriever ran up to us.

"Hey, girl," Jonah said, petting the dog on the head. "Meet a good friend of mine. Melanie, this is Lucy."

Lucy licked my hand. She was beautiful. "I didn't know you had a dog."

"Oh, yeah. All three of us do. We love animals around here."

A cobblestone walkway led to his pool. Lucy walked next to me, her soft fur brushing my leg. A light breeze was blowing, but I wasn't chilly. Still, I thought it might be a little too cold for swimming.

As if reading my mind, Jonah said, "Dip your toe in. You'll see. It's a great temperature."

I did as he suggested, and sure enough, the water was pleasantly warm.

"I swim every morning, even in the dead of winter if I can get out here. As long as we're not snowed in, I swim."

"You mean the water doesn't freeze?"

"When it gets really cold, I cover the pool at night, but remember, it's heated. So, no, the water doesn't freeze."

I didn't even want to think about the electric bill...but Jonah Steel wasn't the kind of man who had to worry about bills.

"I keep my hot tub up and running year-round as well. And Melanie, there is nothing like sitting in a hot tub, with a martini, while snow is falling around you."

I created a visual in my mind as I looked over at the hot tub sunken into the ground next to Jonah's pool. Would I ever sit in the hot tub during a snowfall with Jonah?

Right then, I wanted to more than anything in the world.

"So you feel like a swim?"

"I'm not a great swimmer," I said. "I mean, I know enough not to drown, but I won't win any medals. I mostly just splash around a little."

"That's absolutely fine. Here, let me help you." He untied the oversize silk robe at my waist, shoved it over my shoulders, and set it neatly on a nearby chaise longue.

"So is the water to your liking?"

"Yeah, feels great."

He licked his lips, grinning. "Good." And he pushed me into the water.

CHAPTER TWENTY-SEVEN

Jonah

I hoped I hadn't gone too far, but within a few seconds, Melanie's blond head bobbed up, and she had a smile on her face.

I wondered, then, when was the last time she'd had any fun. Real honest to goodness fun.

And I wondered if it had been before or after I had.

We were both severely lacking in fun in our lives.

I'd make today about fun. I'd set aside the guilt that normally ruled my life and concentrate on Melanie and having fun with her. We could both use it.

I removed my boxers quickly and dived in. When I came up, Melanie was treading water, still smiling.

She moved to the pool's edge and looked to the blue sky. "I can't tell you how good this feels. It's been ages since I've been swimming."

"Yeah, there's something about the water. It just seems to erase the stress away."

"What kind of swimming do you do? You said you swim every day."

"I do some laps. I know most of the strokes. It's pretty much what I do for exercise, although I also get a lot of exercise around the ranch. Most days I'm out on the pastures, walking around and checking things out."

"Well, you look great. Obviously you're getting your exercise," she said.

I stared at her soft body. "I could say the same for you. What do you do for exercise?"

"Not a lot. Although I walk almost everywhere I go in the city. My office, my loft, the places where I shop—they're all within mere blocks of each other."

"Urban living at its finest," I said. "Not that I know anything about that."

"No, you're rural all the way. What was it like growing up here?"

"That's a loaded question."

"I didn't mean to bring up anything bad."

"No, it's okay," I said. "I tend to forget how great it really was. I was only thirteen when Talon got taken, and life after that was...different. It was a cloud that always hovered over us. I never understood why my parents wouldn't allow us to talk about it. They truly swept it under the rug."

"Yeah, Talon and I have talked about that."

"Do you have any insight?"

"No, we really haven't gone into any detail about why your parents did what they did. There are still a lot of unanswered questions."

"You know," I said, "when I look back, I wonder why they didn't try to find those guys then. Especially since Larry Wade was my mother's half-brother. I get that he was family, and that the other guys were after him for letting Talon go. But why would my parents not pursue it? Especially after what he did to their son—my brother? And those other children. Including Luke Walker—" I shook my head. "I forgot. They didn't know what happened to Luke Walker. Talon never told anyone. He only recently told Ryan and me."

"Talon has his own reasons for keeping quiet."

"Yeah, and they're not too hard to figure out, I don't think. What happened to him was probably very humiliating. He tried to block it from his mind. I'm sure I would've done the same."

"People deal with things in different ways." Melanie sighed. "The way Talon was feeling afterward contributed to that, and add to that the fact that your parents were complicit in keeping the whole thing under wraps. It's amazing that he got the help he needed. But I'm so glad he did."

"I'm so glad too."

"You know, Jonah, what happened to Talon didn't just happen to Talon. It happened to you, too. And your brother. And your mother and father. I don't particularly condone how your parents handled it, but I do feel confident in saying that they thought it was best at the time, and they felt they had their reasons."

"I just wish I knew what those reasons were."

"You may never know, and you will have to eventually find peace with that."

I wasn't sure I'd ever find true peace, at least not on land. In water, I got close. I still hadn't told Melanie about what I used to do in those dark alleys on skid row. Or rather, what I used to have done to me. "I do want to find peace with that. But since my parents aren't here to give us any answers, I don't particularly have a choice in the matter."

"That's not true. You have a choice whether to make peace with the fact that you'll never know their reasons."

Melanie raised a good point, but I wasn't quite ready to

give up the fight. I was pretty sure Wendy Madigan, a former news correspondent, had more information than she had told Jade. I intended to converse with her at some point. I just wasn't sure when. I was trying to work through my own guilt and Bryce's father's potential involvement, and when I had a spare moment to think, a certain blond therapist popped into my mind—the same blond therapist who stood next to me now in the shallower end of my pool, her peachy breasts bobbing on the surface of the water.

"I'm not sure that's true," I said.

"Jonah," she said, "there are so many things in this life that we have no control over. Take the control where you have it. The one thing you *can* control is the way you feel about something. Accepting that you may never know the truth of why your parents did what they did is a choice *you* can make."

I gave a small smile. "You know, I think you're the most intelligent, insightful, beautiful woman I've ever had the privilege to meet."

Her beautiful cheeks turned raspberry.

"Oh, come on, don't be embarrassed."

"It's just... No one has ever said anything like that to me before."

"Are you kidding me? Not even loverboy Oliver Nichols?"

She shook her head. "I wasn't lying to you. I didn't ask for that kiss. As far as I'm concerned, he's just a friend."

It hadn't looked like friendship to me, but fine. I'd let it go. After all, she had gone to dinner with me, not him.

"If no one has ever said anything like that to you before, everyone who's met you is either blind or stupid. Or both."

She laughed softly. "Of course they're not, but thank you for saying it to me, Jonah. It means more than you know. On today of all days."

Right, she had come to me because she had been distraught. Something had happened to Melanie earlier today, and like a completely selfish bastard, I had forgotten to ask her about it. Then, instead of making the day about fun as I'd originally hoped to, we'd begun talking about my own issues.

"Tell me what's bothering you today. What brought you to me?" Anything that brought her to me worked in my favor, but I did not want her suffering.

"Oh, nothing really."

I cupped her cheek. "It's not nothing. You don't strike me as the kind of woman who goes running to a man's house unless something is truly wrong."

She visibly swallowed. Then she hoisted herself up so she was sitting on the concrete ledge of the pool, her legs dangling in the water.

I spread her legs and stood between them, rubbing up and down her arms. "You can tell me. I will help if I can."

"I wish you could help. The truth of the matter is, no one can."

"That doesn't sound like the insightful therapist I know."

She let out a sarcastic chuckle and sniffled. "I don't have any insight for myself, I'm afraid."

"Maybe I'll have some," I said. "We Steels have brains, you know."

She smiled. "Oh, I know. A lot of brainpower had to go into making your ranch the empire it has become."

"That was a few generations before me, I'm afraid," I said. "But we do need a substantial amount of brainpower to keep it going. That's for sure."

She nodded, saying nothing.

"Come on, Melanie. Let me help you."

She sniffled again. "I'm going to be taking a little... vacation."

My heart raced. I hoped she wouldn't be gone long. "A vacation? That's nothing to be so sad about. Where are you going?"

"I don't know yet, and I don't really want to take a vacation."

"Then why take one?"

"I don't have a choice. I have to leave my practice for a few weeks. Your brother has probably already gotten a call from Randi canceling all of his appointments for the next three weeks."

I opened my mouth into a circle and then shut it quickly. "I'm so sorry. Why?"

She looked to the sky and then looked back at me. "Someone filed a complaint about me with the medical board."

I shot my eyes open. "Whatever for? You're amazing. Look at what you've done for Talon."

She smiled—sort of. "Talon was one of my success stories."

"I'm sure he's one of many."

She let out a breath of air, the look in her eyes forlorn. "I can't save them all, Jonah. I only wish I could."

"Melanie, no one can save them all."

"I keep looking back, thinking back. What could I have done? How could I have done things differently so the outcome would've been good instead of bad?"

My God. I asked myself the same questions all the time. If only I had gone with Talon that day. If only...

"You have me at a little disadvantage here. I don't know what you're talking about."

"I'm talking about one of my patients."

"What happened?"

She inhaled deeply. "I can't talk about it."

"Of course you can."

"No, I really can't. Doctor-patient confidentiality."

Right. I had forgotten about that. "I understand."

"I wish you did understand, Jonah. I'm just carrying around so much guilt." And then she chuckled. "I can't believe I just said that. You *do* understand guilt, don't you?"

"Yeah, I've had a little experience in that area."

"No wonder I was drawn here. To you. Because you're the one person who might just understand."

I had been hoping she had been drawn to me for reasons other than guilt, but I'd take what I could get. I knew she had been looking for comfort, and I hoped I'd helped give her that.

I tugged on her arms and pulled her down to meet my mouth. I brushed my lips over hers, giving her a few soft kisses. "I will try to help you in any way I can."

"All right." She sighed. "I was kind of fudging about doctor-patient confidentiality. I *can* talk about it, especially under these particular circumstances. I just can't name names. It's just that...I don't really *want* to talk about it. But I know I have to." She laughed a bit. "God, I tell my patients all the time that they need to talk if they want to heal." She shook her head, her wet hair sending a few droplets of water onto me. "I had a patient, Jonah. A patient who...didn't make it."

My heart fell. "I'm so sorry."

"She killed herself. And I've racked my brain, trying to figure out what I missed. I've gone through my notes myriad times. I've gone through the sessions in my head, trying, and failing, to figure out where I went wrong."

"Do you think that maybe you didn't go wrong?"

"But I did. If I had done my job, if I had seen some indication that she was suicidal, I could've saved her. She would be alive today."

"You're putting a pretty heavy burden on yourself."

"Don't you put that same burden on yourself?"

I couldn't fault her perception. She was right. I did. And I'd been lucky. I got my brother back. He hadn't died, though God knew he had spent many years wishing he had.

"Let's not talk about me right now, Melanie. I'm doing fine." A half-truth, but what the hell? "Let's talk about you. You're a professional, and you know how any practice of medicine is. There are some people you can't help. I'm very sorry for your loss. I truly am. But what else is going on here? I get the feeling there's something you're not telling me."

She wiped away a tear that had fallen down her cheek. "I'm telling you all I can."

"Is there anything I can do to help you?"

She laughed shakily. "You can maybe...give me something to do for the next three weeks."

Was she asking me to take her away? To stay with her in the city or for her to stay here? I had no idea.

"I wish I could take you on an extravagant vacation, Melanie, and believe me when I say I would if I could. But this is autumn. It's a busy time for us with the harvest and all and then getting the orchards and vineyards winterized."

She shook her head vehemently. "No, you misunderstood me. In fact, I don't know why I said that. I just wish—"

We both turned our heads simultaneously toward the door to the house, and Lucy bolted to two figures rushing toward us.

Jade and Talon.

Melanie gasped, crossing her arms over her chest and sliding back into the pool.

"Doc?" Talon said.

The poor woman turned beet red.

"What are you guys doing here?" I asked.

"I think I could ask you the same thing," Talon said.

"I'm going for a swim," I said, clenching my teeth. "At *my* house. That's it."

"Sure," he said. "Have it your way."

Melanie was looking down, her arms still crossed over her chest, even though the water was covering her. I got out, naked as a jaybird, and tossed my boxers on. Jade had the decency to look away as she rubbed Lucy behind her ears. I grabbed the robe for Melanie, used it to cover her as she got out of the pool, and then wrapped it around her.

"Do you want to go inside?" I asked Jade and Talon.

"Sure," Talon said. "We have some news."

CHAPTER TWENTY-EIGHT

Melanie

If I'd had one wish at that moment, it would have been for a giant hole to open up right next to Jonah's pool and swallow me. I was completely embarrassed. How unprofessional! I was Talon's therapist, for God's sake. And here I was, naked, and in his brother's pool.

I needed to excuse myself fast. Of course, I wasn't sure what to say, so I walked briskly through the kitchen and back to Jonah's bedroom to put on my clothes...and found that only my bra was on the floor. The rest of my clothes were in the kitchen, strewn on the floor, no doubt being seen by Talon and Jade at that moment.

"What the hell have I done?" I said aloud.

"You haven't done anything wrong." Jonah stood in the doorway, holding my clothes. "Here you go. Get dressed. There's nothing for you to be embarrassed about. Then come out and join us. We're going to have a drink at the kitchen table and look at the new evidence Talon and Jade have."

"This is really none of my business."

"Of course it's your business. You know the whole story. You probably know it better than either Jade or I do. I talked to Talon. He doesn't mind you being here."

I imagined the two of them guffawing and patting

each other on the back, congratulating each other on their conquests. My God, this was so unprofessional.

Joe grabbed a pair of jeans, pulled them on, and then walked out of the room. He turned back to me. "Take your time, but please, don't worry about anything."

What the hell? Right now, I wasn't allowed to practice in my chosen field. Talon probably already knew, had gotten a call from Randi earlier. I took off Jonah's robe and hung it up in his closet to dry out, and then I went to the bathroom and dried myself off with one of his soft cotton towels. My hair was a mess from the earlier shower and now from the pool. I combed through it as best I could and then put my work clothes back on.

"Now or never," I said aloud. I walked out of the room, down the hallway, toward the kitchen.

And then made a beeline to the front door, where I escaped.

★ ★ ★ ★

I didn't particularly want to go back to my loft, so I decided to go into the little town of Snow Creek and do some exploring. The Western slope was home to many little towns, but I usually stayed in the city. I couldn't help but be a little curious about the hometown of one of my most successful patients...and his brother.

Thinking about Talon's healing made me feel a little better, but unfortunately, it wouldn't get me back into practice. I would have to call each of my patients individually, referring them to another therapist while I was taking my "leave of absence." And of course Talon would be on that list. I'd have to find a good fit for each of them. However, there were some—and Talon was in this category—who would be fine going without a session for three weeks. Talon no longer needed weekly sessions. He had come so far. I was proud of him.

A sign decorated with Colorado peaches said "Welcome to Snow Creek, Colorado" as I entered the town. It didn't take long to find the downtown area. There wasn't much parking, so I drove through the little town, which was no more than a few blocks long and housed a mom-and-pop grocery store, several restaurants, a hardware store, a bar called Murphy's, a café called Rita's, a beauty salon—all the small-town essentials.

On the outskirts of town, several roadside stands were set up selling peaches and apples.

I decided to drive back through. Luckily, someone was just leaving, so I found a parking spot on the street. I got out and walked around.

I ambled into Rita's Café and ordered an iced tea. I took it to go and sipped it as I walked down the street, looking in windows. A cute little antique store caught my eye, and I strolled in, perusing their selection.

The woman behind the counter smiled and asked if she could help me with anything, but other than that didn't bother me, which was just as I preferred it. A phoenix figurine caught my eye. Talon had talked a lot about the symbolism of the phoenix during our sessions and how it had become a contradictory image in his mind. For some reason, the little figurine drew me. I wasn't sure why, but I picked it up. It looked fairly new. Why was it in an antique shop?

If only I could be a phoenix. If only I could escape from everything that was torturing me now and rise again.

But there was no escape for me. Gina Cates was dead, and

now it looked as though I was going to pay for it—probably all because I'd made one ill-advised phone call out of guilt, when I knew better.

And the phoenix—it was also a symbol of the man who had stolen Talon Steel's innocence. I swallowed back a lump clogging my throat, put the figurine back on the shelf, and left the shop, taking a business card on my way out.

I kept walking, past a bakery—the yeasty aroma of fresh bread nearly drew me in—a clothing shop, the grocery store, Murphy's Bar. I sipped on my iced tea and crossed the street. The hardware store stood with its door opened, an unassuming little shop nearly hidden. I walked closer and found it was actually a combination hardware and office supply store. I smiled at its small-town charm. I wasn't sure what possessed me to walk in, but I did. I almost felt like the little store needed me.

An elderly man sat behind the counter, helping a customer with the purchase of some rope and duct tape. "There you go, Mayor," the elderly man said.

"Thank you, Gus," the man who was presumably the mayor said. "Always good to see you."

"You too. Have a great day."

The silver-haired mayor brushed past me without a look.

Gus looked over to me. "Anything I can help you with, miss?"

And suddenly I knew why I had walked into the store.

CHAPTER TWENTY-NINE

Jonah

"Anything you want to tell us, Joe?" Talon raised his eyebrows when I walked back to the kitchen.

"Nope."

"Oh, come on," he razzed me. "I knew you had the hots for her."

"I'm not discussing this. And be quiet. She's embarrassed enough as it is."

"I hope she'll join us," Jade said. "I've been wanting to meet her for a long time, to thank her for all the help she's given to Talon."

"Believe me, blue eyes, she knows how much I appreciate it."

"But she doesn't know how much *I* appreciate it," Jade said. "The woman is a miracle worker."

A small smile played at my lips. Melanie Carmichael was special, for sure. Yes, she had worked a miracle with Talon, but right now she was dealing with a patient who hadn't turned out so well. Of course, I couldn't mention that to Jade and Talon, and Melanie would likely be joining us soon anyway.

"She's just getting dressed. She'll be out in a few minutes," I said.

Talon chuckled under his breath.

"Not another word out of you," I said.

"Sure, my lips are sealed." But he was still chuckling.

"So what do you guys have to say that's so important enough to interrupt me in the middle of my swim?"

"Oh, that was swimming? Looked more like skinny-dipping."

"Just show me what you have, Tal."

"They were able to extract enough blood from the business card to get a DNA sample," Talon said.

"That's good news," I said.

"The only problem is we have no idea whose DNA it is. And here's something as well. Jade found Larry's fingerprints in the Colorado attorney database, and they do match one of the three sets that were on Colin Morse's card."

I nodded.

"We can get a DNA sample from Larry easily," Jade said, "If it's his blood, he's probably the one who left the rose. He could have pricked his finger on one of the thorns."

That made sense—which blew my Tom Simpson paper cut theory. Was I totally barking up the wrong tree? Maybe Tom was completely innocent. I'd have to give this some thought. I was certainly glad I hadn't yet voiced my suspicions to Talon.

"Or," I said, "someone planted Larry's fingerprints on the card to implicate him. He's still claiming innocence in the whole Colin matter."

"That's also a possibility," Talon said. "But I don't believe Larry for a minute when he says he's innocent with regard to Colin's disappearance. That man is no good."

"We already know that our uncle is a sick criminal. But remember, the other two beat him to a pulp when he let you go. It's possible they're trying to frame Larry to ensure that he stays quiet."

"Larry is scared to death of those other two," Jade said. "I could see it on his face when he refused to tell me who they were."

"Yeah, Jade is right. Larry won't roll over. He's scared."

"How would you know?" Talon asked.

"I went to see him. Bryce and I."

"Bryce went with you? Really?"

"Yeah, now that this whole thing is dredged up again, he wants to find out what happened to Luke."

"Oh my God, you didn't tell him what they did to Luke, did you?" Talon rubbed at his chin.

"I had to. I hadn't, which was a bonehead move on my part, but he insisted on going with me to see Larry, and Larry mentioned that you knew. Which of course meant that I knew. So I was the one who had to tell Bryce."

"God, I'm sorry, Joe," Talon said.

"You don't have anything to be sorry for. None of us have been through the hell you have. Bryce needed to know. Hell, Bryce *wanted* to know. If I hadn't told him, Larry probably would have."

"It's a nasty situation all around," Jade said. "But now we have to figure out where to go from here. I can get a court order for Larry to take a blood test, so we can check to see if his DNA matches what's on the card. We already know his fingerprints are on the card, so I'm sure Judge Gonzalez will give me the warrant."

"Yeah, let's do that," Talon said. "The next thing I want to try to figure out, while we're dealing with this, is why in the hell Mom and Dad swept this shit under the rug twenty-five years ago."

"I can talk to Wendy again," Jade said. "But Talon, I think maybe you should talk to her. She told me the last time we spoke that there were things she had promised only to reveal to you."

My skin tightened around me. I wanted to know some answers as well. Why in the hell had my father, who was an intelligent and reasonable man by anyone's standards, allowed this to happen?

"I think Jade's right," I said. "And I want to go with you. I think we should visit her in person. We need to go to Denver."

"Jade, you should come along too," Talon said. "After all, you're the one who has the relationship with her."

Jade shook her head. "I've actually been thinking about that. I don't think I should be there. I'm pretty sure she'll only reveal the stuff to you alone, and maybe to your brothers. So yes, take Jonah with you. Maybe Ryan, too."

"Ryan's too busy," Talon said. "He's knee-deep in winemaking and wine-bottling. Busiest time of the year. I wanted him to come over here today and hear about the new evidence, but he couldn't get away."

I nodded. "Understandable. Jade, I understand your reluctance to go as well. But Talon, I do think the two of us should go."

"Will you and Marj be okay at the house with your mom and all?" Talon said.

"Of course." Jade smiled. "With that mega-security system you have installed, no one can get in. My mother is a handful no matter what. But she's got a physical therapist and her nurse to deal with her. I can handle it. Marj can handle it."

"Still, I'm going to have Steve Dugan keep an eye on the place."

"That's fine," Jade said. "When do you guys want to leave?"

"I can go anytime," Talon said. "Axel is used to me taking off by now. He's getting a big raise this year, by the way."

I nodded. "No problem. I can probably get away anytime. I've got guys I trust seeing to the day-to-day stuff, and we'll only be gone a day or two. I just need to have Dolores check my calendar."

"You want to fly or drive?"

I thought for a moment. It was about a four-hour trip. Maybe a road trip with my brother was just what I needed. "Why don't we drive? We won't have to rent a car when we get there."

"Works for me," Talon said. "We'll leave as soon as we can. Check in with Dolores. And oddly, I got a phone call from Melanie's secretary earlier today. Said she had to cancel my appointments for the next three weeks."

I jolted. Of course I couldn't tell Talon anything about what Melanie told me, but the mention of her name stirred me. Where was she? She should've come out by now.

"Excuse me for a minute, guys," I said.

I walked briskly back to my bedroom. "Melanie?" I said softly as I walked in. I checked the sitting area, the bathroom, even the walk-in closet, since I'd caught her in there earlier.

She was nowhere to be found.

I walked back to the kitchen. "Did you see Melanie leave? She's not here."

Both Talon and Jade shook their heads.

"That's strange. Wouldn't we have noticed if she walked out?"

"Maybe not," Jade said. "We were kind of all involved in

the whole blood and DNA thing."

"I don't understand why she would leave," I said.

"I think she was probably embarrassed," Talon said. "I mean, we did catch you guys naked. What was going on here, anyway?"

"That's still none of your business," I said.

"Hey, it's no big deal. She's a great woman. I know you have the hots for her. But...I thought you were seeing her as a therapist."

"I told you, this isn't any of your business."

"Joe, it's okay to date her. Really. I don't mind."

"I wouldn't care if you did mind, Talon, but we're not dating."

"Okay, then I don't care if you fuck her either."

I clenched my teeth. For some reason, the idea that he thought Melanie was just a fuck to me got my ire up. "I'm not fucking her either."

That was one big goddamned lie. But it struck me that I really didn't know what was going on between Melanie and me. Did I want a relationship with her? I wasn't really ready to have a relationship. So why had I started this?

Because something about her drew me. Like we were kindred spirits or something. Both struggling with guilt, both needing an outlet.

Is that what I was to her? An outlet?

She had come to me today, needing comfort. But as soon as things got a little uncomfortable, she had bailed.

The thought slid into me like a knife in the heart. Her embarrassment over the situation had been more important than coming out to meet Jade and to be with me.

What would I have done if the situation had been

reversed?

Truthfully, I didn't know.

Well, it was clear. She wasn't interested in being a part of my life past fucking. I would have to be okay with that. After all, I was pretty much in the same boat that she was.

At any rate, she had made a choice. I would not push it.

No woman was worth that. If she couldn't sit down with my brother, whom she knew, and my most likely future sister-in-law when she was welcome, and neither of them minded, perhaps whatever was between us *should* be over.

I'd let myself get close. But she'd only been using me.

Nope. No more Melanie Carmichael.

I just hoped I could get my body to go along with my mind.

I sent a quick text to Dolores at the office to check on my schedule for the next week or so. She texted back that she could move some things around to free me up for a couple of days.

"Good news," I said to Talon. "Dolores says I'm free. When do you want to leave?"

"How about tonight? We can take turns driving and see Wendy tomorrow morning."

"Works for me." I quickly texted Dolores again, letting her know.

"I just texted Wendy, as well," Jade said. "She says she can meet with you guys tomorrow. I'll get you the address. It's her mother's home in Denver."

"You sure you'll be okay without me for a few days?" Talon said to Jade.

She laughed. "We'll be fine. Marj and I haven't had any girl time for a while. Maybe I'll slip my mother a Valium, and Marj and I can hang out."

"No parties without me, blue eyes." Talon smiled.

And I smiled. Seeing my brother smile warmed my heart every time. I had seen more smiles out of him in the last three months than I had in the last twenty-five years.

Damn, that felt good.

A road trip with my brother was just what the doctor—even though she had disappeared and would no longer be a part of my life—had ordered.

CHAPTER THIRTY

Melanie

It was near six p.m. when I got home to my loft. The package from the hardware store sat on my passenger seat, taunting me the entire way home. I might never put its contents to use. In fact, I probably wouldn't.

So why had I made the purchase?

Maybe as a little bit of a security blanket.

I unlocked my door and walked into my little place. Oddly, my cell phone hadn't buzzed at all since I'd been gone. I'd expected Joe to call me, wondering where I was.

Even though I had left of my own free will, knowing I had been welcome there, I was still crushed that he hadn't called. Maybe I didn't mean as much to him as he was beginning to mean to me. Which is why I needed to let him go. I couldn't get involved with anyone right now, especially someone who had as many issues as I did.

What a mess we would make together. A Freudian nightmare.

What I needed right now was a nice shower. Yes, I'd had a nice hot shower at Jonah's house, and my tiny shower cubicle would never compare to that steam shower of his, but I did have lavender essential oil, and I did need to wash the chlorine out of my skin and hair. Colorado was dry enough on my skin without letting the chlorine sit on it for a long period.

I sighed. I should've stayed. I wished I could've stayed. But it would be better this way. Jonah Steel deserved better than me. He had enough to deal with in his life without taking on a woman with my baggage.

I walked into my bedroom and stripped off the work clothes that had already been off of me today. I spritzed some lavender essential oil into my shower and then turned it on to heat up.

I threw my dirty clothes in my hamper, pausing to smile at how I had picked up Jonah's clothes in his closet that were strewn two feet away from his hamper.

He was definitely a man—an amazing man—and he would be better off without me.

I stepped into the shower and stood under it for several moments, letting the water pelt me, easing the stress away. My back hurt, and my temples had started to throb as I drove home. I took a deep inhale of the relaxing lavender scent. Still, the stress remained. I began shaking, shuddering. My breaths became more rapid.

A panic attack.

I knew the symptoms well. It was part of my professional training, after all. However, panic attacks were not the norm for me. I had experienced one only once before—when I received Gina's letter.

Again I breathed in, out, in, out...trying desperately to will myself out of a panic attack.

But my heartbeat was thundering, nearly pounding right out of my chest.

I looked down. My left breast pulsed with my heartbeat. So fast. So fast.

Not normal. Had to get my pulse down. I inhaled one more deep breath and then sat down on the floor of my shower, the warm water raining over my body.

"Get a grip, Melanie," I said out loud.

But the grip eluded me. Still my heart pounded. Still I breathed rapidly. I stood and forced myself to wash my hair and body. After all, that was why I had gotten into the shower in the first place, to get rid of the chlorine. As I rinsed off, I jerked with a start.

I'd heard something. But I wasn't sure what it was.

I began my breathing again. In, out, in, out. I told myself the same thing I told my patients. *When things get so bad that you think you can't bear it anymore, return to the essential of life. Breathing.*

I hoped my patients bought that drivel more than I did at the moment. It wasn't working, and I jerked as I heard another creak.

My mind could easily be playing tricks on me. Right now, I had to bring myself out of this whirl of panic.

Bam!

I nearly lost my footing on the slick shower floor. Now my panic was real. My bowels cramped and my pulse continued to race.

It hadn't been my imagination before. Someone was in my apartment.

The bathroom door was open. My bedroom door was open. If only I had thought to shut them both and lock them. But that wasn't normal. I never shut the bedroom door and locked it when I showered. Why would I do it today of all days? I stepped out of the shower quietly, leaving the water running. The intruder knew I was in the shower, so perhaps I could surprise him. I wrapped a towel around my wet body and slid quietly out my bathroom door. Someone was shuffling around in the living room. My heart beat rapidly. My purse sat on my dresser where I'd left it, and my cell phone was inside. I crept as silently and quickly as I could, grabbing my purse, and ran into the open closet, shutting the door quietly behind me. The shower was still on, so with any luck, the intruder would look for me there first. In the darkness of my closet, I grappled for my cell phone in my purse. The battery was nearly dead, but I was able to dial 9-1-1.

"Thank you for calling 9-1-1. All of our operators are busy right now—"

Were they kidding me? I ended the call and tried again.

Same message.

I wanted to scream and throw the phone, but that would give away where I was.

As an introvert, I didn't know my neighbors or their numbers. Who could I call?

Jonah Steel. He would help me. So I dialed his number. It rang once, twice, three times... The intruder was in my room now, still shuffling around. The phone was still ringing in my ear. Jonah hadn't picked up, and I dared not leave a message on his voice mail. The intruder might hear me. At least he would see I had called. Maybe he would try to call me back. I put the ringer on silent just in case.

I tried 9-1-1 once more and got the same message. No one was going to help me. I was truly alone.

I would have to help myself. My eyes adjusted to the darkness, and I looked around my closet. There was nothing to use as a weapon except for my shoes. Right then, I wished I were a shoe whore and that I had some sharp stilettos that I could use to gouge an intruder's eye out.

But not me. Not frugal Melanie Carmichael, who wore cotton bras and panties and who thought six hundred and seventy-five dollars was too much to pay for an emerald-green nightgown. Of course I had no sharp stilettos. They were too expensive and nonfunctional.

I grabbed a brown suede pump with a kitten heel. It would have to do. I squeezed my eyes shut, willing myself not to cry.

I had to be strong. I longed to stand and shed the towel that covered my body, to put on some clothes, but I didn't dare move.

I felt exposed, open to violation.

Nine-one-one had deserted me. Jonah had deserted me. Valleycrest Hospital had deserted me.

And now—

The doorknob on my closet door turned ever so slightly.

CHAPTER THIRTY-ONE

Jonah

Talon and I were ready to go before dinner. I drove over to the main house in my BMW. He was packed and ready to go and was giving his dog, Roger, a pat on the head when I walked in the door.

"Don't you guys want to stay and eat something first?" Jade asked.

"No," Talon said. "We just want to get going."

I nodded. "Yeah, now that I know where to go to get some information, I can't wait to get started. We'll pick up something on the way."

"I understand." She gave Talon a quick kiss on the lips. "Drive carefully, okay?"

"We will, blue eyes," Talon said.

My phone buzzed in my back pocket. I pulled it out.

Melanie.

I was no longer interested in what she had to say. She was no doubt calling to apologize for freaking out and leaving without saying good-bye earlier today. I wasn't in the mood to accept her apology. She didn't want to be here with me, and I had no use for her at the moment. Right now, my brother needed me, and I would always have my brother's back. It was the least I could do after failing him that one fateful day.

"You need to take a call?" Talon asked.

I shook my head. "Nothing important. Let's get on the road."

Talon took the first driving shift while I made a call to a hotel in Denver and got a reservation. We would arrive there around midnight. We'd have plenty of time to sleep before we met Wendy at ten o'clock the next morning at her mother's house in Denver.

"Joe?"

I looked up at my brother. He was staring straight at the road. "Yeah?"

"Seriously, what was Dr. Carmichael doing naked in the pool with you?"

I wasn't in the mood to beat around the bush. "What do you think she was doing?"

Talon grinned. "So you and the doc are an item?"

I cleared my throat. "No. I'm not ready for anything like that, and neither is she." Clearly, since she hadn't been able to leave my home fast enough.

"Jonah—" my brother said.

He never called me Jonah. Always Joe. Something serious was about to go down.

"You always try to do what's best for everybody else. Don't you think it's time to do something for yourself?"

"And banging Melanie Carmichael is supposed to be for me?" I rolled my eyes.

"No, I'm not talking about 'banging.' I'm talking about something more. I never thought I was capable of having a relationship, but then Jade arrived in my life like a hurricane. She whirled around me and wouldn't let me go, and she's been the best thing that's ever happened to me."

"I know. I'm really happy for you." And I was. My brother's happiness meant everything to me.

"Good. Be happy for me. And part of being happy for me means you can stop worrying about me. I'm healing. I have Jade. I have a relationship that makes me happy—so happy it's sickening, really. So stop feeling like you have to be responsible for me."

If only it were that easy. Trying to see Melanie Carmichael as a therapist hadn't worked. I hadn't been able to keep my mind on anything other than her.

But maybe I could see another therapist.

And maybe not.

The truth of the matter was, I didn't want to talk to anyone except Melanie, but I feared she had her own issues now. And her behavior today had made it clear exactly what she thought of me. I thought again about the phone call she had made to me earlier. Maybe I should've picked it up. But I was a little too angry with her to deal with her right now.

She didn't want to deal with me when I was angry. No one did.

"It's not that easy, Talon."

"Don't you think I know that? If anyone knows that things aren't always easy, it's me. Believe me, if I can get through this shit, you can."

"If I had been doing my job, you wouldn't have gone through any of it."

"Oh, for God's sake. When was it your job to keep your eyes on me every minute? I had my own mind, you know."

"You were ten. You didn't know what you were doing."

"And you were twelve."

"A few days from my thirteenth birthday."

"So fucking what? You were a kid, Joe. A kid. Get that through that thick skull of yours."

"I was the oldest. I was supposed to keep my eye on you two."

"Says who? Dad? So what? He was far from perfect, and he did a lot of shit that he shouldn't have. Why the hell did he sweep all of this under the rug? If he hadn't, the three of us wouldn't have to be dealing with it now. Maybe Dad didn't make the right decision. Maybe Dad was wrong."

"He wasn't wrong about me being responsible for you two."

"How can you say that? Of course he was wrong. You were a kid. A twelve-year-old kid. No twelve-year-old kid should be saddled with the responsibility of two younger kids. We had a mother. We had a father. It's not like you were all we had. You shouldn't have been charged with our protection. You were one of us. Let. It. Go."

"That doesn't make me feel any better."

"It may not. But Mom and Dad weren't perfect. They failed me. And they failed you, too. For whatever reason they thought they had to, they hid what happened to me and I was never able to deal with it then. It took me twenty-five years. Twenty-five fucking years, Joe, to even admit that this happened, to be able to say the word 'rape' out loud. I lost twenty-five years of my life, and for what? I don't even know why they did it."

"I guess that's what this trip is for—to find out."

"What if Wendy doesn't know? What if she doesn't have the answers we need?"

I sighed. "She may not. But she does have information. She told Jade she did."

Talon nodded, his gaze still on the road. He was clenching

the steering wheel with white knuckles.

"Do you want me to drive for a while?"

He shook his head. "I'm okay."

"It's okay for you to be angry."

"I *am* angry."

"And it's okay to be angry at me." The minute the words left my lips, I regretted them. Because frankly, I worried he would say the words I feared most—that yes, he was angry with me. He always said he wasn't, that he didn't blame me for not being there to protect him, but maybe, somewhere in the back of his mind, he did.

"The only thing I'm angry at you about, Joe, is not letting this go."

"Pull over," I said.

"What? We're on the middle of the highway."

"Take the next exit. We're in the middle of nowhere."

"Why in the hell do you want me to pull over?"

I gritted my teeth. "Because you and I are going to have this out. Now."

"You're not going to suck me into this, Joe. I refuse."

I grabbed the steering wheel. "Goddamnit, I said pull over." I jerked the steering wheel so the car headed onto the off-ramp.

"What the fuck are you doing?"

"I'm getting off the goddamned road. We are getting out of the car, and you are going to punch me in the face."

"Are you crazy?"

Maybe I was. I was feeling crazy right now. I hadn't had a good beating in a while, and my brother, the one I had failed...

And Melanie... I had failed her, too.

She and I were over before we ever began.

I wasn't interested in her apologies for leaving me so abruptly, and I wasn't interested in anything else from her.

She was a mess, and I was a mess. The two of us together were a nightmare. Her, I would let go. I had to let her go. I had no choice. But I could never let my brother go. We were blood. And I couldn't go until he gave me what I deserved.

"Fine." Talon jerked the car to stop. "Let's get this over with."

He got out of the car. I followed. We were on a back road that led into a few small Western slope towns. It was doubtful anyone would come by, and that was exactly how I wanted it.

I stalked around to my brother. "Come on. Take a shot. I know you've wanted to for twenty-five years."

"Oh, hell, no. This is your battle, Joe, not mine. I forgave you a long time ago."

"A-ha. So you admit there was something to forgive."

Talon raked his fingers through his tousled hair. "Jesus Christ."

"Take your best shot, little brother. I'm not getting back into the car until you do."

"You're fighting with yourself. Smack *yourself* around a little. Maybe that'll help."

I advanced on my brother, grabbed him by his shirt collar, and shoved him up against the car. "I've tried everything, you know. You want to know why I ended up in the hospital that time? It wasn't because some thugs randomly jumped me in an alley. I had gone looking for it. I had instigated it."

His mouth dropped open. "I wondered what happened. I know you, Joe. I know how tough you are, how mean you are. You could kick pretty much anybody's ass."

"And guess what? That wasn't the first time. I'd gotten

my ass kicked before, just never bad enough to end up in the hospital. So now you know about the pain that runs through me. And I'm afraid it won't go away until you punch it out of me."

"Why me?"

"You know why."

"You didn't fail me, goddamnit."

"You can say that all day, Talon. You can say it until the end of time, and neither you nor I will believe it."

"Joe..."

"You know I'm right. If I had been there for you, if I had gone with you like you asked me to, those guys never would've gotten you. You wouldn't have been held captive for two months. You wouldn't have been *raped*, Talon."

His cheeks reddened, and his lips trembled. Within a minute, my brother had broken my hold and turned me around up against the car, gripping me as I had been gripping him a second before.

"Is this what you want, brother?" he said, gritting his teeth. "This is what you want? You want me to fuck you up?"

Please, I said inside my head. *Yes, please, that's what I want.*

But even as I thought those words, I knew it wouldn't help to have Talon take a shot at me.

It hadn't helped the other times.

And even though this time, Talon would be doing the beating, it still wouldn't help.

No one could beat the guilt out of me. Melanie had taught me that.

This was so ridiculous, so absurd. I began laughing despite myself.

The only one who could beat my guilt out of me was *me*.

"Now you're laughing?" Talon released me. "Joe, you're going to be the death of me."

I cleared my throat. "You've got a good hold, Tal."

"No more than you do. You can kick my ass, and you know it."

I let out a small chuckle. "Maybe. Maybe not. We're probably pretty evenly matched."

"You were really going to let me kick your ass, weren't you?"

"I sure thought I was." I looked around at the gorgeous mountain scenery. "But I kind of had an epiphany. For some reason, I had the idea that getting my ass kicked would help my guilt. Funny thing though, the guilt never went away."

"What made you think it might be different this time?"

"You're the one I wronged. Maybe if you kicked the guilt out of me, it would take this time."

He leaned back on the car. "Bro, it doesn't work that way."

"Yeah, I figured that out while you were choking me." I looked at him seriously. "Was there ever any time when you did actually blame me? Be honest."

Talon grabbed a handful of his hair. "I've actually thought about that a lot. And consciously, no, I didn't blame you, but I did resent you."

"Why?"

"It wasn't you so much as anybody but me. I always wondered, why me? Why hadn't it been you or anyone else that day? Why did it have to be me?"

"Did you come up with any answers?"

"No. I was in the right place at the right time. Or rather, the wrong place at the wrong time." He chuckled. "You know, I came pretty close to punching your lights out. You were pissing me off. If you hadn't started laughing..."

"I wonder if I would've felt better if you had."

"Maybe for a few minutes. But only a few minutes. The only one who can heal you is you, Joe. Your Dr. Carmichael taught me that."

She wasn't my Dr. Carmichael. She wasn't mine at all.

"Look," my brother said. "You're the toughest guy I know. You always have been. You never took any shit from anyone. You're a lot like Dad in that regard. More so than either Ryan or I are."

I looked down at my feet. "Sometimes I'm not sure that's a good thing. Yeah, Dad did a lot of things right, but he sure gave me a hell of a burden to bear. It was nothing compared to the burden you had to bear, though."

"I won't argue with you there, bro." Talon swiped his forehead. "But maybe Wendy will have some answers. Maybe we can figure out why Dad put those burdens on both of us."

"You want to get going?"

"Sure." Talon adjusted his shirt. "You hungry? We missed dinner, you know."

"Hell, I could sure use a drink. But we're both driving."

"One drink won't hurt either of us," Talon said. "Let's get back on the highway, and the next place we see that has a bar and grill, we'll stop."

"Sounds good." I drew in a breath. "Look, Tal—"

"It's all right. I understand."

His dark eyes were genuine. He did understand. My brother was an amazing person, and he would never have come so far without—

Melanie.

I should've picked up her call.

How could I have thought it possible, mere minutes ago, to let her go? I couldn't allow her to disappear from my life. I needed her. Perhaps she needed me a little too.

Talon jiggled the keys at me. "You want to drive for a while?"

"No," I said. "I have a call to make."

CHAPTER THIRTY-TWO

Melanie

A black mask. Black everything. When the lights in the bedroom hit my eyes, I squinted.

"Get up, bitch," the masked man said.

I trembled, my panic consuming me. Nine-one-one hadn't responded. Jonah hadn't responded. I was utterly alone. Alone and vulnerable, with nothing but a damp towel separating my naked body from the mercy of this man. This had to be a nightmare—a nightmare of jagged glass and broken promises. Exactly what I deserved.

"Who are you?"

"Just somebody who wants to see you punished."

My cold blood turned to ice. "Punished for what?" But I already knew what I deserved to be punished for.

"Did you not hear me the first time? I said, 'get up, bitch.'"

I timidly rose to my feet, holding the brown suede pump behind me. The man was tall and large, dressed from head to toe in all black.

"Y-You've got the wrong person."

"No, I don't. What are you hiding behind your back?"

Without thinking, I lunged toward him with the shoe, but he grabbed my arm, stopping me.

"Feisty, huh?" He took the shoe and then ripped the towel

from me. "I wish I had time to give you a taste of my big cock."

I shrank back into the closet, nausea rising in my throat, but he pulled me forward, right into his body, my naked skin pressed against the black fabric of his clothing.

"Unfortunately, I'm on a tight schedule."

I silently thanked whatever deity was watching over me for this perpetrator's tight schedule. Surely, I would be raped, beaten, or worse, killed, before this was over, but the short respite seemed like a gift from above.

"Turn around," he said.

I didn't, and his fist came into my cheek with a dull thud. Pain surged through my cheek and jaw, and I screamed.

No one had ever hit me before.

I stood, trembling.

"I said, 'turn around,' bitch." He pulled at a length of rope tied to his belt loop.

Rope like I'd seen the "mayor" purchasing at the hardware store in Snow Creek earlier today.

"You want to taste my fist again?" He leered at me.

I turned around slowly, still trembling.

He pulled my hands behind me and tied them together with the rope. I closed my eyes, squeezing them shut. Maybe I was finally getting what I deserved. Whoever this was had probably been sent by Gina Cates's parents. They wanted to see me suffer. They wanted me to pay for what had happened to their daughter and now for what her mother was going through.

In that moment, I made a rash decision—a decision so foreign to me that I became numb to my attacker's touch. I would succumb to whatever punishment the universe had in store for me. It was no less than the punishment Gina had endured. In fact, it wouldn't be nearly as harsh. Maybe I deserved to die, as she had died.

This was my penance for not being able to help Gina. For letting her flounder. For letting her die.

When he was done tying my hands, he pulled me toward him, my back to his chest.

"Do what you want to me," I said. "I no longer care."

Something bit my neck, and I jerked around. His ice-blue eyes stared at me.

Ice-blue eyes.

And then they faded...blurry...wavy...

Until the curtain fell.

★ ★ ★ ★

My mouth was dry. The walls were fuzzy, but appeared to be painted blue—a very light blue. I was on a bed, and my wrists were no longer bound. I was dressed in a sweatshirt and sweatpants, gray, too large. I brought my wrists to my eyes. They were red and chafed from the rope.

Was I in a hotel room?

The man in black sat at a desk, writing something. I closed my eyes. Perhaps it was best to feign sleep. I kept my eyes slitted open enough to see what was going on through my eyelashes.

The man finished what he was writing, stood, and left the room.

I stayed still. What if someone else was here? I had no idea where I was. I didn't even know if this was a hotel room. It could be a room in someone's house for all I knew.

I had no watch, and I didn't have my phone. No clock sat on the nightstand. Was it still dark outside? I looked around the room.

No windows. The light-blue walls were eerily bare. I was in a room specifically designed to keep me in.

I shuddered.

Talon had been kept in a room like this, only he hadn't had the luxury of a bed to sleep on, and his walls were dark concrete, not light blue. Walls that caved in on him...

Like these walls were doing now.

Why had I decided to succumb? That wasn't like me. My mind raced. I had to get out of here.

I stood.

Big mistake. My knees buckled beneath me, and I ended up on the floor. Whatever he had drugged me with was clearly still in my system.

I had to go to the bathroom, so I stood again, more carefully this time. A small door near the front of the room opened to a toilet and sink. And again I thought of Talon. He'd had only a bucket to use...

I quickly took care of my needs and then went back to the bed and sat, still dizzy, trying to figure things out. After a few minutes, I got up and walked around the room, holding on to the wall for support, looking for something, anything, to give me a clue of where I was and how I could get out of here.

I jerked when the doorknob moved.

The black-masked man opened the door and came in, shutting and locking it behind him. "Dr. Carmichael, I see you're up."

I turned and stared. I said nothing.

"I'm afraid you'll be here for a little while. I hope you find these accommodations comfortable."

"I'm sure you really don't care about my comfort," I said.

"Aren't you going to ask me who I am? Why you're here? I figure a shrink like you would be full of questions."

"I don't see the purpose of that. You won't tell me the truth anyway."

He guffawed. "You are a sharp one. I'll give you that."

"I'm hungry," I said. It wasn't true, but I figured if I could get him to leave to get food, I could continue my investigation, once my head was a little clearer.

"I'm sorry about that," he said.

"Your tone doesn't really indicate sorrow."

"All right. I don't give a shit if you're hungry. There, does that make you feel better?"

"So your plan is to starve me to death?"

"No, you'll be fine. But you can't eat for a few more hours. If I gave you food now, you'd just upchuck. You know how these drugs work. You're a doctor."

I had no idea what he had given me, and I wasn't hungry anyway. So I'd cooperate, wait this out, figure out what was going on.

Because I had changed my mind.

I would get out of this mess. I would get out of this mess, and I would apologize to Jonah for leaving him high and dry earlier today. Or was it yesterday? I had no idea.

Somehow, I would get back to him.

And I would tell him that I had fallen in love with him.

CHAPTER THIRTY-THREE

Jonah

Wendy Madigan opened her door. She had aged a few years, but she was still the nice-looking woman I remembered from long ago. Her hair was short now, but her blue eyes still sparkled.

She said nothing for a few moments.

"Wendy?" I said.

She shook her head as if to clear it. "I'm sorry. It's just that...you both look so much like him. Especially you." She nodded to me.

"Like who?" Talon asked. "Our father? I'm Talon, by the way."

"Yes. I recognize you. Come on in." She held the door open, led us to a living room, and gestured for us to sit on a silver brocade couch. "Can I get you anything? I made a pot of coffee."

"How about a bourbon?" Talon said.

She laughed out loud. "That's what your father would've said."

Had our father been a bourbon drinker? He'd rarely drunk alcohol. I looked over at Talon. The inquisitive look on his face told me he hadn't known that either.

"I'm not sure I ever saw my father take a drink," I said to Wendy.

"Really? He did enjoy a good bourbon. I know it's early, but if you want to drink, I do have some good stuff."

"Yes, ma'am, if you don't mind," Talon said. "I know this is going to be a rough conversation."

"What about you, Jonah? You're Jonah, right?"

"Yes, that's me."

"You are the spitting image of Brad. It's almost scary."

I cleared my throat. "People have told me that before."

She looked to Talon. "Not that you don't look like him as well. But wow." She stared at me again.

I squirmed, getting uncomfortable. I had been told before that I bore a striking resemblance to my father, even more so than Talon and Ryan. Why it was making me uncomfortable, I couldn't say. Maybe it was the way she was looking at me, kind of in a wistful yet lustful way. I didn't like it.

"What can I get you, Jonah?" she said. "You want a drink too?"

I shook my head. "Coffee for me. For now, anyway." I wanted to keep my head. I was a little worried about Melanie. She hadn't answered my call last night or this morning.

Maybe that was her way of telling me to fuck off. Maybe that's why she had left yesterday so abruptly. Maybe she just couldn't deal with—well, whatever this was between us.

Fine. I would learn to get along without her. Hell, we'd only known each other a few weeks.

Wendy went to the kitchen and came back a few minutes later with a bourbon for Talon and a cup of coffee for me.

"Aren't you having anything?" I asked.

"Yeah. A stiff scotch. I'll be back."

Stiff scotch? She must have some interesting news to tell us.

I had met Wendy Madigan years ago, when I was a kid. She came around every once in a while, when she was in town. Evidently she had grown up somewhere near Snow Creek and had gone to high school with my father. In fact, rumor had it that they had been an item before he met my mother—a rumor that Jade had substantiated after her talks with Wendy. I still couldn't quite wrap my head around that one.

I hadn't seen Wendy in years, though. Even when she arranged the cover-up of Talon's homecoming and heroism when he'd returned from Iraq several years ago, she hadn't been in town. She had handled it from her base in Denver.

I imagined it had come as kind of a shock to her to see me now, my gray hair starting to sprout at the temples and in my beard. I did look a lot like my father.

She returned with her drink and sat down. "I don't know where to begin."

I took a sip of my coffee. This was Talon's call. I would let him take the lead.

He took a drink of his bourbon and set the glass back down on the coffee table on the coaster she'd provided. "Let me tell you what we know so far." Talon related what we had learned from Larry Wade—that he had helped Talon escape, that Larry was beaten to a pulp by the other two—or so he said—for allowing Talon to escape, and that he was also being held for the murder of Colin Morse, for which he was still proclaiming his innocence.

"He's also claiming he never got paid off by my father to leave the state. But we have a five-million-dollar transfer on my father's accounts that coincides with the abduction. We figure that went to Larry. Can you tell us if that's true?"

"I'm sorry." She stroked her cheek with her index finger.

"I'll tell you the same thing I told Jade. I don't know anything about a five-million-dollar transfer twenty-five years ago."

Jade had believed her. But I wasn't sure whether I believed her.

"All right," Talon said. "I'll accept that for now. But Jade also told me that you have information for me. Information you promised my father and mother you would only reveal to me when the time was right. The time is right, Wendy."

She took another long sip of her scotch and sighed. "It was all such a long time ago, Talon. You really want to go back there?"

"Look," Talon said. "We've already caught one of these guys, and I have an idea who another one of them might be. He's still at large, and we have no idea where he is. I need to know everything that you know."

"I wasn't lying to Jade. I don't know who the other two are."

"The only reason we know one was Larry was because he supposedly helped me escape," Talon said. "How did Mom and Dad find out it was him?"

"It's a long story," she said. "How much time do you two have?"

"As much fucking time as it takes," I said, looking into her tired blue eyes. "We have as much time as it takes, Wendy."

She sighed. "It started with Larry's father. Your grandfather. Supposedly Larry was consumed with guilt. I'm not sure if that was the case. I'm not sure psychopaths ever feel guilt. But that was his story. He went to your grandfather and confessed what had happened. He said he couldn't live with himself, that he had to tell someone, and that his father was the only one he trusted. Well, your grandfather had a few faults. If he hadn't, Larry might have turned out differently. But for the most part, he was a decent human being. So he did what any decent human being would do. He told Brad and Daphne."

"So his father sold him out," Talon said.

"I suppose so. But what would you have done? You were his grandson, Talon, and Daphne was his daughter. Yes, he had to forsake one child for another. I never had children myself, but I can't imagine how hard the decision was for your grandfather. He loved Larry, but he also loved your mother and you."

"Jade said Larry was raised by his mother."

Wendy nodded. "That's true."

"Do you know anything about her?" I asked.

"I'm afraid I don't, other than her name. Lisa Baines Wade. That's all I know."

I remembered the name from Larry's birth certificate that Jade had uncovered. "Did she have any mental ailments?" I asked.

"Like I said," Wendy said. "I really don't know much about her."

I wasn't buying this. Wendy Madigan was a newswoman. Surely she had looked into this back in the day. I wasn't ready to call her on that, though. I had to talk to Talon in private first.

"All right," Talon said. "So my grandfather told my mother and father about what Larry had done. Then what happened?"

"Then it happened exactly as I told Jade. They threatened to have Larry arrested, but before that happened, he ended up in the hospital, presumably beaten by the two other men. At that point, when they realized the danger he was in, they agreed to let him go."

"That's what we don't understand," I said. "Why would

my mother and father have let that happen? My father was a decent, honorable man. He wasn't one to give criminals the benefit of the doubt, especially when the victim was his own son."

"It was your mother," Wendy said. "He did it for Daphne."

"Why would he do that for my mother? And why would my mother have wanted him to?"

"Because she loved her father, and because her father loved Larry."

I shook my head. "None of this is making any sense. My father could've just told my mother how it was going to be, that Larry was going to prison. That's the kind of man my father was. He was domineering and controlling."

"He couldn't do that. Your mother would not have taken it well." Wendy sighed and set her glass of scotch on the coffee table. "You do know, don't you, that your mother was mentally ill?"

Jade had said as much, but she also said that my mother had never been diagnosed with anything. I had been fifteen when my mother took her own life and Talon only twelve. We remembered her as children remember their mother—as a loving, protective woman. Mentally ill? I didn't know. But her half-brother certainly was. Maybe mental illness ran in the family.

"Jade said she was never diagnosed with any mental illness."

"Not that I know of, no," Wendy said. "Your father tried to get her help on several occasions, but she always said no."

Something was wrong with this story. Something big. Talon and I needed to do some investigation on our own and then talk to Wendy again. She hadn't told us anything we didn't already know, except that Larry had confided in his father and that was how our parents found out.

"Wendy," Talon said, "Jade said there were things you promised only to reveal to me. I need you to reveal those things now."

She sighed. "Are you sure?"

Talon leaned forward, his dark eyes brooding. "Joe and I drove most of the night to get here. And now we want the truth."

CHAPTER THIRTY-FOUR

Melanie

Gina Cates first walked into my office on a Friday afternoon. Fridays were tough all around, especially the afternoons. I was tired and ready for the weekend, and so was the patient. But this particular appointment had been my first time available when Gina called Randi to schedule, and Gina had been adamant about getting in as soon as possible.

She was a young and pretty girl, with dark—nearly black—hair cut in a shoulder-length bob, brown eyes, and olive skin. She was shy at first, and I had a difficult time getting her to talk at all. Finally, halfway through the session, she broke down in tears.

"I can't do this."

"You can," I told her. "If you want to heal from whatever is troubling you, you can."

"It's too awful."

"I know. And I'm so sorry about that. But we'll go at the pace you're comfortable with, and anytime you need to stop, you just tell me."

She nodded and stood. "May I? I'm more comfortable standing."

"Of course," I said. "Some people are more comfortable sitting, some lying on the couch. If you're comfortable standing,

I want you to stand."

She looked around my office, her gaze finally resting on the globe on my desk. She walked toward it and lightly touched its surface. "I've always wanted to travel," she said.

"Where would you like to go?"

"Someplace warm, where life is easy. Maybe somewhere in the Caribbean, where I would have no worries."

"You can't run away from your problems, Gina."

★ ★ ★ ★

"He would wait until I was alone and vulnerable. That's how he got close to me. For a while, he would just cuddle me in his lap, telling me how beautiful I was, how he wished he had a little girl just like me."

"Did your uncle have any children of his own?"

"No. He wasn't married."

"How did it feel when you sat in his lap?"

Her lips curved up into a smile but then quickly reverted to the straight thin line I was used to seeing below her nose. "I don't want you to think badly of me."

"I would never think badly of you, Gina."

"You want the truth, then?"

"Yes, I want the truth. The only way we can work through this and get to your healing is if you're honest with me. I won't be able to help you otherwise."

She looked down, not meeting my gaze. "At first...I liked it. It made me feel...special."

"Why did it make you feel special?"

"Someone was paying attention to me."

"Hadn't anyone paid attention to you before?"

She blew out a breath in a whistle, Gina's version of a sigh. "I didn't have any brothers and sisters, and I didn't have very many friends. I was really shy and never made friends easily. My mom and dad both worked. I think they were more interested in their college students than they were in me."

"Did you ever sit in your mother's lap? Or your father's?"

"Very rarely. They weren't very affectionate to me. Or to each other for that matter."

My heart went out to the young girl. Children needed affection. If they didn't get it from their parents, they would go looking for it elsewhere—sometimes a teacher, a friend's parent, a coach. Gina had gone to her uncle.

"Some people just aren't as affectionate as others," I said. Not that I excused her parents' lack of affection toward her. I wasn't quite ready to voice that thought, though. We'd only had a few sessions.

"I know I must sound like a needy little kid," Gina said, shaking her head.

"All children want affection," I said. "There's no reason for you to feel like you were any needier than anyone else."

"I look back..." She closed her eyes, shuddering. "I can't believe I actually liked it in the beginning."

"Gina, you're not alone. You're not the first child yearning for affection who got taken advantage of by an adult you trusted. It's more common than you know, and though I don't expect that fact to offer you any solace, perhaps it will make you feel a little better just to know that you're not alone."

She opened her eyes, tears emerging. "I wish, Dr. Carmichael. I wish it did make me feel better."

"Believe me, it's okay that it doesn't. So you said you liked sitting on your uncle's lap at first."

She nodded.

"What was his name? What did you call him?"

"I called him Tio."

"Why did he want you to call him that?

"I don't know."

"It's Spanish for uncle. Was your uncle Spanish?"

"No. He was my mother's brother. They were both born here."

"All right. What did you do while you sat in his lap?" I cringed inwardly, knowing what horrors might come tumbling out of her mouth.

"He read me fairy tales."

"Oh? And did you like those stories?"

"I did...until..."

"Until when?"

"Until I no longer believed in happily ever after."

★ ★ ★ ★

"Stop it!" Gina, who had been standing as usual, fell to the floor and rolled into a fetal position, her hands covering her ears. "It hurts me, Tio! Stop! I'd rather die!"

I stood and rushed toward her, wrapping my arms around her. Gina was far from the first patient to break down in my office, but this episode nearly cut my heart right out of my chest. She had finally told me about the first time her uncle raped her.

She was eight years old.

★ ★ ★ ★

I jolted upright, my skin clammy with cold perspiration.

Gina.

My God.

I'd rather die.

She'd been flashing back to her abuse, her first rape, and I thought she'd been saying those words to her uncle. She might have been.

But she'd also been saying them to me.

Had she been crying for help? Showing me she was suicidal? And I'd missed it?

I lay back down on the bed, shaking.

CHAPTER THIRTY-FIVE

Jonah

"The truth." Wendy stroked her cheek with her index finger and then took another drink of her scotch. "I had been under the impression that I *was* telling you boys the truth."

"You know what we mean, Wendy," Talon said. "What are the things that you could only reveal to me?"

"I suppose Jade told you that your father and I were... involved."

My nerves jumped a bit, as they did every time I thought about my father being unfaithful. Yes, Jade had told us what she knew, how Wendy claimed to be our father's true love. I was only fifteen when my mother passed away, but I was old enough to remember the looks my parents had shared between them. I had a hard time believing my father had been unfaithful.

"She did," Talon said.

Wendy sighed. "I'm sorry if that was hard for you to hear."

Talon visibly tensed and clutched the arm of the sofa. "Not especially."

He was lying, but I knew why he did it—so Wendy would feel she could talk freely.

"Brad and I were soul mates," she said. "We would've been together if it weren't for your mother."

"Yes, we've heard the story. Mom got pregnant with Joe."

"As far as I know," Wendy said, "they met at a party. It was during one of the 'off' times in our relationship. We were both seeing other people at the time. I was seeing a journalism major. Your father was dating some homecoming-queen type, blond and blue-eyed. Why he hooked up with Daphne that night, I'll never know."

"Well, we're kind of glad he did, or the two of us wouldn't be here," I said.

She smiled. "True enough, and the two of you are dead ringers for him." She nodded to me. "Especially you."

"So you've told me." I drank some coffee, trying not to think about how she was looking at me.

"Anyway, Daphne got pregnant, but of course Brad didn't know that for a little while yet. After that night, he and I got back together and decided to try to make it work between us, even though we were separated and attending different colleges. So all was going fine and well, and then about a month later, your mother showed up saying she was pregnant and it was Brad's child."

"If Dad was the love of your life and you were his, why didn't he just take care of Daphne and the baby but stay with you?" I asked. "He certainly had the money."

"Believe me, that's what I wanted him to do," Wendy said. "But your father was nothing if not an honorable man. He didn't want a child of his growing up without his name. So he decided to marry Daphne, but he and I continued to see each other."

"That doesn't sound very honorable," I said. And I also wasn't buying it.

"No," Wendy agreed. "But you have to understand the

passion and desire we had between us. This may be hard for you to hear, but we couldn't stay away from each other. God knows, we both tried it more than one time. But we always failed. We were in love." She looked to Talon. "Jade has been very frank with me about what you two feel for each other. Trust me when I say your father and I had that same thing. I would've done anything for him, and he would've done the same for me."

"Which is why you helped him cover up my abduction," Talon said.

Wendy nodded somberly. "Please believe me. I tried to talk him out of that, Talon. I knew it would do no good to bury it. I knew you needed help dealing with it, and so did Brad and Daphne." She looked to me. "You and your brother too, probably. The whole family could have benefitted from counseling, but Brad would have none of it."

"Why?" I asked. "That's the thing that puzzles us the most. Why did Dad allow this to happen?"

Wendy downed the rest of her scotch and set the glass on the coffee table, loudly this time. She looked at both of us intently. "What I told Jade was the truth. A lot of it was because of Daphne. She was so unstable, and she had just had the premature baby. Brad didn't think she could handle the pressure."

"So you're saying my father forsook me for my mother?" Talon said.

"In a way, I suppose he did. But he did love you, Talon. Please believe that. He loved all you kids. The four of you were the reason he and I never got together."

"What do you mean?"

"He refused to disrupt your lives. He wouldn't divorce your mother. I also think your father didn't understand the magnitude of what had happened to you. He refused to contemplate it, even acknowledge it. Male-on-male rape, especially on a child, is a hard thing for most men to deal with."

"You don't have to tell me that," Talon said.

"I know I don't. I'm so glad you finally got the help you needed. You and Jade will have a great life together. She's a wonderful girl."

"That she is."

"But understand, what your father did, he did for love. He thought he was doing the right thing for you—for all of you, including your mother."

"There must be more to this, Wendy," I said. "What is it that you're not telling us?"

Wendy sighed. "Your father had some enemies. There was a part of him that thought..."

"Thought what?" Talon said.

"I haven't said this out loud in twenty-five years."

"Now is the time," I said.

Wendy drew in a breath and fidgeted with her hands. "Your father thought it was possible that...you had been taken on purpose."

Talon nearly jerked off the sofa.

I opened my mouth to speak. "That is directly contrary to what Larry Wade says. He told Jade that Talon was never meant to be taken."

Wendy leaned forward. "Do you hear yourself? Who are you going to believe? A psychopathic pedophile or a former newswoman?"

She had a point there.

"Who are these enemies you're talking about?" I asked. "And why would they be involved with taking Talon? And why would they be involved with Larry Wade?"

"About a week before you were found, Talon," Wendy said, "your father received a ransom demand."

"Let me guess," Talon said. "The demand was for five million dollars."

"I don't know. Your father wouldn't tell me the amount, so I honestly don't know anything about the transfer. But that's my guess," Wendy said.

"Why wasn't any of this made public?" I asked.

"For the same reason none of the rest of it was made public. To protect you, to protect your mother, and for some strange reason, to protect Larry Wade."

"How did our uncle even get involved in this?" I asked.

"Your uncle is just a sick man. He got involved with some even sicker people. And when push came to shove, he couldn't let it happen to you."

"Couldn't let it happen?" Talon gasped. "It happened. I assure you."

"But he did get you out of there, Talon. I'm not defending him," Wendy said. "But their plans were to kill you if they didn't get the money."

"Are you saying this whole thing was a conspiracy? To kidnap Talon?"

"I don't think it had to be Talon. It could have been any one of you three. In fact, they probably wanted all three of you, but Talon was the one they got."

"What about the other kids? What about Luke Walker?"

"The other kids were a ruse. They were setting up their MO. That way, when they took one of you boys, the police would assume it was the same kidnappers that were working in the area."

"So Luke's parents never got a ransom note," I said.

"No," Wendy said. "None of the other kids' parents got a ransom note. That would have made the news. Those poor kids were just playthings for these men while they were setting up for the kill."

"And then I was taken, and it never made the news."

"Yes, and I'm afraid I had a lot to do with that. But your mother was pregnant with your sister at the time, and Brad was really worried about her. If she'd had to talk to police officers and reporters... He wasn't sure she could take it. As it was, she went into premature labor and delivered the girl early. Your sister wasn't supposed to live, you know."

"Yes," Talon said, "we know. Thank you for letting Jade know about that. Now at least our sister knows why she has no middle name."

I studied my hands. I remembered my mother having Marjorie. I had just turned thirteen, Talon had been gone for several weeks, and the baby had to stay in the hospital for quite a while. But I didn't remember being worried about it. Heck, I didn't know this new baby. But I knew my brother. And my brother was gone.

More guilt. Just put it in the guilt coffers. Thank God Marjorie had survived, or I'd feel guilty about that too—guilty for not caring about my new baby sister, who was hovering on the brink of death, because I was too wrapped up in feeling guilty about my brother, who was missing.

I shook my head to clear it. "So this whole thing was a sting basically. To get money out of my father."

"That's my take on it," Wendy said.

"Then why not just kidnap the kids?" I asked. "Why molest Talon and kill the others?"

"I can't begin to tell you what makes people child molesters," Wendy said, turning to Talon. "You'd be better asking your therapist about that."

"All right, then," I said. "Who are these enemies that my father had? Enemies so powerful that they would kidnap his son, abuse him, and nearly starve him to death, for five million dollars?"

"I wish I could tell you. I can't tell you how many times I begged Brad to tell me who they were. But he said he didn't want to burden me with it. That as a newswoman, I would be constantly trying to find them, and he didn't want my life ruined that way." She sighed. "His heart was in the right place. His heart was always in the right place. But that doesn't mean he always did the right thing."

"Larry told Jade that he had reason to believe my father was involved in organized crime," Talon said.

"I know. But trust me, Brad would never do that. He had a lot of integrity."

"Then why would Larry say that?"

"Why does Larry Wade do anything? The man's a criminal. A psychopath. Most likely a pathological liar as well. Don't waste your time trying to figure him out. You won't get very far."

"So our father wasn't in organized crime," I said, "but he did have enemies. Enemies who apparently could be appeased for five million dollars."

"Or some other amount," Wendy said.

"And he didn't tell you who these enemies were or why they were his enemies?"

"No, he didn't. Even though I begged him to."

"So my father paid the ransom?" I asked.

Wendy nodded.

"Why, then, did Larry get in so much trouble from the other two by letting Talon escape? I mean, if my father paid, weren't these guys going to let Talon go?"

"I wish I could tell you," Wendy said. "I realize parts of this story don't jell together. I'm only telling you what I know."

"Larry claims he never saw any of that five million dollars. He says none of it went to him."

"He could be telling the truth for all I know," she said, "or he could be lying. We'll probably never know."

"I do remember that he was the follower of the three," Talon said. "The other two seemed to be more in charge. I got the feeling Larry was just along for the ride."

"It's hard to say," Wendy said. "The other two may have approached Larry because of his familial connection. I don't know, and I can't really speculate."

"We need to get on the road soon, Wendy," I said. "Is there anything else you should tell us? Anything you haven't gotten into?"

"Not that I can think of right off hand. It has been twenty-five years." She looked at Talon intently. "I'm so very glad you're okay. Please give Jade my best."

Talon stood. "I sure will. She speaks highly of you. Thank you for the information. If we have more questions, may we visit you again?"

She stood and pulled Talon into a hug. "Of course. Anytime. I want to do all I can to help all of you."

She turned to me, but I held out my hand. I didn't want to hug this woman, and I couldn't put my finger on why. Something bothered me—something I couldn't put into words. As I shook her hand, I said, "Thank you. We really appreciate your time."

"It's nothing." She smiled at me. "I truly wish I could do more."

"I'm sure we'll have more questions for you." I tried to return her smile but wasn't sure if I succeeded. "For now, we'll be heading out. Come on, Tal."

She showed us to the door, and Talon and I walked to the car.

"I'll drive," I said. Once we were on the road, I cleared my throat. "What do you think?"

"Some of what she said made sense."

"Are you still convinced that Nico Kostas is one of the men who abducted you?"

"Honestly, I don't know. If these guys were enemies of Dad, I guess we have to figure out why Nico Kostas would be Dad's enemy."

And Tom Simpson. But I hadn't yet told Talon of my suspicions, and now was certainly not the time.

"If Nico Kostas tried to kill Jade's mother for a million dollars in insurance money, I guess it would make sense that he would demand a five-million-dollar ransom from some rich rancher," I said.

"You don't sound entirely convinced, Joe."

Sometimes I got freaked at how well Talon could read me. "I'm not. And I'm not sure why. Most of what she said made some sense. And although I didn't know Dad had any enemies, I certainly don't doubt that he did. People with money tend to make enemies, even if they don't know it. It could have been a pissed-off employee for all we know. Or a struggling rancher who didn't get business because Dad could bid lower. So yeah, he certainly could have had enemies out there that we never knew about."

"So what bugs you?"

"A couple of things. Things that hadn't occurred to me before today." Mostly because I'd been so focused on Melanie Carmichael and Tom Simpson.

"Yeah? What are those?"

"Well, the whole 'in love' thing. Wendy is a nice-looking woman, but she hardly seems Dad's type. Mom was drop-dead gorgeous, on the other hand."

"Drop-dead gorgeous, but also mentally ill."

I nodded. "There's that. And I know looks aren't everything, but here's the thing."

"What?"

"If Wendy and Dad were so in love, why didn't they get together after Mom died?"

CHAPTER THIRTY-SIX

Melanie

I had no idea how long I had been in the room. The man in black had brought me food once, and though I hadn't been hungry, I ate. I had been over every inch of the room, trying to find an escape, but it was impossible. Whenever I was thirsty, I drank from the sink in the tiny bathroom. I still had no idea what my fate would be.

As if in answer, the man in black unlocked the door and entered. "Good morning, Doctor."

Did that mean it was morning? I had no idea. I had slept...I thought. Or had I just relived sessions with Gina in a semi-hypnotic state?

"Today's your lucky day," he said. "You're getting out of here."

Though the thought should have made me ecstatic, I stood there grimly. The memory of Gina's session—*I'd rather die*—had numbed me again. Had I missed a cry for help? There'd been no other indication that she might be suicidal. She'd held down a job, done volunteer work at a local children's shelter...had been in a lot better shape than Talon Steel had been when he first came to me, and he hadn't been suicidal. To the contrary, his overwhelming will to survive had completely overshadowed his desire to die.

The man in black interrupted my thoughts by pulling me from the bed and turning me around to face the wall.

He bound my hands behind my back, this time with duct tape. "Can't have you trying anything funny," he said.

Anything funny? As if I could. The room held nothing that could be used as a weapon, and this man had already demonstrated that he was much stronger than I was.

"Don't you want to know where you're going?"

"Not particularly," I said.

"Okay. Have it your way."

We walked out the door, and I realized I was in a house. This little room with no windows had been built in the middle of the basement. He led me up the stairs, through a laundry room. To the left was a kitchen. We went to the right. Into the garage. It was a large garage, big enough for three vehicles. However, only one old car sat in the garage.

"This is a very special car, Dr. Carmichael."

It was huge, like an old pimp car from a few decades ago. "It doesn't look that special to me. It looks like a piece of crap."

He laughed. "Yes, it is that. It belongs to someone you knew, and the funny thing about this car is that it's an older model. I can start it and then lock it so no one can get in while the motor is running."

"So?"

And then it hit me.

"No!" I tried pulling away from him.

"So you figured it out?"

He pushed me into the garage, against the car, and then jiggled the keys in my face. "You won't be able to open the door and turn off the ignition without these. And guess what? I'm taking them with me."

My heartbeat raced as cold fear pulsed through my veins. "Let me go! Let me go!"

"I'm afraid not, Doctor. You're going to die. In this garage, at the mercy of this car. Just like Gina Cates did."

CHAPTER THIRTY-SEVEN

Jonah

Still no answer from Melanie.

The next morning, I was starting to get concerned and was getting ready to drive to Grand Junction, when I got a frantic phone call from Bryce.

"I want to go back to Grand Junction, Joe," he said. "I want to talk to Larry Wade again."

"Your timing couldn't be better," I said. "I was just getting ready to drive into the city now. I suppose I could stop and see Larry first. We'll have to take separate cars, though, because I have some things to do afterward."

The two of us made quick time into the city. Before I knew it, we were sitting at the table, the same table we had sat at weeks before, waiting for the guard to bring Larry out.

I looked around the sterile room. And then I snapped my neck to the left. A silver-haired man was leaving the visitation room. From behind, he looked just like—

Tom Simpson.

I couldn't say anything to Bryce. What if I was wrong?

But no, just as with every interaction I'd had with Tom Simpson, I felt knowledge deep within my soul. That was him, and he'd been here to see Larry. I looked around the large room. Sure enough, Larry sat at another table. He stood, and the guard brought him over to us. Too many thoughts were jumbled in my head right now—all that Wendy had told us, what we knew for sure, and then those gut feelings of mine— those gut feelings about Tom Simpson that wouldn't go away.

I turned to Bryce. "Are you sure you want to do this?"

He nodded. "The close call with Henry made me even more sure. Now that I know what happened to Luke, I'm determined to figure this whole thing out. Find out why this happened and who was responsible. Some way, I'll convince Larry Wade to tell us."

I hadn't given Bryce any of the information that Talon and I had gotten from Wendy Madigan. It just didn't sit right with me, and until I had more evidence, I wasn't going to say anything. I also hadn't had the heart to tell Bryce that I thought the third abductor might be his father. How could I tell him something like that? It was hard enough knowing that one of them was my own uncle. But I hadn't known he was my half-uncle. I hadn't even known he existed, thanks to the cover up of the relationship between him and my mother. Bryce had grown up with Tom. Tom was his father, and as far as I could tell, he'd been a good one.

I still didn't know where Tom's birthmark was. What if it was on his arm, like Talon remembered? What were the chances of two men in the same area having an identical birthmark in the same place?

Probably about as good as being struck by lightning.

When Larry sat down at our table, he looked like he had lost weight since the last time I'd seen him. He also had a big bruise around one eye.

"What the hell do you two want?" he said.

"Get into a fight?" I asked.

"What the fuck do you care?"

"I don't. Serves you right, and it's still not even a down payment on what you did to my brother and those other kids. I imagine child molesters aren't looked too favorably upon by other prisoners."

Larry said nothing.

"Today, Uncle Larry," I said, "you're going to tell us the names of those other two abductors."

He shook his head. "Nope. I'm afraid I'm not."

"What the hell do you care? The DA is offering a good deal. And you're already getting your ass kicked in prison. Look at you."

Still he shook his head. "I can't. And I won't."

"What if we're willing to sweeten the pot a little?" Bryce asked.

"With what? If I walked away from the Steels' money, what makes you think you have anything to offer me?"

"My father's the mayor of Snow Creek. He can talk to the governor. Maybe get you a pardon."

I jerked toward Bryce. "What the fuck?" I said through clenched teeth.

"What's the problem?" Bryce said. "You want to find out who did this, don't you?"

"Not at the expense of letting this asshole free. Hell, no."

Larry chuckled. "I can guarantee you one thing, son. Your father won't do shit for me."

"How can you say that? He appointed you as a city attorney when you needed a job."

"There were special circumstances there."

"Like what?" Bryce asked.

"Confidential special circumstances."

"Just as well," I interjected. "Because, Bryce, we're not letting this asshole out. I don't care if the president himself wants to pardon him. I will not let it fucking happen. Absolutely not."

"Calm down, Joe," Bryce said. "I didn't know you would freak out this way."

"This scumbag molested my brother. This scumbag molested and killed your cousin."

Larry started to speak, but I silenced him with a gesture.

"How could you possibly think I would be okay with getting him pardoned? Not only does he deserve to be in prison for life, but also, what if he got a pardon and then he got out and molested another kid? Maybe *your* kid?"

Bryce went pale. "Okay. It was just a thought. My father probably wouldn't do it anyway."

"That's for damn sure," Larry said.

"Just what in the hell do you have against my father?" Bryce demanded. "He's been the mayor for over ten years. Before that, he was a prominent attorney in Snow Creek."

I had to bite my tongue not to say anything. If I'd been alone with Larry, I would've said straight out that I thought Tom Simpson was the third abductor. Of course, Jade had asked him straight out if Nico Kostas was one, and he had given her a poker face. So he would undoubtedly do the same. Time to give it a test.

"I have a name, Uncle. Was one of the men Nico Kostas?"

"No," he said.

One of his eyebrows rose just a bit. Was that a tell?

"Just tell us," Bryce pleaded. "It will be worth your while. You'll get a lighter sentence. And Joe has already offered you money for a lawyer."

Larry looked intently at Bryce. "Why is it so important for you to learn the truth?"

"Because Luke Walker was my cousin. Because Talon is Joe's brother. Because I have a son of my own now, and I would die inside if anything like this ever happened to him. So I want to know the truth. I want to know who those fuckers are so we can get them off the street and they'll never again hurt innocent children like my son."

Larry looked at Bryce, his face stern. "Look, I've got nothing against you, kid—"

"Kid? I'm thirty-eight," Bryce said.

"To me, you're a kid." Larry coughed. "I'm not going to tell you who they are."

Bryce stood. "Then Joe and I will find them on our own."

Still facing Bryce, Larry curled his lips into a sleazy half smile, his blue eyes creeping eerily toward me while his head stayed still. "Keep looking if you want to, kid, but let me give you a piece of advice. The truth is overrated. Once you open the door to that dark room, getting out is damn near impossible."

Jonah and Melanie's story continues in

Burn

Coming February 14th, 2017
Keep reading for an excerpt!

CHAPTER ONE

Jonah

Still facing Bryce, Larry curled his lips into a sleazy half smile, his blue eyes creeping eerily toward me while his head stayed still. "Keep looking if you want to, kid, but let me give you a piece of advice. The truth is overrated. Once you open the door to that dark room, getting out is damn near impossible."

My body went cold. Larry was addressing Bryce, but only I knew what he was referring to.

The truth.

The truth—that Bryce's father was one of the men we were searching for.

The truth was indeed a dark room, and I knew who would have to open that door for Bryce. And it wasn't Larry.

Larry was still being steadfast in his refusal to name the other two culprits. But now more than ever, I was certain of what I had inferred earlier from Larry. Bryce knew one of the abductors.

And that abductor was his own father.

"Tell me, Uncle," I said. "You seem to think that Bryce here knows one of the abductors. Why don't you save him and my brother a lot of heartache and tell us, right now, who it is?"

My demand to Larry wasn't altruistic, and I knew it. If Larry told Bryce about his father, I wouldn't have to.

Larry's expression remained stoic. "I said no such thing."

"Maybe not in so many words," I said. "But you certainly implied it."

"Again, I did no such thing."

Bryce sat next to me, his face pale, his countenance rigid. Larry's words had gotten to him.

"Then what is all this bullshit about the truth being a dark room?" I stared into my uncle's blue eyes.

"Do you really think you can handle the truth?" This time Larry was looking straight at me, not Bryce, whose eyes were focused forward.

"I've been forced to handle things no human being should have to handle since I was thirteen years old." I gritted my teeth. "I can deal with anything you throw my way." Especially since I knew already what "truth" he was referring to.

Larry continued staring me down. "And your friend here? A new father? You think *he* can handle the truth?"

Those words catapulted Bryce out of his stupor, the color gradually returning to his face. "I can handle anything you have to dish out."

"Think long and hard before you go there, kid," Larry said, turning his gaze to Bryce.

"I can handle it," Bryce said again through clenched teeth.

"We're grown men, Uncle, despite the fact that you like calling us kids. Now, do all three of us a favor and tell the goddamned truth. Who were those other two men?"

Larry shook his head, chuckling. He turned to the guard standing next to him. "We're done here."

Bryce stood, his hands clenched into fists. "We're far from done here. You're going to tell Joe and me who abducted his brother and who killed my cousin. Right now."

Larry stood as well, his half smile snakelike. "You two don't hear very well. I'm not going to roll on anyone. That will never change."

MESSAGE FROM HELEN HARDT

Dear Reader,

Thank you for reading *Melt*. If you want to find out about my current backlist and future releases, please like my Facebook page: **www.facebook.com/HelenHardt** and join my mailing list: **www.helenhardt.com/signup/**. I often do giveaways. If you're a fan and would like to join my street team to help spread the word about my books, you can do so here: **www.facebook.com/groups/hardtandsoul/**. I regularly do awesome giveaways for my street team members.

If you enjoyed the story, please take the time to leave a review on a site like Amazon or Goodreads. I welcome all feedback.

I wish you all the best!

Helen

ACKNOWLEDGEMENTS

I enjoyed writing *Melt,* but I have to admit that I missed Jade and Talon. But once I got into Jonah's and Melanie's heads, I knew I had another amazing couple whose story needs to be told. Jonah and Melanie are as alike as they are different, which makes for some fun writing. I hope you all enjoy this first installment.

Thanks so much to my amazing editors, Celina Summers and Michele Hamner Moore. Your guidance and suggestions were invaluable. Thank you to my line editor, Jenny Rarden, and my proofreaders, Amy Grishman, Audrey Bobak, Angela Kelly, and Scott Saunders. Thank you to all the great people at Waterhouse Press—Meredith, David, Kurt, Shayla, Jon, Yvonne, and Robyn. The cover art for this series is beyond perfect, thanks to Meredith and Yvonne.

Thank you to the members of my street team, Hardt and Soul. HS members got the first look at *Melt,* and I appreciate all your support, reviews, and general good vibes. You ladies are the best!

Thanks to my always supportive family and friends and to all of the fans who eagerly waited for *Melt.* I hope you love it.

You know me—I can't resist leaving my readers hanging. But have no fear. *Burn* is coming soon!

ALSO BY HELEN HARDT

The Sex and the Season Series:
Lily and the Duke
Rose in Bloom
Lady Alexandra's Lover
Sophie's Voice
The Perils of Patricia (Coming Soon)

The Temptation Saga:
Tempting Dusty
Teasing Annie
Taking Catie
Taming Angelina
Treasuring Amber
Trusting Sydney
Tantalizing Maria

The Steel Brothers Saga:
Craving
Obsession
Possession
Melt (Coming December 20th, 2016)
Burn (Coming February 14th, 2017)
Surrender (Coming May 16th, 2017)

Daughters of the Prairie:
The Outlaw's Angel
Lessons of the Heart
Song of the Raven

DISCUSSION QUESTIONS

1. The theme of a story is its central idea or ideas. To put it simply, it's what the story *means*. How would you characterize the theme of *Melt?*

2. What new things are revealed about Jonah in this book? About Melanie?

3. Do you think Melanie failed Gina? Why or why not? How do you feel about her not telling anyone about Gina's letter?

4. Discuss the character of Bryce Simpson. What might his childhood have been like? His relationship with his father?

5. Do you think Jonah is right about Tom Simpson being an iceman? Why or why not?

6. Whose blood might be on the business card found in Jade's bedroom? Whose fingerprints?

7. Discuss Jonah's altercation with Talon while they were driving to Denver. Do you think it helped either or both of them? Why or why not?

8. What do you think Melanie bought at the Snow Creek hardware store?

9. Is Jonah letting his feeling of being responsible for everything go too far? Why or why not?

10. Discuss Jonah and Talon's conversation with Wendy Madigan. Do you think Wendy is telling the truth? Why or why not?

11. Discuss the Cates family. What do you know about them so far? Do you think they went after Melanie because of the ill-advised phone call she made? Or would they have come after her regardless?

12. Who do you think is responsible for kidnapping Melanie? The Cates family, or someone else?

13. Where do you think Jonah and Melanie's relationship will go from here? How will Jonah feel once he finds out that Melanie was in danger and he ignored her call?

14. Will we see more of Oliver Nichols? What might his role be?

15. How will Melanie be rescued?

ABOUT THE AUTHOR

New York Times and *USA Today* Bestselling author Helen Hardt's passion for the written word began with the books her mother read to her at bedtime. She wrote her first story at age six and hasn't stopped since. In addition to being an award winning author of contemporary and historical romance and erotica, she's a mother, a black belt in Taekwondo, a grammar geek, an appreciator of fine red wine, and a lover of Ben and Jerry's ice cream. She writes from her home in Colorado, where she lives with her family. Helen loves to hear from readers.

Visit her here:
www.facebook.com/HelenHardt

ALSO AVAILABLE FROM

HELEN HARDT

TEMPTING DUSTY
THE TEMPTATION SAGA: BOOK ONE

El Diablo strikes no fear in the heart of Dusty O'Donovan. The accomplished rider knows life holds much greater fears than a feisty stud bull. Diablo's owner, Zach McCray, is offering half a million dollars to anyone who can stay on him for a full eight seconds. That purse would go a long way helping rebuild Dusty and her brother's nearly bankrupt ranch.

Let a woman ride his bull? Not likely. Still, the headstrong Dusty intrigues Zach. Her father worked on the McCray ranch years ago, and Zach remembers her as a little girl when he was a cocky teen. Times change, and now she's a beautiful and desirable young woman. A few passionate kisses leave Zach wanting more, but will Dusty's secrets tear them apart?

Visit HelenHardt.com for more information!

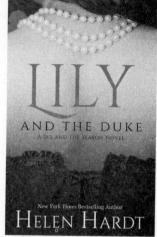

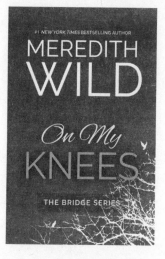